ALPHAS' MATE

Leah Brooke

MENAGE AMOUR

Siren Publishing, Inc.
www.SirenPublishing.com

A SIREN PUBLISHING BOOK
IMPRINT: Ménage Amour

ALPHAS' MATE
Copyright © 2009 by Leah Brooke

ISBN-10: 1-60601-491-9
ISBN-13: 978-1-60601-491-2

First Printing: September 2009

Cover design by Jinger Heaston
All cover art and logo copyright © 2009 by Siren Publishing, Inc.

Printed in the U.S.A.

PUBLISHER
Siren Publishing, Inc.
www.SirenPublishing.com

ALPHAS' MATE

LEAH BROOKE
Copyright © 2009

Chapter One

Lars Tougarret pulled up in his SUV right behind his half brother, Damien. He shaded his eyes, nearly blinded, as the sun reflected off the chrome of the black motorcycle. He got out and approached Damien, extending his hand and chuckling. "How many hours a week do you spend polishing that damned thing?"

Damien grinned and pulled his hair loose from its tail. "Don't be jealous. I look good on it and you know it."

Lars shook his head. "You know when you show up here with that thing, our grandmother is going to lecture you on how dangerous it is."

"I live for danger." He gestured to the car coming up the drive. "Why don't you yell at this asshole?"

Seth, another half brother, pulled up in his sports car and swaggered up to them. "Hey Damien. When are you going to get a real car?"

"Kiss my ass. You'd better worry about yourself and getting control of your pack. Bob and Tim Fields got drunk again and shifted in town. If you can't handle your pack—"

Lars stepped between them, grabbing Seth when he lunged at Damien. "Cool it. If you want to fight, do it somewhere else. Christ, that's all we need. Don't upset Grandmother. You two had better be on your best behavior while you're here, or I'll kick both your asses."

Damien stood with his hands on his hips. "Anytime you feel lucky."

Wes pulled up in his pickup truck. "Jesus, I fucking love these visits. Can't you people get along for a few hours a week?"

He turned and walked into the house, leaving the rest of them to follow.

"He's right," Lars said to both of them. "Grandmother doesn't deserve this from us. We're half brothers, for God's sake. Can we at least try not to kill each other? And you," he pointed at Seth, "get control of your fucking pack or the three of us will take it from you. We don't need to give O'Reilly any more reason to hassle us."

Seth glared at both of them. "I'll take care of it. Just leave me the hell alone. I don't tell you two how to run your fucking packs."

Damien spun and grabbed him by the collar. "Even though we have separate packs, they each affect the others. If I have to kill anyone or scatter my pack because you can't control two drunks, I'm coming after you."

Lars sighed in frustration. Fucking unbelievable. Every damned time they got together lately, he ended up refereeing. Glancing at the window, he pulled Damien's shoulder. "Stop it before grandmother sees you. We'll talk about this later. Give Seth a chance to deal with it."

Seth shoved at Damien to break his hold. "Get the fuck off me, pretty boy, before I make you not so pretty anymore."

Disgusted, Lars pushed between them. "Enough, damn it! Wes is already inside. Grandmother's going to be watching for us. If either of you upset her I'm really going to kick both your asses."

Damien broke Lars' hold and turned away. "Let's get this over with so I can get the hell out of here."

Lars made sure he stayed between them as they walked to the front door. Tension between Damien and Seth seemed to get worse each week. He wished they would just fight it out and be done with it.

Glancing up, he saw his grandmother standing in the doorway wearing a big smile. Not until they got closer did he see the worry in her eyes. He would definitely have to have a talk with the others.

He waited until Damien greeted her and went inside before bending to kiss her cheek. "Hello, Grandmother. You look beautiful, as always. I guess Victor's taking good care of you."

She wrinkled her nose but her eyes twinkled. "He's a nag."

Grinning, Lars walked inside and moved to the sitting room to stand across the table from Wes. He and Wes usually sat across from each other so that Damien and Seth didn't sit together. Thinking about that depressed him.

To distract himself, he looked around. He'd always loved this room. The leader of the pack had always lived here, passing the house and grounds down to the next generation. That had been until their father died before they were born. The mansion their great-grandfather had built over a hundred years ago had, at one time, looked stuffy and formal.

Their grandmother had hated it.

Now, the casual placement of comfortable furniture gave the room a warm, homey feel. He pulled out a chair as she approached. "I love this room."

She poured coffee for each of them as they took their seats. "When your father and his father were alive, they used to have meetings with the pack elders in this room. Of course it's a lot more comfortable now than it was back then. It's a shame this room hardly gets used anymore."

Lars sighed, sorry he'd said anything and shared a look with his three half brothers. "Grandmother, we've been over this hundreds of times." He loved his grandmother dearly, but lately she'd become obsessed with talking about their future, a sensitive subject for all of them.

"Then once more won't make a difference, will it?" Eleanor Tougarret lifted a brow as she sipped her tea from the delicate china

 6

Iment

cup. She looked at each them in turn. "You know that the four of you are all the family I have left in the world. Well, except for little Lacey. I want to see all of you settled and the pack reunited before I go. We've spoken of this many times, I know. I can't believe that you still resist uniting the pack and leading it together."

Lars sighed again, shooting a glance at his brothers. Grandmother wouldn't be happy until all four of them lived at the mansion, leading the pack as one. "Grandmother, all four packs are doing well and prospering. You know that. We're all very happy with our lives and with our packs."

"The Tougarret pack is *one* pack. *One*. Not four. If your father had waited until he found his mate instead of getting all four of your mothers pregnant—"

"None of us would be here," Damien Tougarret finished.

When their grandmother paled, Lars shot him a warning look. Damien had a short fuse at the best of times, but lately he'd been even worse. Out of the corner of his eye, he saw Damien and Seth glare at each other. He patted his grandmother's hand, shifting her attention to him so she wouldn't notice. "Grandmother, we know how hard all of this has been for you, especially dealing with our mothers. But it's different now."

He hid a smile when he thought about the turnaround their mothers had made. They all actually got along now and none would dare go against their grandmother.

Eleanor sipped her tea, her hand shaking, startling the hell out of him. "I don't know what your father was thinking. He gets four women, *pack members*, for God's sake, pregnant. I can't believe he didn't realize that they would turn on each other. Their jealousy of each other and their greed to be the mother of the pack leader made it impossible for you to be close when you were all children. I'll never forgive them for that. Never. You should have been family from the day you were born instead of being encouraged to mistrust and hate each other."

Seth Tougarret leaned forward and touched their grandmother's hand. "And when we got old enough to understand, you put an end to all that. We get along better than we did before. You know we took over responsibility for our own packs years ago. Our mothers have no say in any of the decisions we make. You made us see what they were doing and we'll always be grateful for your support. But you have to accept that there are four distinct packs now, four leaders." He glanced at Damien. "We don't all agree on everything. We're all happy with the way it is now."

Damien flicked him a glance and sat forward, his tight features softening as he smiled at their grandmother. "What is it, grandmother? Why are you bringing all of this up again? Why is it upsetting you so much this time?"

Her eyes flashed in a rare show of temper. "The packs should be joined. You should be family. The Tougarret pack used to be one of the largest and most powerful packs in the world. It could be again. Other pack members used to find safety here. They came to us when they had nowhere else to go." She paused, sighed, then looked up at them worriedly. "I know you all think I'm stupid. You think that I don't know that you only get along when you visit me? Seth and Damien are barely speaking to each other."

Lars rubbed his eyes, not even bothering to look at the others. They'd tried to hide the fact that they didn't spend much time together from their grandmother. Apparently they'd failed. It wasn't because they didn't really like each other. They got along, but each had their own lives, obligations and careers. It suddenly hit him that they'd never really tried to spend any time together.

Once a week, they still came together here, at their grandmother's insistence. They spoke, but had never become really close. They never confided in each other and only came to each other for pack business or their grandmother. It amazed him to realize, that after getting together all these years, they really didn't know each other at all. And it saddened him. When they left their grandmother's today, he would definitely have a talk with his brothers. "Grandmother, we don't fight. We just don't see that much of each other. We're each very busy."

"Too busy. You should never be too busy for family. You need to enjoy life more instead of working all the time and you should make time for each other. I worry about all of you."

Lars smiled at his grandmother tenderly. Family had always been her priority and he knew the lack of closeness between him and his brothers upset her. "Grandmother, we all get along much better than we did before and we all consider each other family. Damien, Wes, Seth and I don't fight the way we used to. Sure, we have disagreements, but don't all brothers? We *are* closer now than we were before. You made sure of it."

Her eyes welled with tears. "Do you realize that's the first time I ever heard any one of you refer to the others as your brothers instead of your half brothers? You are brothers. You should rule the pack together. Even the occasional challenges would diminish. Another werewolf would have to defeat all four of you to claim leadership. The Tougarret pack would again be the largest and most powerful. We could do a lot more to help others."

"Grandmother, we help each other and we all work together," Damien said softly. "We take care of those who come to us for help and take in those who want to join our packs." He slid a hard look at Seth. "We help each other and work together when O'Reilly comes sniffing around."

Wes grimaced. "It's getting harder and harder to get rid of him, especially with some of the other packs growing more violent. They draw too much unwanted attention."

The phone rang, and Lars heard Victor answer from the kitchen.

Damien sighed heavily. "Some packs don't like that we provide a refuge for those who disperse. More and more have come recently because they don't like the violence in their own packs. Most of them come because they want to be allowed to mate. I still don't understand why some of the packs have limitations on when members can mate. They just can't let go of the old ways. They can't get rid of rules that don't make sense any more."

Seth joined in. "Why would anyone want to stay in a pack where no one could mate when the Alphas' mate is pregnant? The packs are much stronger and happier when mating within the pack is permitted at all times."

Their grandmother nodded. "It's true, and you all agree on that. But in the old days, the betas couldn't mate while the Alpha female was pregnant because they may be needed to protect her. The Alpha couldn't take the chance that the others would be more intent on protecting their own pregnant mates. And when food was scarce, the Alphas ate first. A pregnant Alpha female got whatever she needed."

She shot a look at each of them. "You agree on that, just as you agree on many other issues. If the four of you lead together, the pack would be even stronger than ever. And while we're on the subject, are each of you looking for you own mate? Or are you going to follow your father's example? He gets four of his own pack pregnant and is caught with another were's mate and gets killed for it. I loved him but he was never a strong man. Maybe if your grandfather had lived longer..."

Lars grimaced, knowing his grandmother knew that he and the others had always been popular with women. He and his half brothers all shared the same dark looks as their father, black hair, blue eyes and stood well over six feet tall. They kept themselves in good shape. Werewolves generally kept in shape. Their lives depended on it. But knowing about their father, none of them had wanted to be anything like him.

As he and his brothers got older, and none had found their own mates, their frustration grew. Close in age, with only months separating them, they all wondered if they would ever find their true mates or if somehow they hadn't been paying attention and they'd missed out. Since Seth's birthday last month, they all were thirty-four now and anxious to find their women and start their families.

Damien raised a brow. "As soon as I find my mate, grandmother, I promise to latch onto her and never let her go. But you don't expect any of us to settle for anyone other than our true mate, do you? Not after what our father did."

"I hope not. Don't make the same mistakes that he did. I want each of you to find your mate, settle down and have children. Children are important. I still miss your father." When she fell silent, Lars looked helplessly at his brothers as their grandmother's voice lowered. "Roland was such a good little boy. Your grandfather and I were true mates. He said that as soon as he caught my scent, he knew." She laughed softly. "I remember when he first told me that, I got offended. I thought he was trying to say that I smelled bad."

Lars breathed a sigh of relief. He slid a glance at each of his brothers as she sipped her tea, surprised to notice how often they looked at each other for support around her. His grandmother's uncharacteristic moroseness unsettled him, and he could see that it unsettled his brothers as well. He had no doubt that the subject of reuniting the pack would come up again. As would her insistence that they find a mate.

He tilted his head when he heard an unfamiliar car approach. It appeared his grandmother had company. He decided not to mention it and shot a glance at his brothers. Let her guest surprise her. She needed something to cheer her up.

He and the others would have to talk about that.

For now he wanted to distract her. "From what I hear from the other pack members, the scent of a mate is like no other and that you know it immediately." He tried to ignore his impatience at finding his own and poured himself more coffee. Shit. Bad subject. Dwelling on their lack of mates would depress them all. He tried again. "Are you excited about your birthday party tomorrow?"

Her cheeks turned pink and she smiled, shaking her head. Better. "I can't believe you boys went to so much trouble. It will be wonderful to see the pack together again. You couldn't have chosen a finer gift for me. It's been a long time since they all gathered in one place. It will be just like the old days. By the way, I've invited someone I want all of you to meet."

Lars smiled at her excitement. "Who is it, Grandmother?"

She beamed. "It's a surprise. It's someone very special to me. This is going to be so much fun!"

Glad now that they'd decided to throw a big party, Lars sat back, smiling at his grandmother's excitement. He knew how much she loved having all four packs together and was glad they'd arranged the party.

Seth chuckled. "You talk like our pack members never see each other. A lot of them are good friends and see each other all the time. They were happy to be invited to your birthday party. They all love you."

Wes got up to refill his coffee cup. "It's a good thing the house is so big. And the yard. They're going to set up several tables out there. With all four packs together, it's a lot of people."

"Especially with mates and children," Seth added.

"Nonsense. The pack used to gather here at the mansion quite often and there was always enough room."

A few minutes later Victor, their grandmother's butler, nursemaid, protector and everything else appeared in the doorway. In his late fifties, Victor had lost his mate two years ago and had just recently begun to recover.

Still handsome, the ladies clamored for his attention. But still mourning his mate, he had no interest. When they'd asked him to move in here and see to their grandmother, they'd been relieved when he'd accepted. It worked out well for all involved. Taking care of their grandmother gave him something to occupy his thoughts and his time. He absolutely adored their grandmother and had taken to the job like a duck to water. Both had lost their mates, and their grandmother wouldn't let him brood. She and Victor argued constantly, matching wits and both seemed to enjoy it immensely. No one dared to interfere.

"Miss Eleanor, the caterers are here to look over some things and make some last minute adjustments. The florists called to confirm everything. I told them to make sure everything is fresh. We don't want everything wilted and tired looking before the end of the party, do we?"

Lars watched in amusement as his grandmother's eyes narrowed.

"If you say one more word about me taking a nap before my party—"

To his credit, Victor's face showed no expression. "Of course not. I wouldn't dream of telling you what to do. You, of course, know best. I'll be here to the very end of your party and will be more than happy to see to your guests when you get tired."

He ignored her scowl as he refilled her teacup. "Should I call the young girl that does your hair? Perhaps she has some makeup that will cover those dark circles."

Lars and the others lifted their coffee cups to hide their grins. Sliding his gaze to his grandmother, he struggled not to laugh as she glared at Victor.

Victor, apparently unfazed, met her look with a cool one of his own.

After a long silence, she sighed. "Fine. I'll go lie down in my room for a few minutes before the party. But I'm not agreeing to a nap."

Victor's lips twitched. "Of course not."

Lars watched Victor leave and spared a glance at his grandmother. "He knows you well, doesn't he?"

"He's a pain in the butt and I don't know why I put up with him. Do you know what he made me eat for breakfast?"

His grandmother began to list all of Victor's flaws, something she enjoyed doing, especially since she knew Victor could hear her. Usually the games they played entertained him, but not now.

Her voice dimmed. His heart rate sped up as all of his senses went on alert. Every muscle in his body tightened as primal instincts, never too far from the surface rose within him. Heightened senses sharpened even more. Possessiveness, relief, elation, need and fierce protectiveness warred within him, ruthlessly clawing their way to the surface. He could hardly breathe. His skin felt hyper sensitive and the air around him seemed to shimmer.

That scent. He closed his eyes, breathing deeply the most wonderful, captivating scent he'd ever experienced. Clean. Fresh. Sweet. It was a scent he'd never been exposed to before but knew it immediately. It reached out to him, pulled him, as nothing else on earth could have. He wanted to howl.

His mate.

He'd know that scent anywhere and had waited for it forever.

He felt almost dizzy with need, his groin tightening immediately and almost painfully. The scent of his mate brought the beast to the surface and he wasn't at all surprised when a low growl erupted from his throat. He whipped his head around when the same sound came from his brothers.

He was already on his feet, though he couldn't remember standing. He absently noticed his brothers moving beside him as he headed toward that delectable scent. He paid them little attention. He had to get to her. Now. "Stay with grandmother. My mate is here."

"Mine, too," Damien growled.

"And mine," Wes and Seth said together.

Lars glanced at them, not slowing his stride. The surprise on all their faces would have been comical in other circumstances, but not now. Somehow all of their mates had shown up simultaneously. Nothing mattered to him but getting to his.

"They must be with the caterers," he murmured as he hurried toward the doorway.

"Are you saying that *all* of your mates are here?"

Lars spared a look at his grandmother. "Apparently. Sorry

grandmother. I have to go find her."

A clear sweet voice sounded from the doorway. "Surprise!"

Lars stopped as if he'd run into a brick wall. So did his brothers. His mate stood before him, the scent of her wrapping around him, trapping him, as he knew it would for the rest of his life. His breath caught in his throat. His groin tightened even more. She was beautiful. More than beautiful. Gorgeous. Intoxicating. Savage need raced through him. His world spun out of control. Slowed. Centered. Everything in his world suddenly made sense.

Mine!

He looked at his mate for the first time, ensnared by her beauty, her wonderful scent. Auburn hair framed a face so spectacular, it took his breath away. High cheekbones flushed a delicate pink as he stared at her. Little dimples appeared and he ached to trace them with his tongue. Full, pink lips made him tremble with the urge to take them. The full bottom lip just begged to be nibbled, something he would take great pleasure devoting his time to. His mouth watered with the need to know the taste of her. All of her. Every inch.

But her eyes, oh God, her eyes had to be the deepest green he'd ever seen. He could drown in them. He couldn't wait to see them darken with arousal. Look at him with love shining from them.

And he wanted it *now*.

He took another deep breath, craving more of that tantalizing aroma. Paradise. His hands tightened into fists as he fought the almost overwhelming urge to grab her and carry her away.

His gaze roamed her body, need growing with every passing second. She had small, high breasts which his hands itched to cup. Hard little nipples poked at the front of her shirt and made his mouth water even more. His gaze traveled lower to a tiny waist and slim hips that he couldn't wait to grab onto. His nostrils flared as the scent of her slight arousal reached him. He ruthlessly swallowed another growl before it could erupt.

He wanted to bury his face between her thighs and taste the honey he knew he would find there.

His mate. More than he'd ever hoped for. After all these years of waiting, she stood before him and he could hardly contain his excitement, his need to run away with her and make her his. Her captivating scent nearly brought him to his knees. He couldn't wait to strip her naked and explore every inch of her.

"Lacey! You made it!"

Lacey? Little Lacey?

He blinked, trying to tamp down the beast clawing its way to the surface and speared a glance at his brothers, who'd frozen beside him.

Damien's face had tightened like never before, his teeth bared. Wes's eyes glittered dangerously, his hands also clenched at his sides. Seth looked shocked to the core. His eyes had sharpened and low growls kept coming from his throat.

Lars took in their reactions in a glance before turning to watch his mate greet his grandmother.

Two things hit him at once that rocked his world.

Little Lacey, his grandmother's beloved goddaughter was his mate.

And even more amazing, she was also the mate of his three half brothers.

Chapter Two

Lacey Roberts walked into her godmother's sitting room and came to an abrupt halt, her smile frozen in place as lust slammed into her. The sight of the four men who stood just a few feet away, their eyes like blue lasers aimed at her, filled her with such an intense longing, it took her breath away.

This is where I belong.

Before she could process the ridiculous thought, she heard a low dangerous sound come from their direction. She automatically looked down, thinking she'd heard a dog growling. Seeing nothing, her eyes widened when she realized it came from them. *Growls?*

She'd been called pretty, beautiful even but she's never had men look at her the way these men did, as though they would eat her alive. And none had ever growled at her. She felt almost *hunted.*

They had to be Nana's grandsons. She'd told Lacey about them and described them, but had severely understated their dark good looks.

Something about them pulled at her, physically pulled at her, and she was surprised to discover she actually wanted to run to them and throw herself in their arms. Barely resisting temptation, she watched them warily, not at all comfortable with her uncharacteristic response to them. Her skin prickled with awareness and suddenly there didn't seem to be enough air in the room.

Their eyes roamed over her from head to toe, making her skin tingle as though they'd actually stroked her. Her nipples throbbed and pebbled and she had to fight not to cover them. Amazed at the sudden flow of moisture from her slit, she squeezed her thighs tight, her hands fisting on the purse she held in front of her. She looked at each of them in turn, amazed at the low growls that rumbled from their chests.

What the hell? The more they growled, the wetter her panties got. The more her insides fluttered. The hotter she became.

She couldn't speak. She just stood there for what seemed like an eternity, her brain numb as her body came to life. Instinctively, she took a step back, confused, nervous and more than a little overwhelmed.

"Lacey, come here and let me see you," her godmother called out.

She blinked, having completely forgotten her godmother's presence. Shakily, she carefully gave the men a wide berth and deliberately focused on her godmother. She had to clear her throat before she could speak. "Hi, Nana. I hope you don't mind the surprise. I didn't know I could make it until last night."

"Oh, Lacey. I'm so glad you could come. I was afraid you might have to work. It's so good to see you. I've missed you so much."

Lacey could actually *feel* the men's gazes on her, heating her skin and causing curious little tingles wherever they touched. When her godmother released her, she turned, unsurprised to find that all four of them had their eyes on her. She hurriedly sat in one of the vacant chairs next to Nana. As she watched their approach, the possessive looks on their faces puzzled the hell out of her. They hadn't even been introduced yet.

Her godmother's voice bubbled with delight. "Lacey, these are my grandsons. I've told you about them. I'm so excited that all of you finally meet. This is Lars."

When one of the men stepped forward, she hesitantly put her hand in his outstretched one. Heat raced up her arm and she gasped and attempted to pull away, but his other hand closed over hers, holding her trembling one cupped between them. Struggling to breathe normally while her heart nearly pounded out of her chest, she stopped fighting his firm but gentle grip. The large hands holding hers felt hot as he stared at her hungrily, making the casual gesture far too intimate.

"It is a great pleasure to finally meet you, Lacey. You have no idea how long I've waited to meet *you*."

Lacey shivered at his tone, something in it sending up warning flags. She didn't understand his emphasis on the 'you'.

She knew Lars to be the oldest, but remembered that only months separated them in age. Jesus, he had to be one of the most beautiful men she'd ever laid eyes on. Shiny black hair just barely touched the collar of his white dress shirt. The white shirt was a sharp contrast to his olive skin. The way he dressed made her wonder if he was the one with the business interests.

His lips curved, making her long to press her own against them. Her body vibrated with the need to feel his body pressed against hers.

She blinked, dragging her gaze from his and averting her eyes. Finally managing to extricate her hand from his much larger one, she smiled faintly in his direction, fighting the urge to bolt. "It's nice to meet you. Nana has told me so much about all of you."

She glanced at her godmother, trying to shake off whatever hold he seemed to have on her. The older woman looked thoughtful and not just a little unsettled. Lacey wondered what she'd missed. "Have I come at a bad time? If you want me to go—"

"*No!*"

She jumped as all four men and her godmother exclaimed simultaneously.

The older woman reached out and patted her hand. "Don't be ridiculous. Of course we're happy you're here. I wanted my grandsons to finally meet you. What a wonderful birthday gift!"

Lacey looked at each of them warily. "If you're sure I won't be in the way—"

"Of course not. Now let me introduce you to my other grandsons. This is Damien."

Lars looked reluctant to step back as she greeted Damien, even scowling as Damien nudged him aside.

"Hello, Lacey. I'm so glad you're here," Damien told her and she stiffened at the jolt of heat again as he took her hand in his and touched his lips to it.

Trembling, she tightened her thighs against the raging need building inside her.

Jesus, he was potent. His gaze raked over her, heating every inch of her skin in its path. Wicked intent shone in his eyes, making her glad they had an audience. His black hair, longer than the others, hung loose, giving him a wild look. His striking good looks only enhanced the aura of danger surrounding him. She'd be willing to bet that he was the one who played the stock market, the gambler.

She couldn't take her eyes from Damien's face and saw the flare of his nostrils as he breathed deeply again. A low growl sounded deep in his throat and every erogenous zone on her body tingled with awareness.

His mouth curved and she realized belatedly that she'd been staring at his lips. He chuckled, the sound of it sending her heart racing and making her palms sweaty. The knowledge that he knew exactly what he did to her glittered in his eyes. Startled by her reaction, she struggled to gather her thoughts. "I wasn't sure if I would make it. This is the first time I've been able to come for Nana's birthday."

Damien brought her hand to his lips again, his eyes full of sympathy. "Yes, I'm very sorry about your grandmother. We should have come with grandmother for the funeral. But I promise that I'll always be here for you from now on."

Damien frowned when another of the men pushed him aside, and Lacey heard another of those low growls emanate from his chest. "I'm Weston. Wes. I'm very happy to meet you, Lacey. I'm also sorry about your grandmother. Damien's right. We should have been there for you."

"Don't worry about it. You didn't even know me."

Wes's eyes darkened and his voice lowered seductively. "I know you now. I'll know you better. You'll never have to be alone again."

Lacey nodded numbly, wondering at the strange statement, as Wes took her hand from a now glaring Damien. Wes turned her hand over and lifted it to touch his lips to her palm.

The indulgent tenderness in his eyes gave her a warm glow. She couldn't help but meet his smile with one of her own. Although her pulse raced, she felt more comfortable with him than she had with the others. It was as if she'd been wrapped in a warm blanket. She had the most overwhelming urge to lay her head on his chest and feel those strong arms come around her.

The last man took the seat next to her, brushing against her as he reached for her hand, his other arm moving to rest on the back of her chair. "Hi. I'm Seth. Grandmother has told us a lot about you, but I want to hear more. We can have dinner and you can tell me everything."

She had to laugh at his playful grin and cocky manner, relieved to find him a little easier to deal with.

"She just got here, Seth," Lars growled. "I'm sure she wants to spend time with Grandmother. Besides, it appears we have some talking to do before anyone makes any plans that involve Lacey."

Lacey blinked, taken aback at his proprietary tone. Frowning at him, she resisted the urge to ask him who the hell he thought he was. She'd only been here five minutes and already she wanted to fight with one of Nana's grandsons. Knowing how it would upset her godmother, she snapped her mouth closed. She would only be here a few days, long enough to see her godmother and get Sarah settled before she went back home.

A low rumbling came from beside her and she spun to stare at Seth.

"None of that, Seth. You're scaring Lacey."

Seth's tight features softened almost immediately, although Lacey could see it took tremendous effort. "I'm sorry, my m—, Lacey. Your scent is bringing out the animal in me."

Lacey blinked at the outrageous statement. "I stink?"

"Shut up, Seth," Damien murmured softly.

Seth shot a hard look at him before turning back to smile at her. "Just the opposite. You smell delicious." His nostrils flared as he continued to watch her.

The heat from his body and the clean fresh scent of him surrounded her. Dressed in jeans and a button down shirt, he should have appeared non-threatening, but she could see the wildness in him. As a teacher, she'd become very familiar with that 'I'm up to no good' look. His hair, almost as long as Damien's had been pulled back, and she itched to run her fingers through it and loosen it from its band.

Snapping the lid on that thought, she turned back to her godmother, to find her watching her closely. Lacey's faced burned. It wasn't like her to let men distract her and she could only imagine what her grandmother thought of it.

She knew all about sexual chemistry, but the overwhelming attraction to not one, but all four of them, embarrassed the hell out of her. She definitely needed to get laid more often. Of all the men in the world to be attracted to, why would it have to be Nana's grandsons?

She glanced at the others to find all three of them glaring at Seth, every line of their bodies poised threateningly. Seth merely flicked them a glance, keeping his attention on her, his smile cocky.

She looked away, forcing her attention back to her godmother, feeling like the only one in the room not knowing her lines.

Her godmother smiled and sipped her tea, still regarding her thoughtfully. "You must be tired from your trip. You should have called, and I would have sent someone to the airport for you."

Lacey shifted, aware that the men listened to every word. "I didn't fly. I drove."

"What did you say?"

Lacey felt a chill go down her spine at Lars' tone, and glanced over to see the blue eyes that had heated her blood only moments earlier, had frozen into two chips of ice. She shivered at his look, which angered her even more. Why should she care what he thought about it? She picked up her teacup, addressing Nana and trying her best to ignore him. "I didn't want to fly so I drove. I had some things to do before I left and on the way here." She didn't want them to know that she had reason to hide and couldn't afford to have her name appear on a plane ticket.

"You drove here through the night and alone?" Lars asked and this time she had no choice but to face him. "You drove all the way from northern Ohio to southern North Carolina alone? At night? Without telling anyone?"

Lacey bristled at his words even as another shiver went through her at his tone and she struggled to hide both. She wouldn't be here very long and didn't want to upset her godmother by arguing with one of her grandsons. But she wouldn't let him criticize her decisions. She'd taken care of herself and her grandmother a long time and didn't need his advice. "I wasn't alone the entire time, but I'm a big girl. I can take care of myself. As you can see, other than being tired, I'm fine."

Her godmother frowned worriedly at her. "Lacey, I don't like this. Promise me, please, that you won't do anything like that ever again. It's dangerous for a woman alone at night."

Damn, she didn't want to argue with Nana. "But Nana—"

"Promise me, Lacinda Eleanor."

When Nana used her full name and that tone, she knew she'd lost. She smiled at her godmother. "You just like using my full name because I was named after you."

"Who was with you?" Damien demanded.

Lacey bristled. "It's really none of your business." Regretting that she'd snapped in front of her godmother, she turned back to her and smiled apologetically.

When Nana just continued to stare at her, she sighed. She never could pull the wool over her godmother's eyes. "I promise, Nana. If you don't mind, I'd like to freshen up and rest a little."

"Sure, darling. I'm sure Victor already has a room picked out for you. I think you'd like the rose room best, but Victor never listens to me. How long can you stay?"

"You and Victor still arguing?"

"Yes. Now, answer my question. Can you stay for a while?"

The men stilled, and she knew she had their full attention. "I thought I would stay a few days if it's all right with you."

"A few days? That's it? Can't you stay longer?"

"I'm sorry. I have to get back. I have some things to take care of."

Damien sat forward, bracing his forearms on his knees. Although he addressed his grandmother, his eyes never left hers. "Don't worry, Grandmother. I'll make sure Lacey stays for a while. Why don't you show Lacey to her room so she can lie down and rest? Have you eaten?" At her nod, he continued. "My brothers and I have some things to talk about."

Lars stood, nodding at Damien. "We definitely do."

Lacey started to open her mouth to object to Damien's assurance that he could make her stay longer. When he raised a brow, his jaw tight, she swallowed her protest. Too tired to argue, she didn't bother. Why should she? She would leave whenever she wanted to.

Her godmother's smile looked forced as she exchanged a look with each of her grandsons. "That's a good idea. Why don't we go upstairs, Lacey? I'll show you to your room."

Lacey smiled. "Just let me get my bags from the car."

Seth rose. "I'll get them. Did you lock your car?"

Lacey nodded and dug her keys from her purse and handed them to him. Startled at the jolt of electricity that raced up her arm when their hands touched, she dropped the keys in his and hurriedly pulled hers back, not meeting his eyes.

They all started out of the room, the men bringing up the rear with Seth moving ahead to retrieve her luggage. A smiling Victor met them in the foyer. Lacey had met him on the way in and had immediately recognized him from the way Nana had described him. Apparently he and her godmother fought like cats and dogs but had nothing but respect and admiration for each other, which they tried hard not to show.

"Victor, which room did you put Lacey in?"

Victor slid a look at Nana and winked at Lacey. "I've put you in the rose room. I think you'll be very happy there. If you need anything, please let me know."

"Thank you, Victor." Impulsively, she moved close and stood on her toes to kiss his cheek. Hearing low growls coming from behind her, she turned. The growls stopped but all four men scowled at her. What the hell was their problem, and why the hell did they keep growling at her?

Deciding to ignore them, she turned back to Victor and smiled. "No wonder Nana speaks so highly of you. I'm terribly sorry I showed up without calling."

"Nonsense. I'm happy you could be here for Miss Eleanor's party."

"Not as happy as I am." Her godmother smiled distractedly and hugged her again. "Come on. Let's get you settled. You're tired after driving all night. Get some rest and come down to eat whenever you're ready."

Victor nodded. "I'll have something prepared for whenever you come down."

"No, please don't go to any trouble. I just want to lie down for a little while. If I sleep too long, I won't sleep tonight. If I'm still asleep, could someone please just wake me about an hour before dinner? I would appreciate it."

Victor smiled. "I'll be happy to wake you."

Lacey smiled and nodded. "Thanks." She started up the stairs with her godmother, aware of the other men's eyes on them as they stood at the bottom of the stairs and watched them the entire time.

Once they got upstairs and turned the corner, Lacey breathed a sigh of relief. She hadn't realized just how intensely the men's presence affected her until she'd moved out of their sight. Once she got some sleep, she'd be better able to deal with them. She could barely keep her eyes open and it became increasingly difficult just to put one foot in front of the other.

Another hall led in the other direction, and Lacey wondered briefly just how many bedrooms this huge house had. She put an arm around Nana as they walked down the hallway, disturbed by the older woman's silence. Her godmother appeared to be lost in thought, not her usual self at all. "Nana, is something wrong?"

Her godmother blinked, as though she'd forgotten Lacey was there. "No, darling. Of course not. I'm spending my birthday with my grandsons and goddaughter, the people who mean more to me than anything. What could possibly be wrong? I'm just so glad you could make it." They came to a door halfway down the hallway. "Here's your room, sweetheart. If there's anything you need, just pick up the phone and push one. Victor will answer and will be glad to help you. Get a good rest and I'll see you at dinner."

Lacey grinned. "What? No bedtime story? I haven't heard one of your werewolf stories in months."

Nana's smile looked forced. "Maybe later."

Lacey frowned as she watched her godmother turn and walk away. She hoped nothing was wrong and made a mental note to ask one of the men later if she had any health problems or if anything had been bothering her lately.

After losing her grandmother, she didn't know what she would do if something happened to Nana. The two women had always been the center of her world. Losing her grandmother had been agony, even though she'd been expecting it for years. She opened the door and walked into the bedroom, trying to throw off her depressing thoughts.

She paused at the threshold, her first look at the beautiful room rendering her speechless.

Now she understood why Victor and Nana had called it the rose room. The walls had been painted a delicate pink and the curtains and bedspread had tiny little roses on a green background. The room itself was huge, easily double the size of her bedroom at home. The furniture appeared to be antique. The large dressers and bed looked like they must weigh a ton. She couldn't wait to climb up into the high bed and get lost in the mountain of pillows.

Kicking off her shoes, she sank to her ankles in the plush cream carpet, curling her toes, and moaning at how good it felt on her tired feet.

Hearing a sound, she spun to see Seth standing in the doorway, holding her luggage. She couldn't help but admire his lean muscular frame as he carried it into the room.

She couldn't quite come to terms with how strongly all *four* men affected her, especially since they were her godmother's grandsons. Too tired to think about it, she looked away and struggled for something to say. "This is a beautiful room."

Seth placed her luggage in the corner before turning to face her. "I'm glad you like it." He glanced around briefly, his gaze quickly returning to her. "I haven't been up here in a long time. You should be very comfortable here. We'll probably lose you in that bed."

Although his words had been innocent, his tone had been pure seduction. She could easily imagine that low tone murmuring to her in the dark. Shaking her head at her uncharacteristic reaction, she moved to the window, looking out at the huge yard and the woods behind it. "That's right. None of you live with your grandmother, do you?"

Lacey jumped when warm hands settled on her shoulders. Closing her eyes against the rush of pleasure that raced through her, she involuntarily leaned back against him. The heat from his hands spread, warming her all over. "We haven't. But I think that's about to change."

Her eyes met his over her shoulder. He looked momentarily shaken before flashing his cocky grin again. His warm breath brushed against her ear and she tilted her neck automatically as his arm wrapped around her. Warm lips touched her neck. "I have a reason to move in now. I can't believe I finally found you."

Lacey felt Seth stiffen and groan, bringing her to her senses. She straightened and pulled away from him, wondering what the hell had come over her. She looked toward the doorway to see Lars, Damien and Wes storm through it.

All three looked feral, their eyes going to Seth and back to her accusingly. Their nostrils flared, and the glares they shot at Seth looked deadly.

Lars strode toward her, gripping her shoulders, his eyes full of fire. "What the hell is going on up here?"

Fury rolled off them in waves so tangible she could almost see them. She sure as hell felt them. Shocked, she stood there, frozen in place as Damien and Wes leapt at Seth. Their deep growls, inhuman sounds like she'd never heard before, froze her blood.

Seth met their growls with his own, meeting their attack head on. It had all happened in an instant.

Lacey stood there, stunned for several heartbeats before she jumped toward them. "No!" Heavy furniture broke as the three men fought savagely, growling their rage. A vase shattered and she didn't even hear it, their chilling growls and her own screams blocking out the sound. She fought to break free of Lars' grip.

Lars tightened his hold, pulling her against him. "Stay out of it, Lacey. Seth should have known better."

Lacey fought against his hold. She could only imagine what this would do to Nana. "Please. Stop! Oh God. Don't do this. Please don't do this. Please don't fight. This is all my fault. Damn it, I never should have come."

Lars tried to lift her out of the way as the scuffle moved closer, but she escaped his grasp. Even though they didn't speak, the animalistic sounds they made as they fought, forced her to raise her voice to be heard.

"Damn it, stop it! Think of your grandmother." Damien and Wes had Seth on his back on the floor, both going after him. She took a flying leap and landed on their backs, grabbing handfuls of their hair. "Stop it. Why are you doing this? Stop it right now!"

She heard Lars curse and felt him grab at her shirt, but she fell between Damien and Wes and onto Seth's chest before Lars could get a good grip.

She heard more cursing as everyone froze.

A heartbeat later, Seth rolled over her, caging her body protectively beneath his. His lip bled and his eyes had already begun to swell. "Are you hurt, baby?" He ran his hands over her hair, looking down her body as though searching for injuries.

Damien and Wes dropped to either side of her. Wes pushed at Seth. "Get off. Is she okay?"

She heard Lars frantic voice coming from behind Seth. "Is she all right? Damn it, move. Give her to me."

Lacey had had enough of these Neanderthals.

She shoved Seth, who thankfully let her up, and scrambled to her feet, glaring at Lars, Damien and Wes and slapped their hands away as they reached for her. "What's wrong with you? Why did you hit him? What's Nana going to think when she finds out?" She pointed to the door as she knelt beside Seth. "Get out."

With his hands on his hips, Lars stared at her, his eyes narrowed. "He touched you."

Lacey led Seth to the only chair in the room not broken by their fight. "I don't know what's wrong with all of you. Big deal. He put his arms around me. I don't see how you could think it's any of your business. And how did you know, anyway? The door was closed until you three animals came barging through it."

When the three of them just looked at each other and remained silent, she turned her attention to Seth. She brushed her fingers lightly over his cheek, checking out the swelling and bruising. He didn't look too bad, considering, but she didn't want Nana to see him like this.

"Damn, you're going to need some ice. Come downstairs with me and I'll put some on it. I want to get some of the swelling down before Nana sees it." She helped him to his feet, turning to glare at the others. "Get this cleaned up before your grandmother sees what you did."

Still shaking, she led Seth from the room, very afraid that she'd made a big mistake in coming here.

Chapter Three

Damien sat with the others in the study, glaring at Seth. His brother sat slumped in one of the leather chairs, the makeshift ice pack Lacey had made for him balanced on the arm. Damien, along with Lars and Wes had cleaned up the bedroom the best they could while Lacey had tended to his brother's injuries. Damned wuss. It pissed him off that his brother had taken advantage of Lacey's sympathy— who was he trying to fool? Jealousy ate at him that she'd been so attentive to Seth while all but ignoring the rest of them. She'd seen Seth as the victim.

He'd have to remember that.

Damien's jaw tightened when he thought of the way his mate had looked at him when she'd come back into the bedroom. He was her *mate*, damn it. Not only that, but an *Alpha*. She shouldn't glare at him like that. It pissed him off that he hadn't taken care of it right then and there, but the thought that his woman, his *mate* had finally come into his life had his senses reeling. For her to have the damned audacity to *glare* at him made him almost wild with the urge to put her over his knee.

After they'd cleaned up, she'd kicked them all out, not wanting to hear any explanations. Seeing that fatigue had nearly drained her, they left without protest. They would have it out after she'd rested and he and his brothers had a chance to talk.

Damn, she was something else. His fiery mate sure did have a temper. It made him wonder what other passions he could arouse. His groin tightened just thinking about it.

He rubbed his jaw where it had begun to ache. His lips twitched and he winced when it stung. Seth had snuck in a good one. It would have been nice if his damned mate would have cared enough to put ice on it.

Damn. Now he acted like a wuss. Fuck. He'd better get himself under control if he intended to have any kind of authority over his mate.

He sobered when he remembered the rage he'd felt when he caught the scent of her arousal. Knowing she was alone with his brother had set his quicksilver temper off like nothing before.

"I can't share my mate," he told the others now. "She's mine. There's no way I'm going to allow anyone else to touch her." He shot a glance at Seth. "You're lucky I'm not feeding your balls to you."

Seth flew to his feet. "I'm not standing aside while you or anyone claims my mate. She's mine."

Damien saw red and leapt at Seth, but Lars jumped between them. "Stop it, both of you. Don't you think Wes and I feel the same way? Beating the hell out of each other isn't going to solve anything."

Victor opened the door and escorted Rolph, one of the pack elders, into the room. Damien pulled out of Lars' grip, scowling at him. "She's mine, damn it." Glaring at both of them he moved away to greet Rolph. They would have this out after the elder left. "Hello, Rolph. It's good to see you."

Damien put some distance between him and his brothers as they each greeted the older man. Victor left and when he came back with a tray of coffee and tea, Damien grimaced. "Don't tell me. The tea's for Grandmother. She's joining us."

Victor nodded. "She's the one who called Rolph. As soon as she finds what she's looking for, she'll be down."

Of course, she would know. Victor knew everything that went on in the house and kept their grandmother informed. Christ, they'd been so loud, she'd probably heard them, even though they'd been in the other wing.

As Victor poured coffee, Damien moved to sit across from Rolph.

"Did Grandmother tell you what's happened?" He tried to keep his tone friendly while fighting the urge to howl his rage at the thought of sharing his mate.

Rolph nodded and smiled. "Yes, God it brings back memories. I haven't heard of this happening for at least, oh, about forty, forty-five years."

Damien automatically glanced at his brothers to see the incredulous looks on their faces. "You've heard of this, Rolph? You've heard of pack members sharing a mate?"

Rolph sipped the coffee Victor handed to him and nodded. "Yes, several times, but, like I said, not for years." He frowned thoughtfully. "But I've never heard of it happening to the Alpha. And now that there are *four* Alphas, well, to my knowledge that's never happened before."

Lars, who sat next to Rolph, leaned forward. "I know. I know. You want the pack reunited, too. It looks like you and grandmother will both get your wish." He sobered. "How does it work out? Sharing mates. How do they get along?"

Rolph chuckled. "I guess it must have been difficult at times, but the men were always very happy. The women loved it. They were the happiest women I've ever seen and always well protected. It would be suicide to go after a woman with more than one mate. Hmm, and yours will be the Alpha female. Isn't that something?" He smiled broadly. "This is a cause for celebration!"

Celebration? He wanted to rip somebody's throat out. Damien wanted something stronger than coffee and, before he realized what he did, he'd poured a shot for each of them. "How the hell are we supposed to mate with her if she's the mate to all of us?"

"You'll have to mate her together."

They all turned at the sound of their grandmother's voice. Damien had been so preoccupied with the conversation that he hadn't even been aware of her approach. Christ, Lacey had turned him inside out and left him floundering. Being an Alpha, he took pride in being centered and in charge. He didn't care for the fact that a tiny little woman could undo him so easily. "What are you talking about, Grandmother?"

She moved forward and placed a very large, very old book on the desk. Damien and his brothers all gathered around it, looking at their grandmother expectantly.

"What's this?"

Their grandmother ran her hand reverently over the huge leather book. "This book belonged to your father, and your grandfather before that. And his father and grandfather. It's the pack leader's journal and gets passed down along with the house and grounds." She stared down at the book and whispered, "It belongs to all of you. You'll have to share it."

Damien grimaced. "Apparently we'll be sharing everything now." He hoped he sounded more confident than he felt. The thought of sharing his mate made his stomach burn. Jesus, he wanted to hit something.

His grandmother's smile fell and he smiled at her apologetically, reaching out to stroke her arm. "Everything will work out fine, Grandmother, as soon as we figure all of this out."

She nodded and looked back down, stroking the worn leather. "I can remember your grandfather sitting at the desk writing in it. He always used to say how important it was for the leader to write down anything that would help his successor." She looked at each of them. "When I saw how you all reacted to Lacey and realized that she's the mate for all of you, it reminded me of something your grandfather told me many years ago. It's written in the journal along with details and notes for all of you to read."

Seth led his grandmother to a seat. "What is it, Grandmother?"

"I'll get you some tea," Victor said and stood.

"No. Victor. Please sit down. I want you to hear this, too. My grandsons are going to need all the help and guidance they can get. With my son gone, you and Rolph are the only ones I trust to see them through this. I would consider any advice you could offer my grandsons a personal favor." She patted his hand in a rare show of affection.

Lars frowned. "What are you talking about, Grandmother?"

Damien's gaze kept sliding to his brothers. Whether they liked it or not, they were all in this together. Used to being in charge of his own pack, his own destiny, to think that he now had to share decisions with others didn't set well with him. He turned back, alarmed to see that his grandmother's eyes had filled with tears. She took a shuddering breath, alarming Damien even more. "Your grandfather told me something a very long time ago that I'd completely forgotten until this afternoon."

She took a breath and leaned back in her chair. "As all of you know, weres mate for life." She glanced at Victor in sympathy before continuing. "After the mating, a were's mate carries his or her scent, which warns off other weres. Most weres respect it and very few actually have the courage to touch another's mate. Unlike your father."

A ghost of a smile curved her lips. "But I remember shortly after we were mated, I teased your grandfather. I asked him what would happen if another werewolf showed up at the door, claiming that he caught my scent and that I was his mate also. I thought he would laugh about it. Instead, he took my question very seriously. He told me that in very rare instances, more than one were would claim the same woman as their mate. In every case his ancestors had written about, the werewolves had common blood."

"Like us?" Damien asked gently, amazed that he'd never heard of this until today. How the hell had he missed this part of pack history? If his father had been able to keep his dick in his pants, maybe he would have lived long enough to share this.

"Like you," their grandmother smiled and nodded. "The only ones that would have heard about this would be the pack elders. I never knew the weres it happened to before. They left the pack before I could meet them." She smiled at Rolph. "Anyway, years ago they would fight to the death and the winner would claim the woman as his mate. And every time that happened, those involved suffered. No children came out of the union and both ended up unhappy. But several times pack members shared a woman."

"What happened?" Wes asked.

She gestured toward the book on the desk. "According to that, they were all very happy. Your grandfather told me that after the initial mating, it was good for all involved. Children came out of the union and the men and their mates have all been deliriously happy."

Damien scrubbed a hand over his face, hardly believing any of this. As a pack leader, shouldn't he have known this kind of thing? Ever since Lacey had walked through the door he'd been floundering, something that didn't sit well with him at all. Because of being raised separately from his brothers, each dealing with only their own individual packs, none had ever seen the whole picture. Suddenly, everything became clear. The only way they would be able to successfully lead the pack, would be to do it together, the way they handled O'Reilly. He turned back to the others, not wanting to miss anything. As soon as they finished here he needed to go for a run to get rid of some of this restlessness.

Rolph nodded. "It's true. It's a good sign. Good fortune has always come to the pack when a mate is shared, especially if the mate is not were."

Wes nodded and frowned at his grandmother. "What did you mean, after the initial mating?"

Their grandmother blushed. "That's something you're all going to have to read for yourselves." She stood and they all automatically followed suit. "I'm going to leave the book with you. It belongs to all of you now. I assume you'll reunite the pack and lead it together?"

"So much for our birthday surprise," Lars grumbled.

She laughed delightedly. "You couldn't have given me a finer present." She sobered and looked at each of them in turn. "I know what happened upstairs. Please don't put too much pressure on Lacey. She's been through a lot. With her parents dying before she was born, her grandmother raised her. Poor Lacey stayed home to look after Lily and didn't get to go out and have fun like the others her age. Then, just as she gets a good job and gets her life together, her grandmother dies, leaving her all alone. Poor thing."

Damien gaped at his grandmother. "Poor thing? She ripped us a new one and kicked us out." Surprised to realize that he was filled with pride at how well his mate had handled all of them, he couldn't keep from grinning. That didn't mean he still didn't want to paddle her ass. Christ, he got turned on just thinking about it.

Wes chuckled, while Lars just stared at their grandmother incredulously.

Seth laughed outright and put an arm around her. "Don't worry about her anymore. I promise you, we'll take good care of our mate."

Lars sat, frowning thoughtfully. "I'd forgotten that she never knew her parents. Wasn't there some kind of accident?"

Damien listened with interest, realizing just how little he really knew about his mate. Their grandmother had spoken about her for years, but he didn't realize until now just how little attention he'd paid. Christ, what the hell had he been doing all these years? This had been a hell of a wake-up call. Frustration at his own stupidity ate at him. Their grandmother had been right all along. By not leading the pack together, they'd missed so much. Too much. He'd been sent into a tailspin by all of this and needed to get it together.

Their grandmother nodded sadly. "There was a car accident. Lacey had to be taken by cesarean when her mother died. I flew out there to be with Lily who suddenly had a newborn to take care of and two funerals to plan. We were all little Lacey had. Now that Lily's gone, I'm the only family she has left."

Damien smiled and shook his head at the 'little Lacey'. For someone so small, she packed quite a punch. He should have known by all that red hair. Everything would change now. His life. His home.

His—*their* pack. He and his brothers would figure this out. How? He had no idea. But somehow he would have his mate and find his footing again. He hated being unnerved this way, hated the uncertainty of the entire situation. But he did his best to reassure their grandmother. "You're never going to have to worry about Lacey being alone again, grandmother. We're her family, too. We'll figure this out somehow."

Lars sighed. "Well, it appears you get your birthday wish all around. We *have* to get along and this means we'll all be spending quite a bit of time together. I'm moving in today."

Wes went to their grandmother and kissed her cheek. "We're going to make mistakes, Grandmother. But I promise you, we'll do whatever we have to in order to work this out. Don't worry about it anymore."

Damien grimaced. Jesus, what a mess. He murmured his agreement along with the others, trying to show a confidence he didn't feel. He just wanted his mate, damn it.

Grandmother smiled. "I've told her stories about werewolves since she was a baby. She thinks that's all they are. Stories. I'll talk to her. I'll explain everything. Now I'm going to leave you alone to figure all this out amongst yourselves. Read the pages I've marked." She started for the door, turning when she reached it. "And put some ice on those bruises."

They watched her go, Victor and Rolph, right behind her. As soon as everyone left, Damien and his brothers crowded around the book.

Lars began flipping pages. "Let's see what the hell grandmother was talking about."

* * * *

Damien rubbed his burning eyes. It had taken almost an hour to finish reading everything their ancestors had written about pack members sharing a mate. They made it sound not only possible, but like Rolph said, something to celebrate. Amazing.

He closed the book and dropped into a chair. "Damn it. We're going to have to explain all of this to her and go really slow. I'm sure she doesn't have any experience with having four men make love to her at once," he added sarcastically. He fought off images of his brothers touching her when it only stirred his anger again. Fuck, he needed to run.

Lars ran his hand over the leather. "What choice do we have? Now that we've found her, none of us is willing to live without her. *We* have to figure out how we're going to get along well enough to make this work."

Wes bit off a curse. "So, the first time, we have to mate with her together, make sure that our seed mixes inside her. This is going to be hard for all of us," Wes said as he refilled drinks. "But according to the journal, we can't take her separately until her body has adjusted to all of us. If one of us does, the others won't be able to truly mate with her. She wouldn't carry the other's scent, for one thing. Her true mate would also be the only one with a strong bond to her."

Bile rose in Damien's throat at the mental image of his brothers touching his mate's naked body. "We have no choice, if we're agreed that she'll belong to all of us." Damien tossed back his whiskey, and slammed the glass down, surprising himself by shattering it. He took several deep breaths, forcing himself to calm down before speaking. "I hope like hell we can do this. We've never been real enemies but we've never really been close. Now it looks like we'll be sleeping in the same bed, sharing a woman, raising children together. How the hell are we supposed to know who the father is?"

Lars turned from the window, his expression fierce. "It won't matter. It can't matter. We're all in this together, no matter what. Every child she bears will belong to all of us."

Wes stared down at his glass. "We're going to have to make all decisions together. We can't fight around Lacey like we did earlier. She has to believe we're in agreement. We can't give her conflicting instructions or send mixed messages. We all have to be on the same page with her. She has to know that we all know what's best for her. And we have to make her feel comfortable coming to any of us. If we do what we did earlier, she's never going to let any of us near her."

Damien understood the worry he saw on his brother's face. This certainly wasn't what he'd envisioned when he thought about taking a mate. Mating by vote. Christ. "We're all in agreement then. But I'm going to be honest. I don't know how in the hell I'm going to be able to watch all of you touch my mate without wanting to rip your fucking throats out." Just thinking about it made him crazy.

Seth opened the book again, flipping back through the yellowed pages. "It says in here that after the mating, she'll carry the scent of all of us. I've never heard of such a thing."

Lars chuckled. "It's certainly going to warn other werewolves off. With her carrying the scent of all four of us, she should be much safer from any advances or threats. The warning scent she'll give off would be overwhelming."

Seth curled his lip. "It's a good thing. I'm going to have enough trouble with the three of you touching her. If someone else tries, I'll kill them."

Lars nodded. "We're going to have to talk to her when she comes down. We'll have to explain that's she's mate to all of us, and assure her that what happened earlier will not be repeated." He raised a brow when Damien shot him a dirty look. "We'll all have to spend time with her alone, but not now. This is too important to mess up."

Wes grimaced. "She still doesn't know we're werewolves. It might be a bit much to put on her all at once."

Damien scrubbed his face. "We're going to have to tell her about that, too. I want everything laid out so Lacey knows what to expect. No secrets. Let's put everything on the table with her and with each other right up front, or this is never going to work."

Wes leaned forward and dropped his face in his hands, and groaned. "I can only imagine how she's going to take all of this.

Hopefully better than we did."

* * * *

Lacey woke, filled with a sense of anticipation and at first couldn't remember why. She blinked her eyes open and sat up quickly, as it all came back to her that she was now at her godmother's house. Remembering the fight, she blew out a breath and sank back against the pillows.

Wonderful. Only hours after arriving and already her visit had caused trouble.

She threw off the quilt and headed for her suitcase. Too bad. They would have to just get over it. She hadn't done anything wrong and wasn't about to let them ruin her visit to Nana. They would just have to get over themselves. Why the hell would they get so mad because Seth put his arms around her? They had acted like a bunch of Neanderthals and she wouldn't put up with it. Now that she didn't feel so groggy, she felt better able to handle them.

Grabbing her clothes and heading for the bathroom, she promised herself that she would lay into them if they started that nonsense again. They didn't live here, and she doubted they would be around much. Wait, what had Seth said about moving in here?

Shampooing her hair, she tried to remember but couldn't. She'd been so damned tired at that point, she hadn't paid much attention. Plus, once he'd touched her, her mind had turned to mush.

As she got dressed, her stomach growled, reminding her just how long it had been since she'd last eaten. She glanced toward where she'd seen a clock before. Gone. It must have gotten broken in the fight. Picking up her watch from the dresser, she grimaced. She'd missed lunch but was too hungry to wait for dinner. Slipping on her sandals, she glanced at her laptop. No. Checking her email would have to wait. Her stomach growled again as she stepped out into the hallway.

Once she got downstairs, she heard voices coming from the back of the house. Assuming the kitchen would be in that direction, she started back, nearly jumping out of her skin when Seth called out. "We're back here, Lacey."

She hadn't made any noise and wondered how he'd known of her presence. Her stomach growled again and she giggled. If she didn't eat something soon, they'd hear her stomach back in Ohio.

Thinking of back home made her angry so she determinedly pushed those thoughts away. Walking into the kitchen, she saw Lars, Damien, Wes and Seth all sitting around the table. Her breath caught at the way their gazes all zeroed in on her.

"Where's Nana?"

Seth smiled at her. "She had last minute instructions for the caterers and had Victor drive her into town. I think she's adding your favorites to the menu."

She moved toward him. "She didn't have to do that. Look at you." She brushed his hair back from his forehead, wincing at the cut she saw there. "Does that hurt?"

* * * *

Seth wasn't a stupid man. He hid a grin at his brother's glares and allowed Lacey to tend to him. He didn't tell her that the bruising and cuts would all be gone by the time he woke up in the morning. His groin tightened at the first touch of her soft hand on his face. Breathing in her scent had his cock coming to attention and he had to fist his hands on his thighs to keep from reaching for her. He bit back a moan as she traced the bruising around his eyes.

"We should put some more ice on that. Jeez, Nana's gonna love you showing up at her party with two black eyes."

Seth watched her tight ass as she rummaged through the drawers for a towel. He watched the sway of her hips as she moved to the freezer. When she came back with the ice filled towel and placed it over his eye, he couldn't take his eyes off of her breasts only inches away. When he noticed that her little nipples poked at the front of her cotton shirt, a groan escaped before he could prevent it, earning another look of concern from her and scowls from his brothers. He lifted his hand to hold the towel, but also to hide the grin he shot at his brothers, barely containing his laughter as Damien flipped him off.

"I want to know why all of you acted like a bunch of bone heads and started fighting."

Lars said softly. "There are some things we need to talk to you about."

Seth obediently held the ice in place, coughing to hide his laughter as Wes angled his face so Lacey would also notice his black eyes.

Seth grinned when she ignored Wes completely. Apparently, she only tended to the victim, not the one who'd caused the fight to begin with. He'd have to remember that.

"I can't believe you all fought that way, like children. If you did it because of me, you're way off base. Seth held me, but I really don't see that it's any of your business, especially since it won't be happening again."

Like hell it wouldn't happen again.

Grateful that his thought hadn't come spurting out of his mouth, Seth dropped the ice pack on the table. "Sit down, Lacey. Please. We want to explain some things to you."

Wondering how she would take this knotted his stomach. Once she was seated, he glanced at each of his brothers before beginning. "The others were pissed off at me because I'd touched you." When her face tightened and she opened her mouth to speak, Seth lifted a hand. "Wait. Let us explain some things to you. When we're done, we'll answer all your questions."

When Lacey nodded and sat back in her chair, Seth continued. "We've known about you your entire life. Grandmother talked about you a lot over the years, but I have to admit I never paid much attention. But when the four of us met you yesterday, each of us knew right away that you're the woman we want in our lives."

Lacey flew out of her chair. "What? All *four* of you decided- Are you crazy?"

Lars reached for her hand, holding onto it when she would have pulled away. "We thought the same thing. We couldn't believe that the same woman was our—that we each wanted the same woman. We already know a lot about you from our grandmother, and I know you know a lot about us."

"Yes, but that doesn't mean we know each other well enough to make a decision like that. And, I'm sorry, I can't be with all four of you."

"Why not?" Damien asked quietly. He stood and moved closer to her. "Lars, Wes, Seth and I have never really been close. We fought the idea, but decided that none of us is willing to be without you." He held up a hand when she tried to speak. "I know we just met. The reason we fought earlier was jealousy. We just want you to know that it's no longer an issue."

Wes leaned forward. "We knew that after that fight, you wouldn't want any more to do with us. We all want, very much to spend some time with you and we knew you wouldn't even give us a chance if you thought it would cause another fight or any kind of trouble between us."

Seth gripped her hand, desperate to get through to her. "We just want you to know that we're not going to compete for you. We *all* want you. I know it's too soon for you, but all we want is for you to give us a chance. We'll go slowly, but please don't worry that spending time with any one of us will cause another fight. It won't."

Lacey pulled out of his grip and stood, moving several feet away and leaning back on the counter. "You're all crazy. You're my godmother's grandsons. What would she think if she knew all of you want me in your lives?"

Seth grinned. "She already knows and is thrilled."

Lacey arched a brow. "Really?" She shook her head. "Look, I

don't know anything about your lives, but I can't even imagine having a relationship with four men. Plus, like you said, we hardly know each other. And I won't be here long. I have to work. I have bills to pay."

Lars stood and moved to her. "You don't have to work." He raised a hand when she opened her mouth. "I didn't say you can't, I said you don't *have* to. If you're going to live here with us, believe me, you'll have enough responsibility here to keep you busy."

Lacey's eyes narrowed. "Did Nana put you up to this? She always says I need to find a man, someone to take care of me. And she keeps asking me to move in here. Oh, I see. She wants all of you to spend time with me and the one that I fall for has to convince me to stay here with him. You'd probably even marry me to please Nana, wouldn't you? Then I'd be stuck with a man who didn't love me and only married me to please his grandmother. Look, I appreciate your concern for Nana. It's really nice. But I'm not falling for this. Nice try, though."

Damien leapt to his feet, spinning her around when she would have walked away. "You think we're going crazy, wondering how the hell we can all have you, all to please our grandmother? We're talking forever here, Lacey. I love my grandmother, but I'm not willing to sacrifice my life just to relieve her worries about you."

Lacey stared at them in disbelief. "Do you hear what you're all saying? You met me *today* and you're talking about commitment with not one, but all *four* of you. One woman with *four* men. I don't even know you and you certainly don't know me! I'm a teacher, for God's sake. I can't do something like that."

Seth wondered at the look that passed over her face, but it disappeared as quickly as it had come.

"Besides, how the hell can I have a relationship with all of you? I'm assuming we're talking forever and babies, not just sex."

Damien gripped her chin. "Sex, forever and babies. All of us. Together and separately. Forever." He pulled her against him, wrapping his arms around her and covering her lips with his.

As much as Seth wanted to look away, he couldn't. Jealousy stirred, but he couldn't keep from smiling. He knew Damien's reputation with women. Hell, all of them had always been very sexual people. Werewolves thrived on sex.

The sounds she made went straight to his cock and he watched, amused as Lars and Wes both shifted in their seat, obviously similarly afflicted. Neither could take their eyes off of them.

Lacey ripped out of his grasp and Seth knew it was only because Damien allowed it. His brother usually had a short fuse and he could see just what this cost him. He knew Damien well enough to know that he wanted his woman, and he wanted her *now*. Surprised to find he knew more about Damien than he'd thought, he stood, moving between them, to give his brother a chance to regain control.

Seth took Lacey's hand, pressing her palm to his chest, barely biting back a moan at the jolt of electricity that went through him. His cock pushed painfully at his zipper and he shifted uncomfortably. He couldn't wait to get her under him, couldn't wait until they could mate with her. Then she would belong to all of them forever. "Lacey, we know this is a lot to take in. I know you're wondering how we could possibly know that we want you on such short acquaintance. I'll have to ask you to just trust us in that for now. Just know that we won't change our minds. We know what we want. It's you. It won't change tomorrow or next week, or next year. We want you to believe that and know that we have every intention of making you our woman."

He leaned down and touched his lips to hers, with the intention of letting her see just how serious they all were about sharing her. He and the others had stood by while Damien had kissed her, and he wanted her to see that the others wouldn't interfere while he did. His intentions went right out the window as soon as his lips touched hers. He forgot everything but getting closer to her. He cupped her head, angling it to give him the best access to her delectable mouth. Deepening his kiss, he pulled her against him, letting her feel his hardness pressing against the zipper of his jeans. God, he'd never experienced a kiss like this before. She tasted like sin and sunshine. He wanted to consume her. Feeling her breasts pressed against his chest, a low rumble escaped from his throat.

The scent of her arousal drifted to him and every muscle in his body tightened as he fought the primal instinct to mate. The need to rip her clothes off her body and plunge into her became almost unbearable.

When he finally lifted his head, both of them fought for air. Now he knew what Damien had experienced. *Jesus.* What he'd heard about it being more intense with your mate didn't come close. She'd turned him inside out with only a kiss. He could only imagine what fucking her would be like.

He fought every possessive instinct as Lars came close and raised a brow at him. Nodding reluctantly, Seth handed her over to his brother.

Seth moved to lean against the doorway. His cock had gotten so hard, he knew he couldn't sit. He watched as Lars tugged a dazed Lacey into his arms and pulled her head against his chest, bending to touch his cheek to the top of her head.

"We won't rush you, baby. We just don't want you to avoid being alone with any of us, fearing that the others would be upset. We know how you feel about our grandmother. Believe me, she's thrilled with our decision. The only thing preventing our being together is you."

Lacey leaned back to look up at him, blinking as though trying to focus. "And the fact that I don't love any of you any more than any of you love me."

Lars kissed her lingeringly. "All of that will come in time. We belong together. We already know it. You soon will, too."

Wes stepped forward and Seth couldn't take his eyes from the sight of him taking Lacey into his arms and kissing her hungrily. Holding her and kissing her this way hadn't been planned, but he was glad that they'd done it. Maybe now she would understand and see that none of them got pissed off or territorial.

Wes ended the kiss and trailed a hand down her arm, looking more than a little unsettled. "All we ask is that you give us a chance. There's no rush. We just wanted you to know how we feel. Give us a chance to show you how good it'll be."

Lacey looked at each of them in turn, releasing a shuddering breath. "This is beyond crazy. There's no way I can be with four men. I can't even fall for one of you, let alone all four. This can never happen." She turned and walked out the way she'd come in.

Damien started after her, but Lars pulled him up short.

"Let her be. Give her a little time alone to think about what we've said. I don't want any of us to pressure her. She's already skittish and I want her to calm down so we can tell her the rest of it."

Seth scrubbed a hand over his the back of his neck. "At least she listened. I just wonder what's going to happen when we *do* tell her the rest of it."

Wes reached into the refrigerator for a bottle of water. "We should each spend some time alone with her, talk to her. I think it'll make her a little more comfortable with us if she gets to know each of us a little better."

Lars nodded and started out of the room. "Yeah, and I'm going to go after that mouth again. Damn."

Damien called after his brother. "As long as that's as far as you go."

Seth looked at the others, still fighting to cool down. "We're going to have to trust each other not to take her alone. We're in this together, remember?"

Wes chugged his water and tossed the bottle toward the recycling bin. "God help us."

Chapter Four

Lacey grabbed her purse and keys and went out the front door, anxious to get away for awhile. Her rumbling stomach reminded her that she hadn't eaten, so she got into her car and headed for the town she'd driven through yesterday. With Nana away, she didn't trust herself or them enough to stay.

She started down the long drive, her body still humming and her mind spinning. She still couldn't believe the conversation they'd just had. Could they possibly be serious? Her senses went on overdrive, just imagining the possibilities.

"Stop it, Lacey. Don't even think about it."

She pulled out onto the road and headed toward town. She had to get her head together before she went back. She felt as though she would wake up any second to find that this entire day had been a dream.

They didn't even know her. Today she didn't feel like she even knew herself.

She'd felt a little off ever since she got here. She was usually opinionated and outspoken, something that had just recently gotten her fired. She had a temper, but didn't often lose it. She had today. Their fight and arrogant attitudes had infuriated her.

What they'd said and done to her in the kitchen threatened to bring her to her knees.

The effect all four of them had on her astounded her. Her body still hummed with an arousal that went all the way to her core. It shook her, how quickly the need had built inside her. And they'd only kissed her.

She had no experience with need like this. When Damien had kissed her, shock had kept her immobile until it was too late to stop him. After the first touch of his lips on hers, she couldn't have stopped if she'd wanted to. He'd pulled her under, drowning her in sensation with just a kiss.

She'd stood there, stunned as each man kissed her, each differently, yet all with the same effect.

Their techniques and their tastes had been as different as night and day. But each one took her to a place she'd never been before. Each one drew something from her she hadn't known she possessed, gave her something she hadn't known she needed. They made her feel like for the first time in her life, she didn't know herself at all.

It unsettled the hell out of her. She'd always been in control of her life every step of the way. Knowing she could never be what they apparently wanted from her did nothing to alleviate the feelings that bombarded her.

Lust. Need. Desire.

Denial. Fear. Disbelief.

As she drove, she went over what they'd said to her over and over and still couldn't process it. How could they possibly live the way Lars, Damien, Wes and Seth proposed?

Why did it tempt her so much to try?

What the hell was she thinking? Of course it would never work. They hardly knew each other. Sure, they sort of had a history because of her relationship with their grandmother but she'd only met them *today.*

She had to just put it out of her mind. Yeah, right.

She would spend the next few days visiting her godmother, send out resumes and then she would leave. Jeez, she must be even more frazzled than she thought, just to entertain such an idea.

She reached town only minutes later and parked in front of a small diner.

She got out and looked around, smiling. Several small businesses lined one side of the street, including an ice cream store. Maybe she would bring Nana to town for ice cream. They could spend some time alone here, away from the far too distracting presence of her grandsons. Hearing children playing, she looked across the street and saw a small park she hadn't noticed when she'd driven through earlier.

Aware of the stares she drew, she went inside the diner. She'd just finished ordering when a man walked in that drew her attention. Tall, leanly muscled, with short black hair, he looked around briefly before his gaze settled on her. Blue eyes. Jeez, did men who looked like this grow on trees around here?

She had the strangest feeling that he'd been looking for her. Her suspicions were confirmed when he walked straight toward her table.

"May I join you?"

Lacey sighed. "Look, I'm not looking for a—"

"Please, I'd just like to talk to you for a minute or two. You're Eleanor Tougarret's goddaughter, aren't you?"

"Yes, I am. Who are you?"

"Oh, I'm sorry. My name is Steven Galbraith. Can I talk to you for a minute?"

He looked so much like Wes it amazed her. That, and the fact that she sat in a crowded diner and he apparently knew her godmother, had her nodding. Once he'd taken his seat, she couldn't help staring at him. "You look a lot like Wes, my godmother's grandson. As a matter of fact, you look like all of them. Do you know them?"

Steven chuckled. "No. I know *of* them. But we've never met."

After the waitress left, she turned back to him. "How did you know who I was, and why did I get the feeling you were looking for me when you came in?"

Dimples slashed his cheeks. "Everybody around here knows about you already. It's a very tight knit community. So this is your first visit here?"

Lacey nodded. "Yes, I couldn't come before. My grandmother

couldn't travel. Do you live far from here?"

"No, I only live about five miles from here."

"You only live five miles away but you've never met the Tougarret men?"

He smiled sadly. "They've never lived at the mansion and we do our best to avoid each other."

Lacey frowned. "And already you've heard about me? That's a little odd, don't you think?"

Steven shrugged. "Like I said, we all know what goes on around here."

"So what are you doing here today?"

"I came to see you."

"What? You were coming to the house?"

He threw back his head and laughed. "No. Your men are very protective of you and wouldn't have allowed me to meet you. I had every intention of driving past the house to see if I could get a glimpse of you. I had a description of you, and when I saw a redhead on the sidewalk, looking around the way a tourist does, I took a chance. I'm glad I did."

"Look, I thought you were friends of theirs. Maybe you'd better go."

Neither said anything as the waitress brought her order, giving Steven a dirty look.

"Brushing me off, huh?" He shook his head. "Listen, I know you don't know me, and I know all of this might sound a little strange to you. There are a lot of things you don't know, but if you ever need a friend, I want you to call me. My office and cell phone numbers are on the card." He pulled a card out of his pocket and offered it to her.

Lacey stared at the card for several seconds before accepting it. She had no idea why she'd taken it, but thought it couldn't hurt. "I don't know what it is you want from me. I won't be here long and doubt if I'll call you."

He sighed. "I've looked for something for a long time and when I heard about you, I wondered— Forget it. Listen, there are a lot of strange things that go on around here. If you ever feel you need a friend, someone to talk to, I want you to call me. I'd like very much for us to be friends."

"What kind of strange things?"

Steven shook his head. "Things about your men that I can't tell you. Things about the town that I don't have time to explain. Things about me. Just remember I'll be here for you if you need someone."

"Are you coming to Nana's birthday party tomorrow night?"

Steven threw back his head and laughed, before sobering and smiling sadly. "There's nothing I'd like more. I'd love to be friends with your men, but it's just not possible. They hate my father for something that he did years ago. I can't blame them. But, because they hate my father, they hate me. They don't realize that I'm as much a victim as they are." His eyes sharpened. "But if you ever need anything, anything at all, I want you to call me. If you get scared or sad or just need someone to talk to, you can call me. I have a law office in the next town."

"You're a lawyer?"

He smiled again. "Yeah, trying to make things right where I can. Now, I've got to go before your men get here." He gestured toward the waitress. "I'm sure Ida called them. They won't like it that you talked to me. I'm sorry if it causes any trouble for you. I just had to know."

Lacey blinked. "Had to know what?"

"If you were the one," he smiled sadly, turned and walked away.

* * * *

She had only taken a couple of bites of her lunch when a squeal of tires made her look out the window. A huge SUV, taking up two spaces had been parked haphazardly next to her car.

Lars got out of the driver's seat, his brothers each slamming their doors, their faces grim, as they got out and followed him into the diner. Lacey looked back down at her plate with a sigh. She had no idea why they were acting this way, but she had to put a stop to it. What she did was none of their business. Having already seen their tempers, she shoved the card Steven had given her into her pocket, not wanting to give them fuel for their anger.

All four stormed into the diner, somehow managing to do it gracefully, but she winced when the door hit the wall behind it. They looked furious as they strode straight to her table. Lars nudged her aside and slid into the booth next to her, Damien and Seth across from her. Wes stood at the end of the table.

Lars leaned close, his arm resting on the back of her seat. "What do you think you're doing?"

Lacey blinked, ignoring the glares from the other men. "Excuse me?"

"You were talking to Steven Galbraith. You had lunch with him."

She gestured toward her plate. "I had lunch. He didn't."

The waitress hurried over and brought coffee for all the men, smiling and greeting each of them, all the while shaking her head at Lacey.

When the waitress left, Damien leaned forward, pushing his coffee aside. "We know he followed you in here. What did he say to you?"

Lacey reached for her iced tea. "Nothing. He just introduced himself, that's all. Said he wanted to meet me. What's the big deal if I talk to someone?"

Lars took the glass from her hand and set it on the table with a thud and gripped her chin. "You stay away from him. If you see him, you run like hell, do you understand me?"

"Run? Are you crazy? He's a nice man. Why the hell would I run from him?"

Wes leaned over the table. "Do you have any idea just how much danger you were in? He could have killed you in a heartbeat, and we wouldn't have been around to help you."

"Killed me? You people are crazy. Listen, I don't know what kind of game you're playing—"

Lars clenched his jaw. "You think this is some kind of a fucking game?" He pulled her against his chest, wrapping his arms around her, almost desperately. "When I think about what could have happened, Jesus." He released her and pulled her hand, dragging her from the booth. "Come on, we're taking you home."

Wes reached for his wallet, but the waitress stopped him. "It's already been paid for."

"Damn it," Wes muttered. "I don't even want this guy buying her lunch."

Lacey opened her mouth to ask what the big deal was, but when he shot an icy glance at her, she snapped her mouth shut. She didn't want to argue in the diner. Already several of the patrons stared at them, smiling and shouting greetings to the men.

When they got outside, she pulled out her keys, jerking them out of Seth's range when he reached for them. "I'm driving my own car back."

Seth clenched his jaw. "Fine, I'll ride with you."

Lars opened the driver's door of the SUV. "We'll be right behind you."

Driving back to the house, Lacey turned to Seth. "Why are all of you acting this way? Why would you say something like that about Steven? What's going on around here? Why in the world would you think that he would hurt me?"

Seth sighed. "Lacey, there's a lot you don't know. Everything has happened so fast. When we get home, we'll try to explain all of this to you, but you're not going to want to believe us."

"What are you talking about? What am I not going to want to believe?'

"Not now. Wait until we get back. But Lacey, no matter what, I want you to remember that my brothers and I would do anything to protect you. We know what's best for you, and you're just going to have to believe that."

Insulted, Lacey snapped. "You know what's best for me? Listen, you and your brothers better get a grip because if you think you're going to tell me what to do while I'm here—"

Seth's own temper flared. "You're not leaving here, Lacey. This is where you belong. All of us will do whatever it takes to keep you here."

Furious, Lacey glared at him. "Who the hell do you think you are? I'm leaving here in a few days, and none of you are going to stop me. I can't believe any of this."

"We're your mates, damn it! And we'll never let you go. Get that idea out of your head right now."

Lacey could do nothing but stare at him and almost missed the turn to the driveway. She said nothing until she pulled up to the house and shut the car off. Slowly, she turned to him. "Mates? Did I hear you right? Did you say that I'm your mate?"

Seth sighed and rubbed a hand over his face. "Yeah. I wasn't supposed to tell you that until we were all together. You're my mate, and my brothers' mate."

Rendered speechless, Lacey just stared at him.

The men got out of the SUV and came up beside her car. Wes opened her door and offered his hand. "Come on, let's go inside."

She ignored him and turned back to Seth. "The only time I've ever heard anyone talk about *mates* is when Nana tells her stories about werewolves. Seth, you do know that they're just stories, don't you?"

Lars cursed. "Seth, what the fuck did you say?"

As Wes helped Lacey out of the car, Seth scrambled out on the other side. "Shut up. She was talking about leaving. She thinks we're all crazy. It slipped out."

Victor opened the door as they walked up to it. "Your godmother is in the sitting room. She asks that you join her." He looked at the men. "You, too."

A glance at each of the men found them all watching her, frustration and anger clearly apparent on their faces. She looked away from them and walked across the foyer to the sitting room to join Nana. She sighed, resigned, when they followed her.

* * * *

Steven could feel the tension before he even walked into his parents' house.

"Stop nagging me and clean this mess."

Steven winced at his father's tone. Perhaps the time had come again to try to convince his mother to leave her husband. She hadn't listened so far and wondered what the hell it would take to convince her to go.

Walking into the house, he went straight back to the kitchen, fighting not to show any emotion. He knew his father would smell his anger, though. The scent of his father's anger reached him, a scent he'd become very familiar with. And the scent of his mother's fear, another scent he'd grown up with.

He nodded toward where his father sat drinking coffee. "Hello, father."

"What are you doing here?"

Accustomed to his father's deep, angry growls, Steven didn't even flinch. His father, a big, burly man, had always been a fearsome and respected leader of the pack. His father was an Alpha who never backed down and never, ever, changed his mind about anything.

Aaron Galbraith was a hard man, a man filled with bitterness, rage and self-pity.

And as far back as Steven could remember, his father had hated his mother. And him.

His mother, washing dishes, beamed when she saw him.

"I came to see mother. Hello mother." He bent to kiss her cheek and leaned against the counter next to her. "What's he pissed off about this time?"

Glancing nervously toward the table, she shook her head. "It's nothing. Your father's a busy man. He has a lot on his mind and I was bothering him. Why don't you sit down and have a cup of coffee with him? Have you had lunch?" Her hands fluttered, splashing dishwater and she talked too fast, the way she normally did around her husband.

Steven spared her a glance and shook his head. "I'm fine."

She glanced toward the table again, not meeting her husband's eyes. "Your father's meeting with some of his key advisors. Maybe you should join them."

His father growled. "I don't want Steven at the meeting. Jesus woman, you're a fucking nag. If I had wanted him at the meeting I would have ordered him to be there. This is none of his business. Or yours."

Steven met his father's eyes squarely, allowing himself a small smile. "You only want me around when you need legal advice, right? Well, I'm too busy today anyway. When you need me you'll have to make an appointment."

His father sat back and scowled. "I hear the Tougarret pack has company. They're not going to find it easy to reunite their pack."

Steven felt a heavy weight settle in his stomach. He shrugged, trying to appear nonchalant. "They can deal with whoever tries to stop them. They'll be much stronger now. You won't find it so easy to cause them trouble anymore."

As he'd hoped, his father slammed his cup down and shot to his feet, knocking his chair over in the process. "Fuck both of you." Scowling at both of them, he stormed out of the kitchen and out the front door, slamming it behind him.

Steven turned to his mother. "Why the hell do you stay with that asshole? You don't have to live this way. Go pack and I'll get you out of here."

Drying her hands on a dishtowel, his mother turned away. "You know your father would never let me go. I'm the Alpha female. Besides, I would be lost without him. He's still a little upset with me, that's all. Once he gets over it, everything will be back to normal."

Fighting his anger, Steven gripped her arms. "He's been *upset* with you for thirty-five years. This *is* normal."

His mother frustrated him even more when she patted his hand. "Nonsense. He just has a lot on his mind. Why don't you try to spend some time with him this week? He's really agitated. He doesn't like the idea that the Tougarret pack is uniting again."

Steven sighed and muttered under his breath. "How can you tell?"

His mother waved that away. "Tell me what happened. Did you see her?"

Nodding, he opened the cupboard and grabbed a cup. Now that his father was gone he'd sit with his mother for a bit. "I saw her."

She took the cup from his hand and poured the coffee herself, nudging him toward the table. "And?"

Steven took a seat and accepted the cup. "She's beautiful. She's got red hair and gorgeous green eyes. And no, she's not my mate."

* * * *

Lacey stared at her godmother in shock. "Nana, what do you mean, all those stories you told me are true? There's no such thing as werewolves."

They had all gathered in the sitting room. Victor had just walked in the room with a pitcher of iced tea when her godmother made her startling statement.

Her godmother smiled gently. "I assure you, every story I ever told you was true. There's nothing to fear. Especially for you, sweetheart. Do you remember the stories I told you about werewolves finding their mates?"

Lacey couldn't believe any of this. "I feel like I've been dreaming since I got here. You don't really expect me to believe this is true, do you?"

Victor had stayed behind after placing the tray on the table, and stood behind her godmother's chair. He looked at each of the men in turn. "You're going to have to show her."

All four men stood. Lars held out an arm. "Not all of us. She's going to get scared. Damien and I will shift."

Lacey's stomach turned over at his tone. She'd already begun shaking nervously, as the atmosphere in the room became surreal. Wes and Seth came to stand beside her chair as she slid forward.

"There's nothing to fear, I promise," her godmother said softly.

Lacey slid a glance at her but kept her attention on Lars and Damien. They toed off their shoes and stripped off their shirts, their eyes never leaving her face. In a blink of an eye, two large black wolves stood where they had been a split second earlier. Shaking off the rest of their clothing, they moved closer. She yelped and started to bolt, but Wes and Seth held her in place with a hand on each arm.

Both knelt at her knees. Seth rubbed her arm and frowned. "You're shaking. There's nothing to be afraid of. It's Lars and Damien. They would never hurt you."

Lacey couldn't take her eyes off of the wolves. Both were completely black and had blue eyes. They stayed several feet away, watching her and remaining completely still. "It's not possible." Her words came out in a whisper. "Werewolves don't exist."

Wes lifted her hand to his mouth, kissing her knuckles. "You saw it yourself. If you don't trust us, at least you trust Grandmother. Do you think she would lie to you?"

She looked up to see her godmother and Victor both watching her. "It's all true?"

Nana smiled. "Yes, honey. And nothing could make me happier than learning that you're the mate to my grandsons."

Lacey looked back at the wolves. "How can I be the mate to four men?"

Her godmother stood and came close, leaning down to kiss her cheek. "It's happened with the pack before, although not with the Alphas'. You'll be the Alpha female of the pack. It will be so nice to have you living here. I've missed you so much. Now, Victor and I will leave all of you alone. Victor's going to drive me to Sheila's. We won't be home until dinner."

Lacey watched in disbelief as Nana and Victor left the room. The click of the closing door sounded loud in the dead silence as they left her alone with the men.

Four werewolves, who considered her their mate.

Chapter Five

Lacey trembled as the wolves approached. Even though she'd seen for herself that it was Lars and Damien, she couldn't stop shaking. How could she? Struggling to believe the unbelievable, she couldn't help but grip Wes and Seth's hands as the wolves slowly moved toward her. She couldn't think of them as Lars and Damien. She thought of them as dangerous animals, and she was afraid to move.

"Go ahead and pet them," Wes urged.

Lacey gulped. "Pet them?"

Wes and Seth both laughed. "It's Lars and Damien, Lacey. They would love if you pet them."

"Can they understand us?"

Seth patted her hand. "Of course they can. When any of us shift, we can't speak, but we can still communicate with each other, and with you when you learn to understand us."

Intrigued now, Lacey looked at Seth. "Show me."

Seth grinned. "Okay. First, do you see how they're standing?"

Lacey looked back at the wolves who now stood only about two feet away. "What about it?"

"See how stiff they are? See how their tails point straight out?"

"Yes. What does that mean?"

Wes laughed. "They're either tense or aroused, or both. Right now, I would guess tense. See how they both look as though they're ready to pounce. I think they're afraid you'll take off, afraid they frighten you. Reach out and pet them. Remember it's Lars and Damien."

When she put out her hand, they both moved closer. She petted them both, amazed at how silky their coats felt. "Their tails are wagging. Does that mean they're happy?"

Wes chuckled. "I would be happy, too, if you petted me like that."

Both wolves moved even closer, putting their heads on her knees as she continued to stroke their soft fur. "I should be running out the door screaming my head off. As unbelievable as all of this is, I guess growing up with all Nana's stories has made it a little easier to accept."

She stopped petting them and sat back, looking down to where the two of them still rested their heads on her knees. "It's still going to take some getting used to. And even though I'm starting to believe all this, I can't be your mate. It's not possible. There has to be some kind of mistake."

Wes leaned close, crowding her. "It's not a mistake." His mouth covered hers, his lips soft, but firm as they moved on hers, his tongue pushing past her lips to sweep inside. His hands warmed wherever they touched. When he covered her breasts, a whimper escaped as her nipples pressed into his palms.

When he lifted his head, her eyes fluttered opened. His hand caressed her jaw before settling there and running a thumb over her lips. "It's definitely not a mistake."

Lacey moaned when his mouth closed over her breast, and she hated that her shirt and bra kept her from feeling the moist heat on her bare skin. She gripped his shoulders, her eyes going wide to see Lars and Damien shift back, both *very* naked and *very* aroused.

Both men moved gracefully, their bodies leanly muscled, their chest lightly sprinkled with silky looking hair. Their cocks stood thick and long, rising toward their stomach, the large heads dark and menacing.

Damien's smile was lethal as he watched what Wes did to her. He and Lars moved toward her, stroking their cocks as Seth turned her head and captured her lips with his.

"I'm not mating with her in a damned chair," Lars muttered.

Seth nibbled at her lips, stroking them with his tongue. "Let's go upstairs. We're going to need the room." He deepened the kiss just as Wes lifted her shirt, unfastened her bra and ran his thumbs lightly over her nipples.

"Look at how beautiful our mate's breasts are. Small, firm and pretty pink nipples." She felt his mouth on her bare breast, licking at her nipple teasingly and making her cry out.

Seth swallowed her cries, angling her head to his liking and sweeping her mouth again, tangling his tongue with hers as she whimpered.

Another mouth closed over her other breast, the sensation nearly overwhelming. It felt incredibly erotic to have three men's mouths on her at once. While Seth kissed her with long, drugging kisses that made her limp with need, Wes teased a nipple. Running his tongue over it teasingly, he occasionally scraped it with his teeth, making her cry out each time.

Another mouth, she didn't know whose, nibbled his way around her other breast, not touching her nipple at all. She arched, desperate to have him touch her there.

Her hands gripped Wes's shoulder and Seth's, fisting the material of their shirts in her hands as she struggled to get closer. The pleasure amazed her. Overwhelmed her.

Seth lifted his head and she looked down to see that it was Damien who used his mouth on her other breast, teasing her so erotically.

Damien slid his arms under her and lifted her from the chair. He carried her effortlessly, staring down at her, his eyes darker than they'd been before. Laying a hand on his chest, she smoothed it over his hot skin, fascinated by the way the muscles bunched and shifted under her hand. The smattering of dark chest hair felt as silky as it had when he'd been in wolf form. Just thinking of it made her tremble with need. The other three followed them out of the room and they moved quickly up the stairs and into her bedroom.

Lacey looked over as Lars and Wes stripped the covers from the bed, leaving only the sheet. She opened her mouth to speak, not quite sure what she would say, but before anything came out, Damien covered her mouth with his.

Knowing what was about to happen, Lacey's trembling increased. She'd never done anything like this before. Who had?

Even though she'd just met them, and after what she'd heard and seen downstairs, it still felt so right. Being with them this way felt like coming home, giving her a sense of belonging exactly where she found herself. In their arms.

She couldn't fight the pleasure. Never had her body spiraled so out of her control before. As Lars and Damien lay on either side of her, touching her with their hands and mouths, kissing her until she couldn't breathe, she lost more of the ability to think.

She felt her cotton pants being removed as Lars pulled her shirt over her head and Damien divested her of her bra. Hands covered her breasts, tweaking at her nipples as she heard a rip and felt her panties being pulled off of her.

Hands and mouths touched her everywhere, all at once.

Strong hands moved over her thighs and abdomen. Someone licked her toes. Open-mouthed kisses rained up and down her legs. Lars cupped a breast, his thumb moving over her nipple, while he nuzzled her jaw. Damien interlaced his fingers with hers, lifting her arm over her head as he sucked a nipple into his mouth, scraping his teeth over it.

Drowning in indescribable sensation, she gave no thought to objecting. Her cries and moans filled the room as they gave attention to every inch of her exposed flesh.

She heard low growls coming from each of them. Instead of scaring her, they only aroused her more. She'd never felt so primal, so needy that nothing mattered except the pleasure. With her legs spread wide, she knew Wes and Seth looked at her slit. She could actually feel their gazes caressing her swollen folds. She couldn't keep from crying out when she felt her pussy lips being spread.

"I've got to taste her," she heard Wes say in a voice that made her shake even more. "Her scent is driving me crazy."

Her juices literally flowed from her now, her clit so needy that even Wes's warm breath caressing it felt like a stroke.

Lars lifted his head and looked down at her, his face a mask of tortured need. He spoke to his brother but his eyes never left hers. "Hurry up. I can't wait to mate her. Her scent is making me so crazy, my dick is going to explode."

Damien lifted his mouth from her breast and nipped her bottom lip. "One day soon, I'm going to spend hours just feasting on you."

"We all are," Lars growled, smoothing her damp hair back from her face. "You belong to us. Once we mate you, everyone will know who you belong to. We'll never let you go."

"No, I don't, ohh!" Lacey's moans and cries got louder as Wes lifted her bottom and buried his face between her thighs. "Just sex," Lacey screamed as Wes drove her relentlessly over the edge. All orgasms she'd ever had paled in significance to what he did to her now. He used his lips, his tongue, his teeth, to make her come so hard and so fast, it left her breathless.

"Just sex?" Damien growled at her and pinched a nipple, sending a jolt of pleasure through her. "You're ours forever, mate. We'll make sure you don't forget it."

Lars rubbed her abdomen where it tightened painfully. "Yes, my mate. Come for us. Wes, take her, damn it."

Lacey shuddered expectantly when Wes lifted his mouth from her and poised the head of his cock at her opening. Holding onto both Lars and Damien, she moaned as he began to press into her. It had been quite a while for her and her body struggled to adjust to his thickness as he continued to press forward.

Lars kept rubbing her abdomen as he and Damien alternated between watching her face and watching where Wes filled her.

Lacey tried to tilt her hips, but Wes held her firmly. "Oh God. Oh! Condom. I'm not on the pill."

Lars stroked her hair again. "You're fine. Trust us. Just enjoy."

Lacey groaned as Wes slid to the hilt inside her. She could feel her inner muscles milking him, but could do nothing to stop it. "Pregnancy."

Damien nipped her jaw. "You can't get pregnant this time, not until we all mate you. Our seed has to mix inside you. But we're going to get you pregnant as soon as possible."

Lacey didn't understand about their seed mixing, but couldn't form the words to ask. So lost in sensation her mind couldn't keep up, she kept a tight grip on Damien and Lars so she wouldn't be swept away. "No, I can't stay. I, ahhh, I have to go home."

Wes slid out until only the head of his cock remained inside her and surge forcefully into her again. "You are home, my mate."

He began thrusting in earnest now, his eyes fierce as he watched her face. "So fucking tight. So good. Never like this before."

Seth stood next to the bed, watching her face as he caressed her thigh and stroked a breast. "You are so fucking beautiful." His hand moved close to Lars' hand on her stomach.

She tightened on Wes as he stroked his cock over sensitive flesh, each stroke bringing her closer and closer to another orgasm. Wes's hands tightened on her buttocks as his thrusts came even harder.

Lars leaned over her, his hand moving lower. "Come again."

She had no choice, as he slid a finger over her clit as Wes's thrust continued. Again, she exploded. Fire raced through her as she came, even harder than last time, her inner walls clenching repeatedly on Wes's cock.

"Fuck, so fucking incredible." His voice had become so deep she barely recognized it. With a last hard thrust, he came, holding himself deep.

Lacey gasped as his cock pulsed, shooting his hot seed into her. Her pussy tingled and warmed even more. "What's happening? It tingles. It's hot. Oh God," she groaned as the hot tingly feeling set off another mini orgasm.

Wes released her buttocks to rub both hands over her lower abdomen. "We're mated. Your body is adjusting to my seed. Jesus, we're mated."

"Get your ass out of the fucking way so I can mate her, too," Seth growled at him.

Wes scowled at his brother, but reluctantly withdrew, pushing Damien out of the way to lie beside her. "My mate," he murmured softly before his lips captured hers in a kiss so possessive, it curled her toes. Her lips tingled where he touched them and her head spun, making her dizzy.

Seth took Wes's place between her thighs, lifted her as Wes had and began to press inside her. "Her cunt is so fucking hot. Fuck, it's like little sparks all over my cock. Damn it, I'm never gonna last."

Wes caressed her breast as he kissed her, his fingers plucking at her nipple, shooting more arrows of pleasure pain straight to her pussy. His touch affected her even more now, almost completely overwhelming the others. Lars used his mouth on her other breast, nipping her over and over. The differences in their touch nearly drove her mad. One gentle and one aggressive. She realized that the more aroused they got, the rougher their lovemaking became. She loved it.

Her clit felt swollen and far too sensitive. Her hands fisted in the pillow when she saw Seth moving his hands toward her slit. "Come mate, I can't last. You're too fucking hot."

With a roar, he held himself deep inside her and she could feel his seed hit her inner walls, making them tingle and get even hotter. Her pussy clenched on him, burning her even more as he stroked her clit. Her body bowed, bucking as if to throw him off as she came yet again.

Her screams of release mixed with the low growls coming from all of them. But she could actually *feel* Wes and Seth's growls vibrating through her. She panted, squeezing her eyes closed as more pleasure than she could have ever imagined raced through her.

Damien quickly took Seth's place, sliding into her with one breathtaking thrust. "Fuck. Fuck. *Fuck.*" Damien began thrusting almost immediately, lifting her into them. "I've never felt anything like this before. It's like fucking electric shocks on my cock."

Lacey squirmed, her cries hoarse now, as the tingling heat spread, causing a series of small orgasms. "It's too much. I can't—"

"Yes, you can," Lars tortured voice sounded next to her ear. "We can't stop now, not until all of us mate you. Let go. We've got you, my mate. Just feel."

Lacey opened her eyes to see Lars almost savage look as he continued to watch her, his hands moving over her, firing her blood even more with his devastating caresses.

"Look at me!" Damien demanded, his hands tightening on her hips even more.

Lacey looked down, her pussy clenching at the raw lust on his face. Holding onto Lars and Wes, she rocked her hips, panting and whimpering. "Don't stop. More."

"I'll give you more." He slid his hands under her legs, lifting them onto his biceps, spreading her high and wide. Leaning forward, he pressed his entire length into her, so thick and hot, she moaned as her inner walls stretched. One hand covered her lower abdomen while the other reached for her slit.

Lacey held her breath for his touch. When it came, she felt as though she'd shattered into a million pieces.

He pinched her clit, something she'd never before experienced. Her screams of pleasure pain nearly drowned out his roar of release as his cock pulsed inside her. The heat of his semen and the clenching of her pussy, made her burn hotter and set off another of those little orgasms that made her crazy, not satisfying her hunger, just making her want more.

Lars and Wes held onto her, speaking softly, Wes's voice low and rough against her neck, Lars' rumbling from deep in his throat. She had no idea what they said, but just the sound of their voices became enough.

When she began to come down, her body still trembling, Damien kissed each of her thighs before releasing her to Lars. Lars kept her legs high, sliding his thighs under hers and sinking into her soaked pussy with a groan. Unlike the others, he lay over her, his weight pressing her into the mattress.

Wrapping her legs around his waist and her arms around his shoulders, she buried her face in his neck. Breathing in the clean, masculine scent of him, she dug her heels into his taut butt, lifting into his slow, steady thrusts. Gripping his shoulder more tightly, she began kissing his neck and shoulders as the steady climb to orgasm began yet again.

Exhausted, but energized by need, she raced to come. As she got closer, her kisses became rougher and more aggressive. She'd never been this crazed by lust before. Lars growled when she bit him, cupping the back of her head and holding her close, while his other arms slid under her, cupping her bottom and lifting her into his thrusts.

She felt the others touch her, heard their voices, but she focused on Lars. Surrounding her with his heat and strength, he filled her, holding her tightly against him. Digging at a spot inside her that drove her wild with slow smooth strokes, he took his time, driving her to the peak more slowly than the others had, but no less thoroughly.

Even after all the pleasure she'd already had, she still wanted more, *needed* more from Lars. His slow strokes drove her crazy. "More, damn you. Harder." Digging her nails into his shoulders, she astounded herself by biting him, sinking her teeth into shoulder.

A loud, deep growl, followed by a sharp warning nip on her own shoulder had her releasing him with a gasp.

Lars lifted his head to stare down at her, his look dark, menacing and sexy as hell. "I bite back, my mate." The hand on her bottom shifted, and his thick finger pressed against her puckered opening threateningly. His voice had become so deep and animalistic, it probably would have terrified her under other circumstances. But he held himself still, his cock like hot steel inside her, an unfamiliar and highly erotic touch at her bottom hole.

"You'll have to learn to be good, my mate, or pay the consequences. Be good for me now. Come."

Lacey bristled at his words, but that low tone and the heat in his eyes had her gripping him tighter as his strokes resumed, hard and fast and she flew.

More heat. More tingling. Almost unbearable pleasure.

The deep growl in her ear only added to the sexual atmosphere, making this surreal experience even more unreal. The heat in her pussy burned even hotter, but not enough to cause pain, just an extreme sizzling awareness.

Lars lifted her face, his searching gaze apparently finding what he looked for. He smiled down at her indulgently, tracing her cheek with his finger. "My mate."

Still trembling when he withdrew and lay beside her, she shuddered when Damien lay on the other side. "You're our mate. It's done."

Preparing to argue, Lacey tried to sit up, but Lars and Damien wouldn't allow it, pushing her back down to the pillows. Lars rubbed her stomach. "You have to lie down for a little while and give our seed a chance to mix inside you. When the heat stops, the mating is complete."

Lacey lay back against the pillows, too tired to get up anyway. Seth and Wes sat on either side of her knees, caressing her thighs. The heat inside her warmed her as drowsiness settled over her. "Not mated. I'm leaving."

She felt Lars breath on her cheek. "You're not going anywhere. Your home is here now, with us."

She could barely keep her eyes open. "No. Hafta go in a coupla days."

Finally the weight of her eyelids became too much and she let them close. The men's low voices surrounded her, but she was just too tired to pay attention. She snuggled under the quilt they placed over her, smiling as lips touched her hair and then nothing.

* * * *

Dinner with her grandmother was a quiet affair. She tried to convince herself that she felt relieved that the men had all gone, but failed miserably. At least they could have been around when she woke up.

After she'd showered and dressed, she'd checked her email and had been looking for someone to expend her anger on. While showering, she thought about all that mate stuff and their chauvinistic attitudes. Who the hell did they think they were to tell her she couldn't leave? She couldn't regret the sex, even though it had happened way too fast. She couldn't blame them. She'd been a willing participant in the single, most erotic experience of her life.

But then again, having four werewolves make love to her would be hard to top.

Determined not to let it ruin her time with her godmother, they talked over dinner, laughing and catching up. Not until they moved into the sitting room for coffee, did Lacey fall silent. She listened to her grandmother talk about people she would introduce to her at her birthday party the next night, but Lacey could only stare at the spot where Lars and Damien had turned into wolves right before her eyes.

They'd turned into wolves right in front of her. Werewolves.

"What is it, Lacey?"

"Werewolves, Nana? Why doesn't that scare me to death? Why do I believe it so easily?"

Her godmother smiled. "Ever since you were a little girl, I knew how sick Lily was. I always worried that I would get a phone call, telling me that she was gone. I would have immediately come to get you and brought you back here. You would have found out and you would have been frightened, especially on top of losing your grandmother. So I started telling you the stories. So you wouldn't be afraid. So you would accept."

"Did grandma know?"

"No, sweetheart. Lily's heart could never have handled it."

"They say I'm their mate."

"Nothing could make me happier."

"I have to go. I can't stay here."

"Why not? You can find a job teaching here."

Lacey sighed. "Nana, this can't work. I mean, they didn't even stick around after, um…"

"After they mated you." She came to sit next to Lacey on the sofa. "I'm sure it was too soon for you, but after the scare they had this afternoon, well, one thing you'll learn about weres is that they are extremely protective of their mates. You were in danger, and they needed to prove to themselves that you're all right. They needed to mark you, mate you so you carried their scent, in order to protect you."

"But I don't need protection, especially from someone like Steven."

Her godmother looked extraordinarily pleased with herself. "Protecting you and your children will be my grandson's first priority for the rest of their lives. They won't take any chances with you."

Lacey set her coffee aside and stood, the words coming out before she could stop them. "Well, they sure took off in a hurry."

"Yes, they did. Right now they're meeting with pack members, informing them that their four packs will now be reunited into one. It turns out my birthday party will be a bigger celebration than we thought. They're gathering their things to move in here tonight. They don't want to be apart from their mate. And if you look outside, there are a dozen pack members guarding the house until they return. Word is spreading fast that the Alphas have found their mate and that the pack is reuniting. Our enemies are not going to be happy. Since you're the link that unites all of us, you'll be a constant target."

"A target?"

Her godmother nodded. "You're their weak spot now. There's nothing my grandsons or the pack wouldn't do to protect you."

Chapter Six

The number of guests who continued to arrive amazed her. She had no idea her godmother even knew this many people. But Nana greeted each person by name and every single one of them seemed to adore her.

And every single one of them was a werewolf, or mate to one.

Werewolves. Unbelievable.

She looked over to see her godmother laughing up at something Seth said to her. She'd been amazed this morning to find all of their injuries had healed overnight. When they'd explained how quickly werewolves heal, she'd been shocked. When they'd told her that now that they had mated her, the same would be true for her, she'd been stunned.

She'd slept alone last night, purposely gone to bed early, partly because she'd still been tired from her trip, but mostly because she didn't feel up to dealing with any of them. After Nana's bombshell, she'd gone upstairs and asked not to be disturbed. Thankfully, they'd respected her wishes.

Helping herself to an hors d'oeuvre, she jumped in surprise when a hot hand settled on her lower back. Little tingles of pleasure radiated throughout her body, making her tremble.

"Are you having a good time, sweetheart?"

She shivered as Wes spoke softly in her ear, sounding far too intimate for such an innocent question. His warm breath skimmed over her neck, reminding her too much of how it had the day before as his hands roamed over her body.

She had to clear her voice before speaking, keeping her back to him as she spoke over her shoulder. "Yes, thank you. I'm having a great time. I had no idea Nana knew so many people."

Wes chuckled and wrapped his arms around her from behind, and she bit back a moan as his heat surrounded her. "Grandmother is well loved around here. You will be, too. It won't be long before you know everyone here by name. Have I told you how beautiful you look tonight, my mate?"

She'd worn a long, emerald green dress that was almost exactly the same color of her eyes. She knew she looked good in it, and wanted to look nice for her godmother's party. Almost Grecian in style, it didn't reveal much, just the curve of her breast, but standing here with Wes, she felt nearly naked. "Thank you. Yes, you and your brothers have all told me." She frowned up at him. "Stop calling me your mate."

"But 'my mate' is a very common endearment among weres and can only be used by one mate to another. It's not like, 'darling, or sweetheart' that can be used all the time. We've never said it to another woman before and we like it. Get used to it. With four mates, you'll be hearing it a lot."

Lacey kept her back to him, facing the back yard. It had filled with people and she smiled as she watched the children run around. She looked over her shoulder at Wes. "Well, don't call me any of that. Yesterday was a mistake. I was kind of," she waved her arm, "bowled over by the passion. It's not normal behavior for me, but it happened. I see now that staying here wouldn't work. I thought a lot about it last night. For some reason, you and your brothers decided that all of you want me and want to keep me here. But, that's not what I want. I want a man who loves me and that I love. I'm not your *mate* and don't want to be."

Wes gripped her arms when she would have walked away and bent and touched his lips to her bare shoulder. "Too bad. You are our mate. If you think I or any of my brothers will let you walk away, you don't know us very well."

Lacey sighed. "That's what I've been saying." Pulling out of his grip, she made her way through the crowd to get another soft drink. Wanting to keep her wits about her, she'd opted for non alcoholic drinks tonight.

Even though everyone smiled and greeted her by name, the men gave her a wide berth, stepping aside whenever she walked near, even if their backs had been turned. A sudden thought occurred to her and she walked up to her godmother, bending down to whisper in her ear. "Nana, when you said they wanted to mark me, did they? Do I smell like them now?"

Her godmother smiled and patted her arm. "Since I'm not a were, you smell the same to me. But if you've mated with them, you won't smell *like* them but you'll carry their scent. Don't ask. I never completely understood it myself."

Lars gripped her arm and pulled her with him to the makeshift dance floor. "Come and dance with me."

"But—"

He lifted her arms around his neck, pulling her close, his hands moving seductively over her back. "Grandmother is surrounded by people and is fine. Victor will be watching her like a hawk. What's this about you not being our mate?"

Lacey slid her hands to his chest and pushed. "You're holding me too closely." She looked around to see that others watched them, smiling indulgently.

He didn't budge at all. If anything his arms tightened even more. His breath felt warm on her cheek as he bent over her, leaning close. "I don't think there's any such thing as holding your *mate* too closely."

Lacey struggled just to breathe. His touch, his scent, his heat surrounded her. She trembled in his arms, the combination of sensations robbing her of all rational thought. Never had a man affected her the way these men did.

She said nothing, looking around at the others, as they danced under the twinkling lights that had been strung up. Four large tents set up beyond the patio where they danced, had the same twinkling lights strung all around them, looking like millions of fireflies in the darkness.

Finally, she looked up at him, unsurprised to find him staring down at her. "I'm not your mate. I know you think I am, but when I decide to be with a man, it'll be *my choice*. Just because you and your brothers think that I'm supposed to be with you, doesn't make it true for me. I want a man who loves me. You don't even know me."

Lars leaned close and lightly bit her earlobe. "I would say I know you intimately."

Lacey shivered, her face burning and she pushed against his chest again, not budging him at all. She kept her voice low. "Like I told Wes, that was a mistake. I can't believe I went to bed with four men. That kind of thing doesn't happen to me. And it can't happen again. You're just going to have to accept that."

"Oh, it's going to happen again, my mate. All four of us, in various combinations and alone. None of us is willing to give you up. You're just going to have to accept *that*."

Lacey held herself stiffly in his arms as they continued to dance. One song ended and another began, but when she tried to step away, he kept her firmly against him. She started to push at him again, but saw Nana watching them, smiling happily. Damn.

Not wanting to ruin her godmother's happiness at her birthday party, she forced herself to relax in Lars' arms.

The more she relaxed, the more she felt drawn to him. He felt so warm, and it felt so good to be held this way. And those damned tingles were nearly impossible to resist. Thinking about the way he'd been as he and his brothers made love to her the day before, she couldn't help but lean in closer as his arms tightened even more around her, and he began to caress her back. They danced in silence for several minutes, hardly moving at all. Her body relaxed, and she melted into him more and more as he continued those long, firm strokes on her back.

It felt so good just to lean this way against him. Her eyes had drifted closed but a niggling sensation made her open them again. When she did, she found herself immediately caught in Wes's gaze as he watched them from where he sat, not far away. He looked tense, but smiled when she looked at him. How could his smile warm her while she danced wrapped in his brother's arms?

Troubled, she looked away. Pushing against Lars' chest again, she leaned back to look up at him. "You know that it can never work, right?"

He kept one hand at her back and reached up with the other to touch her cheek. "It can work. It will work. My brothers and I will do everything in our power to make it work."

She shook her head. "I don't understand why any of you would even want to do something like that. Why would you want to share a woman instead of each of you having a woman of your own?"

Lars smiled and touched his lips to hers. "We don't just want *any* woman. We want you, and we'll all do whatever's necessary to have you. You feel it, too, Lacey. Don't try to deny it."

Lacey sighed. "We met *yesterday.* I can't deny that I'm attracted to you. And to your brothers. But I could never be involved in a relationship like that even if I fell in love with all four of you."

"Lacey, all that we ask is that you give us a chance."

"I think the best thing we can do is to stay away from each other. I'll be leaving in a few days and I don't want any hard feelings when I go. I'd like to be able to come and visit my godmother, and when I do, I'd like for us to be friends."

Lars pulled her close again and gripped her chin. "We'll never be just friends, Lacey. Just relax and enjoy the party. We'll talk again tomorrow and maybe you'll understand a little better."

"Understand what? That you want me without even knowing me? That you expect me to fuck you and your brothers whenever the hell you feel like it?"

His face hardened to granite, making her shiver as a chill went up her spine. "If I ever hear you talk that way again, I'm going to turn you over my knee and beat your ass. You sound like we expect you to be little more than a whore for us. If I wanted just sex, I could get that anywhere. I never planned on sharing my mate, and it's something that a little hard to get used to, but you're the mate for my brothers, too. It was meant to be. The sooner you accept that, the better it will be for all of us."

"And the sooner you accept that I won't be your mate and I won't allow four men to pass me around like candy, the better it will be for all of us, too."

Lacey didn't even have time to gasp as her took her mouth with his, kissing her so deeply, so possessively, it curled her toes. Gripping his shoulders for support, she leaned into him, gasping when her nipples brushed his chest. He used it as an opportunity to deepen his kiss even more.

Ending the devastating kiss, Lars ran his lips over her jaw and down to her neck, leaving a trail of fire behind. The scrape of his teeth over her shoulder weakened her knees.

She would have fallen if not for the strong arms supporting her. She shivered when his lips touched her ear. "You're mine, Lacey. Ours. There's nothing we won't do to keep you." He leaned back, gripping her chin and lifting her face to his. "I've never in my life wanted anything as much as I want you. You'll never get away from me, and I'll do whatever I have to do to keep you with me."

"No Lars, I can't have a relationship with four men."

"You will. Don't worry about it tonight. Just enjoy the party. We'll talk about it again when everyone's gone."

She felt a wall of heat at her back a second before warm lips touched her neck. A jolt of electricity shot through her. "You look beautiful, my mate." Damien nipped her neck. "It seems we have some things to discuss."

"You can't bite me every time you don't like what I say."

His lips touched her ear as his arms went around her, pulling her back against him. She could feel his erection press into her lower back and fought the images that went through her mind of what it had felt like to have it inside her.

"I can do a lot more than bite you. How would you like it if I scraped my teeth over your red, shiny clit, enough to keep you begging to come, but not enough to let you? Weres have many ways of punishing and pleasing their mates, Lacey."

Fire raced through her as Lars hands moved to her hips, lightly caressing. She felt as though she floated, feeling nothing but their touch, heard nothing but the sounds of their breathing. Her own breath came out on pants and gasps as they caressed her, their lips moving over hers and her bare shoulders.

When Lars lifted his head, her eyes fluttered open to see that they now stood around the side of the house, apart from the others. She hadn't even been aware of moving.

Damien's hand pressed against her abdomen, pulling her back against him. "How does it feel to have your mates surrounding you? One in front of you and one behind you?"

Her head fell back against his shoulder as Lars cupped a breast. "I can't, it's, ohh."

Damien cupped her other breast as he tilted her head and scraped his teeth down her neck. "You went wild in our arms when you had all four of us touching you. Naked. All of us using our hands and mouths on you."

She moaned at the erotic memories. "Never again. It's not right."

Damien pinched her nipple through her dress. "It's perfect for all of us. You're perfect for us."

Lacey gripped their arms. "Oh, my God." She felt them all around her, their hands and lips moving over her with increasing fervor. Whenever they touched her, she forgot about everything else.

The hands on her breasts teased her nipples, stroking and lightly pinching them through the fabric. She knew she would have fallen if they hadn't been holding her. Her panties had long ago become soaked, and she wanted them to make love to her right here, right now. "Please, I can't stand it."

Lars lightly bit her lip. "We've only just begin, sweetheart. Now tell us you don't want us."

"What the hell's going on out here?"

Lacey jumped, turning at Seth's harsh tone. Gulping in air, she trembled at the inhuman growls that came from both Damien and Lars. Lars lifted his head, baring his teeth at Seth, and Damien whipped his head around. Lacey pulled from their arms and shakily backed away.

Seth strode to his brothers. "What the hell are you doing?"

Wes came up behind Seth, grimacing. "Damn it, Seth." He turned to Lacey, smiling apologetically. "I'm sorry. I guess we're just not used to this yet." He tried to put his arm around her, but she moved away.

"No." She put even more distance between them. "I'm going back to the party. I told you this would never work." She met Lars' and Damien's eyes. "I'm sorry. I shouldn't have let it go so far. I'm not like that. I don't know what happened. I'm sorry."

Lars and Damien looked downright furious, their jaws clenched as they looked back and forth between her and Seth.

"Don't ever apologize for that," Lars deep voice sounded raw. "You're our mate, damn it. There's nothing wrong with getting pleasure from our touch."

Lacey gritted her teeth. "I'm not your mate."

Lars mumbled something under his breath that she couldn't hear. Damien looked like he wanted to say something, but then turned away, running his hands through his hair in frustration.

More than a little aroused, she wrapped her arms around herself. "I'm going to go check on Nana."

Lacey walked away, rubbing her arms as another shiver went through her. She turned the corner to see that the party was still going strong. Several more people had started dancing, and everyone appeared to be having a good time. She forced a smile as she passed people that she'd met earlier, looking around for her godmother.

Not seeing her outside, she walked back through the open French doors and into the house. Something niggled at her and she turned to see several of the people become very still, lifting their noses as though sniffing the air. Several of the men in the house began rushing outside, while others looked around and when they spotted her, moved closer, hustling her further into the house.

What the hell was going on?

Through the throng of people heading for the door, she saw her godmother standing on the other side of the room, looking worried. Nervous now, she moved through the crowd, several men surrounding her, frantic to make sure Nana was all right. She'd just reached her godmother when she heard a woman's horrified wail, coming from out back.

"She's dead! That poor woman's dead."

Chapter Seven

Wes and his brothers had just rounded the corner of the house when they heard the scream. His first thought was of Lacey. Not of his pack. His mate. He stopped in his tracks and breathed deeply, searching for her scent. He had to find her.

"Fuck. Do you smell that?" Damien's voice held a hint of panic that Wes had never heard from him before.

All four moved in sync as they caught the scent of the unfriendly, neighboring pack. "What the hell? Why would someone from the Galbraith pack be here? Shit, Steven came after Lacey." Horrified, he whipped his head around, frantically searching for her.

The need to shift became almost overwhelming, but with all the caterers and musicians present, he couldn't. A woman came flying past them and tripped on the edge of the stone patio. She would have fallen if Lars hadn't caught her in time.

"It's awful," she sobbed. "A wolf attacked a woman and ripped out her throat. So much blood. So much blood."

Fear like he'd never known slammed into him as he and his brothers moved to where the others had gathered around on the other side of the house. The scent of it combined with the scent of his brothers' had the members of their combined packs shifting uncomfortably from where they'd gathered around the woman. Had Lacey come here to have a few minutes alone? They parted as he and his brothers approached. He heard someone calling an ambulance and then nothing as the roaring in his ears drowned out everything else.

Three of their pack members, the doctor included, leaned over the body. As they approached, the doctor looked up at him and shook his head. All three moved away from the body and for the first time, Wes could see her.

The sight of red hair nearly brought him to his knees. "No. Oh God, please, no."

"It's not her. No green dress." Lars' voice was barely recognizable. "Thank you, God."

The roaring diminished as he watched Lars move close to the young woman's body. Now that he knew it wasn't Lacey that lay dead, his mind started to function again. He, Seth and Damien spread out and had the other pack members block the view of the body from the others.

Seth and Damien kept looking toward the house. Wes felt the same need to make sure Lacey and their grandmother were unhurt. But he didn't know if she was even *in* the damned house. He looked around, trying to catch a glimpse of her.

Lars leaned close to the woman's throat, his nostrils flaring. When he stood, his face had become a mask of fury.

Nearly knocked back by the scent of Lars' rage, Wes looked at him questioningly, but Lars shook his head. He looked over his shoulder at one of his pack members, noting that he and his brothers had each been surrounded by members of the now united pack. "Ethan, get the women and children inside."

"It's already been done." He looked at the woman, his face hardening. "How the fuck did a were from the Galbraith pack slip in and nobody noticed?"

"I don't know, but whoever did this is going to pay. I've got to go check on Lacey."

Ethan placed a hand on his shoulder. "Your mate is inside with your grandmother and is well guarded. She's had men surrounding her since the scream."

He breathed a sigh of relief, but knew he wouldn't settle until he saw her, touched her. He spared a glance at Damien and both took off toward the house.

* * * *

Lacey sat with her godmother on the sofa, watching, amazed, at the flurry of activity around her. Men shuffled women and children out the door and into cars, speaking under their breath as they were quickly hustled out. Each time she started forward to help, they sent her back to the sofa. "Please stay with Miss Eleanor." By the time an ambulance and the police arrived, only the men remained.

Lacey couldn't help but notice that all the men that stayed behind were both young and fit. All the teens and older men had been hustled out with the others. She looked up as Victor appeared with a glass of water for Nana. "Victor, I can't believe this. A woman was killed at the party? Why? How? By whom?"

She helped her godmother hold the glass. Nana shook so badly, she would have spilled it all over herself otherwise. "Where's the doctor? I want him to come in and take a look at Nana."

One of the men that had stayed behind came over to kneel in front of them. He looked to be in his thirties and had the same lean muscular build as the others, with brown hair and gentle hazel eyes. "The doctor will be in soon." He smiled at her godmother tenderly. "Miss Eleanor is tough. She's going to be just fine. It's a terrible thing. But I want you to calm down. Everything is under control and there's no danger."

Lacey blinked as Nana composed herself before her eyes. When the older woman rose from the sofa, the man stood, offering her support.

She handed the glass back to Victor and looked at the younger man. "Del, I want to know who that young woman was. Now that the pack is together again, it shouldn't be too difficult to find out who did this and make sure something like this never happens again. My grandsons are going to need everyone working together."

The other man smiled. "Yes, together we'll get to the bottom of this. I don't want you to worry. The Alphas won't rest until they find out who's responsible. And they won't be very happy if you collapse. Please sit down and wait for the doctor."

"I can't believe this," Lacey murmured. "Nana, you stay right here. I'm going to go out to see what happened and if anyone knows her."

Del moved to block her. "You can't leave." He gestured to the half dozen or so other men in the room. "We're here to protect you until your men finish their duties and can get to you."

"Protect me? Why in the world would I need protection? Just stay here with Nana." Lacey started to go past him, and again he blocked her.

"I'm sorry. I can't let you leave. Your men would skin me alive if I do."

Her godmother patted her arm. "Lacey, sit here with me while I wait for the doctor."

Resigned, Lacey nodded and sat down. "I just feel terrible about this. Why would this happen? It's like something out of a movie. It had to be some kind of an accident."

Wes and Damien came running into the room, their eyes wild.

Damien got to her first and lifted her off the sofa, surprising her with his strength and pulled her into his arms. Burying his face in her throat, he held her, his arms like steel bands around her.

Stunned, Lacey slid a hand down his hair. "Damien, what is it? Are you okay?"

He set her on her feet and cupped her face with both hands, touching his lips to hers. "We thought it was you. I've never been so fucking scared in my life."

Wes stood beside her and pulled her to him, much like Damien just had. "My heart stopped. Thank God it wasn't you. I couldn't stand it."

They both moved to hug their grandmother, speaking to her softly, and apparently answering her questions. Lacey couldn't hear the conversation, but all three of them looked grim.

Lacey rubbed her chilled arms. "Who was the woman? Was she a friend of yours?"

Wes came to stand behind her, replacing her hands with his and running them over her arms to warm them. "She was one of the catering staff. We don't know what happened yet."

Lacey watched the men that had remained in the room. They all kept glancing at Damien and Wes uneasily. She noticed that they all seemed to be guarding the doors and windows. She leaned back against Wes and asked softly over her shoulder. "Why did all these men stay behind instead of leaving with the others?"

If she hadn't been watching, she would have missed the fact that several of the men's lips twitched at her question. Could they hear her?

Wes wrapped his arms around her, and she couldn't resist the warmth his embrace provided. "They stayed to make sure you and grandmother were looked after."

As Lacey watched, the men in the room seemed to come to attention as Wes tightened his hold on her and rumbled in her ear. "Shit. Just what we need."

Damien started for the front door, just as Lars and Seth came in the back. Wes released her as Lars pulled her against him, with Seth moving in behind her.

They held her, kissed her and buried their faces in her throat almost desperately, the same way Wes and Damien had.

"Which one of you fucking animals killed that woman?"

Lacey froze at the deep bellow. Seth and Lars straightened, but didn't release their hold on her as she craned to see who had spoken. She blinked, shocked that every man in the room stood between the man who'd spoken and her and Nana.

She stood on her toes to whisper to Lars, tugging at his shoulder until he bent to listen. "Who is that man? Why did he say that? Why does he think somebody here killed that poor woman?"

He ran a hand down her back and sighed. "That man is a government agent. Nobody here killed that woman, but he'll try to prove that one of us did." His arm around her waist tightened. "No matter what you hear, I want you to trust us. He's chased us for years. But he can't prove anything. No matter what he says, and he'll try to scare you, don't believe him. No one here would ever hurt you, my mate."

She could hear the loud man issuing orders in his booming voice and barking out questions. The men in front of her kept sneaking glances at her over their shoulders.

Seth reached over and rubbed a hand down her arm, smiling at her reassuringly.

Lars kissed her hair. "We can smell your fear. Please, don't be afraid. We won't let anything happen to you."

Lacey looked over to see Nana watched her expectantly. She leaned toward her. "Nana, are you all right?"

The older woman smiled sadly. "Yes. I just keep thinking about that poor woman. Lacey, do you trust me?"

"Of course."

"Then no matter what these men say, I want you to remember that. I want you to trust me and trust my grandsons."

"Okay, Nana. But I don't understand any of this."

Her godmother shook her head sadly. "You will."

The men surrounding them looked reluctant as they parted to let the agent through.

Lacey noticed that the agent seemed surprised to see her there, but quickly recovered. He looked to be in his late forties, and had a few strands of gray shining in his dark brown hair. He stood almost as tall as the men, but looked much heavier, a slight paunch hanging over his belt. His sharp eyes went over each of them before coming back to settle on her. "Who are you?"

Lacey bristled at his rudeness and felt the men stiffen beside her. "You're very rude, aren't you? Even my students know better than to talk to someone that way. The polite way would be to introduce yourself first."

Out of the corner of her eye, she could see the smiles of the men surrounding them, which they made no attempt to hide. The agent looked disconcerted for just a moment, before his jaw clenched. "Listen, young lady. I ask the questions around here." Folding his arms over his chest, he waited expectantly. She gave him her best 'teacher to naughty student look'. She heard chuckles all around them. Ignoring them, she waited. Finally, he sighed. "I'm Agent O'Reilly. Who are you?"

Lacey nodded. "Not great, but much better." She stuck out her hand and felt Lars, Damien, Wes and Seth move closer. "Hello. I'm Lacey Roberts, Eleanor Tougarret's goddaughter."

The agent had no choice but to shake her outstretched hand before turning to her godmother. "Hello, Mrs. Tougarret. Do you mind if I ask why your house is full of people?"

"Yes."

Lacey blinked in surprise at Nana's curt reply. Apparently, she didn't care much for the agent. Looking from one to the other, she felt like an outsider, which she was. They all seemed to be privy to information she didn't have.

The agent's look hardened. "Well, I'm going to have to ask you anyway. It seems very suspicious that this woman was killed here while so many of you are present."

Nana sat back down on the overstuffed sofa and sighed heavily. "If you must know, it's my birthday and my grandsons threw a party for me."

"Very convenient," the agent murmured. "I've already seen the body and will read the coroner's report, but we all know how she died, don't we? I have the woman's ID and will be checking her out, but we all know that the only reason she was killed is because she came here, exposing herself to indiscriminate killers."

Lacey gasped. "What the hell do you mean by that?"

He ignored her and yelled over his shoulder to his men. "I want these six questioned separately." He gestured toward Lacey. "I'll take her."

"Over my dead body." Damien shot forward as Lars pulled her back against him.

Lacey watched in stunned disbelief as the agent and all the other officers pulled out their guns and trained them on Damien. "No!" She struggled against Lars' hold.

Lars tightened his grip. "Stay out of this, Lacey."

Lacey watched with a sense of disbelief as the men around them looked at Lars questioningly. None of this made any sense. "Stop it right now. I don't mind answering the agent's questions." She looked up at Lars and touched his face. "I don't know what you're getting so upset about. I'll be fine, I promise."

Lars touched his lips to hers. "Remember what we told you."

Lacey smiled at him reassuringly. "Let me talk to him and then maybe he can figure out who killed that woman." She turned to the agent, still rubbing her arms. "How about the kitchen? I could use some coffee. I've been cold ever since I heard that scream."

Victor moved across the room. "I'll go up and get you a sweater."

* * * *

Lacey sipped her coffee, arching a brow as Agent O'Reilly continued to stare at her. "Was there something you wanted to ask me?"

He pulled out a notebook and a pen and took a sip of his own coffee. "I've never heard of you visiting here before. Why not?"

Lacey wrapped her hands around her cup to warm them. Even wearing the sweater Victor had brought her, she still felt chilled. "My grandmother had been in poor health ever since I can remember. She was never able to travel. We only saw my godmother when she visited us."

"And how often was that?"

Lacey shrugged. "Usually she came for two weeks in the summer. She came here and there when my grandmother took a turn for the worse or for a special event."

"Special event?"

"My high school graduation, college graduation. She came up for my sixteenth birthday party, my prom, things like that."

"So you two are very close?"

Lacey nodded. "Yes, even when we didn't see each other, we talked on the phone at least two or three times a month."

"So you knew what went on in each other's lives?"

Lacey nodded. "Pretty much. Of course we couldn't know everything, but the important things, yes. Why?"

"So what do you know about her grandsons? Have you known them all your life, too?"

"I met them for the first time yesterday. They have lives, Agent O'Reilly. Responsibilities. They wouldn't have gone with their grandmother while she visited an old friend. I knew about them, of course. They knew about me. But we didn't meet or even speak to each other until yesterday."

"Don't you think that's a little strange?"

"No. I guess I never really thought about it before. But I would have been surprised if one of them had come. They all have careers and busy lives."

"Do you know what they do?"

"Of course. I told you that Nana, my grandmother and I talked about things that were important to us. Nana loves her grandsons. I would have thought it strange if she didn't talk about them."

"So you know that they're werewolves?"

"Excuse me?"

"You heard me. Don't try to play stupid. You had to know."

She kept her face expressionless and her voice cool. "Agent O'Reilly, I thought you had some serious questions for me. There's a woman dead and you want to sit here and play games. You asked if I knew what they did. Lars is in real estate. Damien's a whiz at the stock market. Wes paints and Seth sculpts."

She stood, hoping she looked indignant and angry and walked to the sink to look out the window above it. She could see the police milling around, taking pictures and questioning several people. "A woman is dead and you want to talk about werewolves!" She purposely frowned at him. "Have you been drinking?"

His face hardened. "Do you know how the woman died?"

Lacey shook her head. "No." Why hadn't anyone mentioned it? Why hadn't she asked? Wait a minute. She had asked, and Wes had told her that no one knew what happened yet. Not knowing if Wes had known or not, she didn't want to contradict anything. "We hadn't really had a chance to talk. The men came running inside to make sure that Nana and I were all right. You came through the door right after that. How did she die?" A sudden thought occurred to her. "How did you get here so fast?"

"Please sit down. We'd heard that a lot of people had started showing up here and made sure we were in the area."

"You had us watched?"

The agent looked up from his notes angrily. "Do you have any idea of the animals who live around here? Do you know that these men and women have killed? That woman's throat was badly damaged, bitten. No human being did that."

Lacey stared at him in horror. "Something bit her?"

"You said it. Not someone, *some thing*. If I were you, I would be careful. That woman had red hair, not as dark as yours, and she had about the same build. That girl got called at the last minute to be here because someone else didn't show up. I'm going to check on that. But she wasn't supposed to be here. I think she was killed by mistake." He leaned forward. "I know the men can hear me with that animal hearing they have. If they didn't do this, they might want to look inside their own pack for the murderer. Because I think the murderer missed. I think it was supposed to be you lying dead out there."

Lacey tightened her hands on her cup so he wouldn't see how badly she shook. Why would this government agent believe in werewolves? What did he know? She forced herself to look at him as she would one of her students when she knew they were lying. "Agent O'Reilly, I only got here myself yesterday. No one here even knew I was coming. There's no reason for someone to want to kill me." She shoved aside thoughts of back home. It wasn't possible. "But if that woman was killed because of me, I want the truth. And I don't have much faith of finding the truth with a man who believes in *werewolves.*"

* * * *

Lars eavesdropped unashamedly on the conversation taking place in the kitchen and never felt so helpless. He wanted to be with Lacey as the agent questioned her, but she seemed to be doing fine on her own. With no small amount of pride, he listened as Lacey asked the agent if he'd been drinking and then questioning his ability to find the murderer, insinuating he might be less than competent because of his belief in werewolves.

She was spectacular.

"We might have more questions for you so don't leave town."

Lars raised a brow at the arrogant tone of the cocky young cop and got a small amount of satisfaction when the cop swallowed heavily and looked away. Without a backward glance, he left the study and went back into the living room where he knew they'd been questioning his grandmother. They hadn't allowed her to be questioned until the doctor had checked her out.

The other pack members had been questioned and sent home. But Lars could hear and smell them, and knew they waited outside for the agents and police to leave, watching them and for whoever had done the killing. The agents and cops would never see or hear them.

His brothers sat with their grandmother, each looking toward the kitchen. Only bits of pieces of the conversation between Lacey and the agent could be heard now as the voices of the other cops gathered around continued to get louder.

Lars knelt at his grandmother's feet. "Grandmother, why don't you go up to bed? We'll take care of everything down here."

She smiled faintly. "I'm so glad that you've all moved in. I'm worried about Lacey. She's been in there a long time. He's going to do his best to scare her so she tells him something."

Lars smiled and took his grandmother's hand. "Yes, he is. But I overheard part of the conversation and Lacey is holding her own." He chuckled. "When O'Reilly brought up the subject of werewolves, Lacey asked if he'd been drinking. Then she basically told him she didn't hold out much hope of a man who believes in werewolves finding the killer."

She smiled, as he'd hoped she would, while his brothers chuckled. "Our Lacey is something, isn't she?"

"Yes." Lars nodded and kissed her cheek. "She's incredible."

"I couldn't imagine a better mate for my grandsons or men more suited to taking care of my Lacey. And for her to be the mate to all of you, well, it's more than I could have hoped for."

Lars turned to see Lacey standing in the doorway. He could smell her fear and see her confusion. Wes moved toward her, his arms outstretched. She deftly avoided him and moved to sit beside their grandmother, not looking at any of them.

"Are you okay, Nana?"

"Oh, Lacey. I'm fine."

"We're leaving now. Stay available. I'll be back," the agent boomed and walked out, his men following.

Finally alone, Lars reached for Lacey's hand, gripping it when she tried to avoid him. "Are you okay, sweetheart?"

"I'm fine. Nana, it's after two o'clock. Why don't you let me help you to bed?"

Lars clenched his jaw when Lacey continued to avoid looking at them as she led their grandmother upstairs. He knew she'd already been through a lot today and didn't want to upset her, but they needed to talk.

Halfway up the stairs, she turned. "Don't even think it."

Lars blinked and stared after her, before turning to his brothers. "I don't think she understands what it means to be mated."

Damien nodded, staring off into space.

Wes sighed. "Let's let her get settled. Once she's asleep, we'll go sleep with her. Since only two of us can sleep next to her at a time, we'll have to bring two more beds into the room. We'll do that tomorrow. I know sex is out of the question, but we can't leave her alone."

Seth walked to the window. "Why the hell did someone from the Galbraith pack come here tonight and kill that woman?"

"I almost lost it when I saw the red hair," Wes said softly and slumped on the sofa. "I thought it was Lacey, and we'd lost her."

Lars poured each of them a drink. He knew that after the night they'd had, he needed one. He passed them around. "There's something you all should know. The scent of the Galbraith pack wasn't the only scent on that girl. I got a good whiff of where that bastard ripped her fucking throat out. I also smelled Tougarret."

Damien, leaning back in his chair, lurched forward. "Someone from our pack had something to do with killing this woman?"

Lars took a healthy swallow of his drink. "I don't know what the hell's going on. All I can tell you is that the open wound had the scent of both packs."

Each lost in their own thoughts, no one spoke for several minutes. Finally Lars stood and went to the window, looking out to the front lawn. "I heard the conversation between Lacey and O'Reilly in the kitchen. She played it off, told him he was crazy to believe in werewolves, but she believed him when he told her that woman was killed by a werewolf. She was scared. She was also lying. I smelled the lies but don't know if it was just because of the mention of werewolves or, I don't know, something."

Damien leaned back and closed his eyes, rubbing them tiredly. "Did O'Reilly tell her that she was the real target?"

"Yeah, but I don't think she believed him."

Damien leaned forward. "I hate to scare her but we have to make her believe it. I want her to be on her guard."

Lars put his empty glass down with more force than necessary. "Yeah, and we have to protect her while we figure out who the hell is trying to kill her. Christ, she's only been here a day and nobody knew she was coming."

Seth looked at the others. "She had to be the target. Word is already out about the pack uniting and I've already heard that some in the Galbraith pack are furious, especially Aaron Galbraith. The pack leader, I'm told, is not happy at all to have the Tougarret pack together again."

Lars heard the others moving outside and went to open the door. "Someone wants Lacey out of the picture. They probably figure, with her gone, we have no reason to join the packs again."

Damien opened his eyes. "When I find out who, he's dead."

Chapter Eight

After taking a long bath to help her relax, Lacey had hoped she would be able to sleep. Two hours later, she gave up. Turning on the bedside lamp, she got up and retrieved her laptop. If she checked her emails and went over her resume again, that should put her to sleep.

A few minutes later, she was even more wide awake and furious. "You son of a bitch." She got up and started pacing her bedroom. "Call me a bitch? I'm glad your wife left you, you worthless piece of shit."

Knowing she wouldn't be able to concentrate on her resume or get back to sleep, she turned off the laptop. With the intention of going downstairs and fixing herself a cup of hot chocolate, she pulled on her robe and slippers. Opening the door, she yelped. All four men stood outside the door, and Seth had his hand raised as if to knock.

He brushed past her and walked into her room. "Who the hell were you talking to?"

Surprised, she spun to face him. "No one. Myself. How could you hear me?" She shook her head, flicking her hand. "Oh, I forgot. It's that werewolf hearing. Well you're not sleeping here. Excuse me. I'm going downstairs."

She walked past them and went downstairs and into the kitchen, aware that they followed her. She got out a pan and turned. "Why are you all down here? I'm just getting some hot chocolate, and I'd like to be alone."

Lars took the pan from her. "Sit down, honey. I'll fix your hot chocolate."

Lacey sat at the table, determined to ignore them.

"We know it's been a hell of a day for you," Wes finally said. "Is there anything you want to talk about? Anything you want to ask us?"

"No."

Damien reached for her hand, holding it in his when she didn't move fast enough to avoid him. "There's something we want to talk to you about."

Lacey tried unsuccessfully to pull her hand back. She was so physically tired, she could hardly move but her mind continued to race. It *had* been a long day. A woman had been killed right outside only hours earlier. The asshole back home had decided that since she'd ruined his life, he would return the favor. She'd lost her job, and she'd been mated by werewolves.

The last two days had been far from normal. She wondered if she'd ever feel normal again. The knowledge that werewolves not only existed, but surrounded her should have been scared to death. But, because of her godmother's stories, it hadn't.

Until that woman had been killed.

She'd thought about the stories her godmother had told her over the years while she'd soaked in the tub. All of the stories had to do with werewolves' day to day life. No mean vicious attacks like most werewolf stories. These stories had been about how good a werewolf's hearing and sight were. How they stayed together in packs for protection and companionship.

And about how they cherished their mates.

She'd always liked that part of the stories. It had sounded like a fairy tale where everyone lived happily ever after. But in real life, she couldn't imagine how men could claim to want to spend the rest of their lives with her, when they'd only just met her.

She wanted, *needed* to be loved and wanted for herself.

Not because of how she smelled.

Lars put the cup of hot chocolate on the table in front of her. "I can smell your fear. Your anger. Why won't you talk to us?"

When Damien released her hand she wrapped both around the

mug to warm them, wondering if she'd ever feel warm again. Staring down into her chocolate, she told them softly, "I don't know what to say. I can't think." Silence reigned for several minutes as she sipped her cocoa. "Was that woman really killed by a werewolf?"

Lars moved close and before she knew his intentions, he'd lifted her into his arms and sat down in the chair she'd been sitting in and settled her on his lap. "Yes, she was. One of our enemies killed her. We think it was supposed to be you."

The fairy tale turned into a nightmare. To think that a young woman had been killed just because someone, a *werewolf*, had mistaken the woman for her scared the hell out of her. "That's what Agent O'Reilly said. But why would anyone want to kill me?"

She tried to get up, but Lars kept her in place with a hand around her middle while he began stroking her back. Long, firm strokes loosened her knotted muscles.

Damien sighed and stood. "They think that getting rid of you will keep us from reuniting the pack. They're wrong, but you're our weakness and they know it. If they kidnapped you, we would do whatever they wanted to get you back. If they killed you, it would destroy us."

"I want to be wanted for myself, not because you think I smell good."

Lars' strokes became firmer and she slumped against him. "Animals have instincts. People do, too, but they don't always listen. You've heard of pheromones, haven't you?" At her nod, he continued. "Nature has a way of making sure that species reproduce. Werewolves just realize sooner who the mate for them will be just by their scent."

Lacey arched a brow. "I'm not a werewolf. It doesn't work that way for me."

Damien knelt in front of her and reached out to rub her knee through her robe. "It's not going to be easy at first. Our main priority right now will be to protect you and to find out who's trying to kill you. You'll be guarded twenty-four seven until we do."

Wes cursed. "Why don't you just scare her to death, Damien?"

Damien shot him a dirty look. "I want her to be scared. I want her to be alert. I don't want her to trust anyone but us, Grandmother and Victor."

Lacey felt her eyelids begin to droop as Lars' strokes lulled her, and she struggled to keep them open. "I guess Victor knows you're werewolves."

Seth chuckled. "He's one, too, and protects grandmother."

Lacey digested that, forcing her eyes open. Lars hands worked magic, his firm kneading turning her into putty. "What are you going to do when you find out who killed that woman? If Agent O'Reilly has been trying to prove all of you are werewolves for years, and you turn the killer over to him, he'll know the truth. What will he do to you?"

Lars hugged her and kissed her hair. "Agent O'Reilly wants to put us in a cage. He says that's where all animals belong. He won't get the chance."

Damien sank back into his chair and reached for her hand. "When we find the werewolf that killed that woman, we'll take care of him within the pack."

Lacey looked from one to the other. "What do you mean, take care of him?"

Lars stood, holding her against his chest. "We're the Alphas of the pack, Lacey. It means that we deal with problems within the pack. You're the Alpha female, our mate. Do you really think that we're going to let anyone hurt you?"

"But—"

He strode from the room, the others following close behind. "Don't worry about it. You'll learn more about how the pack works over time. Now it's time for your mates to tuck you into bed. Christ, I can feel your exhaustion."

That woke Lacey up. She tried to scramble from his arms, but being so tired made her clumsy. Even if she'd been in peak form, she doubted if she could have escaped his hold. Although he didn't hurt her, he held her easily, his arms much stronger than she'd anticipated. "You're not sleeping with me."

"Oh, yes, my mate. I am. Only two of us can sleep with you tonight. Tomorrow we'll have a room prepared for all of us. Your days of sleeping alone are over."

Lars took Lacey back to her room and put her on her feet next to the bed. "Get into bed, honey. We'll be back in a minute."

Bewildered, Lacey watched all four men go out into the hallway, closing the door behind them. With a shrug, she took off her robe and slid between the sheets as a heated discussion took place outside her door. After only a minute or two, they came back in, Wes and Seth looking less than happy.

Wes leaned over her, dropping a kiss on her forehead, her cheeks, her lips. "Goodnight, sweetheart. I'll see you in the morning." With a last lingering look at her, he directed a glare at Lars and Damien and stormed out.

Seth grimaced and leaned over her, kissing her lingeringly, soft slides of his lips on hers before lifting his head. Straightening, he sighed and without a backward glance, walked out of the room.

Watching Lars and Damien undress, Lacey began trembling. "I want to sleep alone."

Damien tossed away the shirt he'd just removed. "No."

Nerves and need quickly wiped away all traces of fatigue as they stripped out of their clothes and slid into bed with her, one on either side of her. Lars reached out and turned off the light before turning back to her.

She gripped the covers tighter. "No."

Damien wrapped his arm around her waist and pulled her back against him, his lips skimming over her shoulder as Lars took her mouth in a quick kiss.

Lars lay on his side facing her and pulled her thigh over his leg, his warm hand holding it in place. "Go to sleep, my mate. You've had a long day."

Lacey lay stiffly between the men and waited. Lars hand moved over her thigh, the long, firm strokes becoming shorter and shorter until they stopped altogether. His hand rested there, warm, heavy, unmoving.

Damien hand pressed against her stomach, holding her against him as his breathing evened out. His cock pressed against her bottom, and Lacey held her breath as it seemed to grow even larger.

Several minutes passed and no one moved. Lacey stayed perfectly still as she listened to their breathing, afraid that by moving, she would wake one of them up. Gradually, she could feel herself relaxing, bit by bit. Listening to their breathing, feeling their warmth surround her, her eyes closed again.

* * * *

Damien heard Lacey's breathing even out and felt her body go limp against his. Holding her in his arms, he simply breathed her. Muscle by muscle he finally began to relax.

His entire body had been taut with fear ever since he'd heard the scream.

When he'd first seen the body of the woman who'd been killed, a horror like he'd never known had nearly consumed him. He'd thought it was Lacey. For the first time since he could remember, his first thought hadn't been of the pack. It had been for her.

He knew how important a mate was to a male werewolf, but he'd never thought…He felt as if he would die right then. Mind numbing pain kept him frozen until he'd heard Lars say that it wasn't her. Only then did he breathe again.

Racing inside, he'd grabbed her, just needed to feel her in his arms, just *breathing* her. How could he have lived without that beautiful smile, those adorable dimples?

Yesterday, he'd been scared when he found out Steven Galbraith was with her, but that fear had been combined with anger. He'd needed to get to her, to assure himself of her safety. Making love to her had been inevitable for all of them, a were's need to mark his woman, to be as close to her as possible after being so afraid for her.

What he'd felt tonight had been more, much more.

He'd always thought his mate would be someone who would bear his children and live her life under his protection. He'd heard from his friends in the pack just how much better sex is with one's mate and the incredibly close bond that forms between them.

But he'd never experienced anything like what he felt tonight.

He had always been a man who loved sex. Hell, all werewolves did, but he often took it beyond the norm. He loved wild, rough and kinky and made no apologies about it.

With his mate, it had been different. Yes, the sex had been incredible, especially mating a woman instead of just having sex. Knowing it would be forever had added another element that had been missing from sex in the past. Every sound she'd made had spurred him to even greater need than any he'd ever experienced before.

Those seconds when he thought Lacey had been killed, he hadn't thought of the sex at all.

He thought of her smile, that he would never see again, her dimples that he would never get to explore with his tongue, the silkiness of her hair. Breathing deeply, he filled his lungs with her scent.

"It's more, isn't it?"

Damien opened his eyes and looked across at his brother. Lars had kept his voice low, but Damien had no trouble hearing him. Just as he had no trouble seeing him in the pitch black room. Knowing exactly what his brother meant, Damien tightened his hold on Lacey, forcing himself to relax again as she groaned in her sleep. "Yeah," he replied in the same low tone. "Much more. It's more than I expected."

They both lay silent, watching their mate sleep. Finally Damien murmured, "Wes and Seth don't feel it."

Lars sighed. "No, not yet. That's why we're the ones with her tonight. She needs us."

"If they don't, I'm not sharing her with them. She deserves mates who lo—, have feelings for her."

"They will. Besides, she's already mated to them, too."

"I'm not used to feeling this way about a woman."

Lars folded Lacey's hand in his and kissed her fingers. "She won't believe us if we tell her. We'll have to take it slow. Get her used to us. She doesn't understand our ways yet."

Damien watched Lacey's face as she shifted in her sleep. "I'm going to kill him."

Lars lay back, holding Lacey's hand over his chest. "Not if I beat you to it."

* * * *

Lacey rolled to her back and stretched. As memories of the previous night came back to her, she looked to either side of her, surprised to find herself alone. Trying to push aside the feeling of disappointment, she hurried to shower, not liking to admit how anxious she felt to see everyone.

Once dressed, she checked her email again. Her eyebrows rose at the more creative threat, but she knew he could do nothing to her, at least while she stayed here. She'd deal with him when she went home.

She smiled when she opened the next email. Sarah had emailed her that she and Christina were doing well. She'd even found a job. Scared that her husband would find her, she asked if Lacey could please find a way to get some information for her. She wanted a restraining order, a divorce and she needed to get into their joint bank accounts.

Lacey emailed her back, her mind racing as she thought of how she would handle it.

Walking into the kitchen, she bent to kiss her godmother's cheek as Victor greeted her and poured her coffee.

Seth and Wes both rose, grinning, and quickly came forward. Wes lifted her against him and bent his head. Oblivious to their audience, he kissed her deeply as his arms tightened around her. Held against his strong body, she felt delicate and incredibly feminine. His strong arms provided security and surrounded her with heat. By the time he lifted his head, she felt dizzy with need.

She groaned as he slowly lowered her to her feet, the friction of his chest against her breasts causing an erotic pull from her nipples to her slit.

She didn't even have a chance to catch her breath before Seth moved in to take his place. Seth's hand curved at the back of her neck, while the other at her lower back pulled her firmly against him. He kissed her roughly, hungrily, his tongue sweeping through her mouth possessively again and again. His rough playfulness contrasted sharply with Wes's smooth, almost reverent kiss, the combination sending her senses reeling. Hearing his grandmother's chuckle, he lifted his head and grinned down at her, making her stomach flutter.

He helped her to her seat, which she appreciated. Her knees shook so badly, she didn't know if she could have made it without help.

When she reached for her coffee, she was not at all surprised to see that her hands shook.

As Victor came forward with a plate of bacon and eggs, Wes leaned forward. "How would you like to spend the day with us, honey?"

She shook her head. "I can't. I'm sorry. I'm going to spend the day with Nana."

The older woman waved her hand. "Don't be ridiculous. We'll have plenty of time to be together, especially when my grandsons convince you to stay. Have a good time with Wes and Seth. Go see their studio. We'll all have dinner together later."

"But I wanted to see about that woman, the one who died."

Wes leaned forward and touched her hand. "We're taking care of it. The best thing we can do for her and for her family is to find the person that did that to her and to make them pay. We will. Now, no more talk about it today. Seth and I have some things to finish setting up in our new studio, and we thought it would be a good idea for you to think about something else for a while."

Lacey sighed. "I would like to see your studio. Nana's told me a lot about it and she said that you did beautiful work." She looked at Wes. "Are those your paintings all over the house?"

Wes nodded and winked at his grandmother. "Grandmother hangs all of the paintings I give her. She's going to run out of places to hang them before too long."

Nana laughed. "If we ever go broke, I have a fortune in W. Tibbs paintings and Seth Lonewolf sculptures."

Lacey frowned. "I don't know a lot about art, but I've heard those names before." She looked at her godmother. "You took my grandmother and me to an art gallery once and we saw them there. Oh my God. That's you?"

At their nods, she gasped and looked at Wes. "Those landscapes you paint are breathtaking. There's so much color and they make you feel like you could reach out and touch the sand, the trees. They had one there of a storm, and I would swear I could feel the air swirling around."

Wes grinned. "Thanks. I'm glad you liked it. I've never done portraits, but I'd like to paint you."

Lacey laughed happily. "I'd love that. What an honor. You wouldn't sell it though, would you?"

Wes sipped his coffee. "Not a chance. It goes over the fireplace."

Her godmother clapped her hands. "Wonderful! I can't wait to see it."

Lacey turned to Seth. "They had two wooden sculptures you did. One was of a family of rabbits and they looked so adorable. Their fur looked so real."

"Thank you. If you'd like, I can make you one."

"Oh, no. I couldn't ask you to do that. I could never afford one of them. I know your work is in high demand. I'm sure you have orders. But I would love to see your studio. Watch you work."

Seth shook his head and chuckled, glancing at his brother. "She still doesn't get it, does she? Lacey, you're our mate now, our responsibility. We'll do whatever we need to keep you happy."

Lacey shot to her feet, bristling at being considered a 'responsibility'. Amending what had been about to come out of her mouth when she remembered her godmother, she glared at him. "I'm not your responsibility. I have some things to do. I won't have time to go with you, after all."

She strode from the room and went upstairs to grab her cell phone. If she went outside where no one could overhear her, she could call Steven and see if he would help her with Sarah. Damn it. She wouldn't be anyone's obligation.

When she got to her room, she went straight for her purse, shrieking when an arm caught her from behind.

Seth growled in her ear. "You *are* our responsibility and the sooner you accept that, the happier you'll be."

Lacey fought until he released her, lost her balance and landed on the bed. She hurriedly scrambled off the other side. Wes stood next to Seth on the other side of the bed, both men standing with their hands on their hips watching her. "Look, I didn't want to fight with you in front of your grandmother, but I'll be damned if I'm going to be your *responsibility*. I'm not your damned mate. We had sex, that's it."

Seth leaned toward her, his tone low and seductive. "I ought to paddle your ass. I'll show you just how a werewolf punishes his mate for defying him."

Moisture flowed from her despite her fear, angering her even more. She crossed her arms over her breasts to hide the fact that her nipples had hardened. The erotic threat hung in the air as she struggled for something to say. "You've got a lot of nerve. Punish me? I'm not a child to stand in the corner because I don't agree with you."

Seth's evil smile made her panties even wetter. "Werewolves don't punish their mates by making them stand in the corner, my *mate*."

She glanced at Wes, who merely raised a brow. Seeing no help there, she clenched her jaw as she turned back to Seth. "I. Am. Not. Your. Mate. Fuck you."

Seth started to move around the bed when Wes stepped forward to stop him. "Leave her alone. She doesn't understand all of this yet. We agreed to give her some time."

Seth tried to shake his brother off, but Wes held firm as Lacey scrambled across the bed. "She's my mate, too, damn it. Get the fuck off of me!"

They went down in a tangle of arms and legs. Lacey used the opportunity to escape. Racing out into the hallway, she ran straight into Lars.

"What the fuck is going on?" He grabbed her as she tried to run past and pulled her against him. He lifted her face to his as Wes and Seth appeared at the doorway. "The scent of her anger and fear is all through the fucking house. What are you two doing to her?"

Lacey had had enough. Pulling away from Lars, she pointed at Seth and Wes. "Seth has decided that I need to be punished because I have a brain. He claims I'm his *responsibility* and wants me to meekly follow his orders like a damned puppy or something. If I don't, he says he's going to *punish* me. He came at me, and Wes stopped him."

She ignored the concern on Damien's face as he came racing up the stairs. "I don't need this shit. I want all of you to leave me the hell alone."

She ran down the stairs, passing Damien, who looked mad as hell and headed for the back of the house. If they all thought they could treat her as if they owned her, they could all think again. How many times did she have to tell them to leave her alone?

Furious and aroused, damn it, she strode through the kitchen and out the back. Not until she got there, did she realize she still had her cell phone in her hand. Forcing herself to calm down, she pulled Steven's card out of her pocket and dialed. Who knew when she'd have this chance again?

* * * *

Lars watched, resigned, as his furious mate ran down the stairs. Sharing a look with Damien, he turned to Wes and Seth and sighed. "We have to talk."

Behind the closed study door, Lars paced, hoping like hell he could get through to Seth. "We have to do this slowly. Seth, you're going to make Lacey bolt if you don't calm the hell down."

Seth bared his teeth. "Don't you fucking tell me how to deal with my mate. What the hell is wrong with all of you? You know damned well that I have every right to punish my mate if she defies me. You're all turning into a bunch of fucking pussies." He turned to Damien, jerking a thumb at Lars. "Him I get. But you? Since when do you act like this? I've seen the way you are with your women. You're in charge, and they have to do what you say. This is our *mate*, and you're turning pussy with her. What the fuck is your problem?"

Damien leaned forward, resting his elbows on his knees and looking down at his hands. "She's more to me than other women."

Seth's eyebrows went up. "Of course, she's more. She's our mate."

Damien shook his head and looked up at Seth. "When you saw the dead woman yesterday, what was your first thought?"

Seth frowned at him. "I was pissed off that someone had come here, on our land, and killed. I thought it was Lacey, and it pissed me off more. We'd just found her, and some asshole thought they could get away with killing our mate. I was sad that she was gone. She's supposed to be ours now, and I wanted her back. I want a mate, kids.

Why? What was yours?"

Damien leaned back, and Lars saw the remembered horror on his face. Glancing at Seth, he could see the surprise on his, along with dawning realization. Damien let out a shuddering sigh. "At first I didn't think anything. It just felt like someone had slid a knife between my ribs. I'd never see her smile, those dimples again. Hear her laugh. Hold her close. Life was over." He stood and walked out the door, closing it quietly behind him.

No one said anything as they all absorbed the implication of Damien's words. Finally, Lars touched Seth's shoulder. "Damien and I already have strong feelings for her. If it's not love, it's damned close. I got to her first and caught her scent. All that I kept thinking was 'It's not her. Thank God it's not her.' I didn't even think of the pack. All I could think about was her. She's not used to any of this, and we can't lose her. I know you don't feel yet what we feel for her, but please ease up. Right now we have to make her as comfortable as possible, get her used to being the mate to four men, werewolves, and find the person who wants to kill her. It's a hell of a lot for her and for us to get used to. Just ease the fuck up. Let her settle."

Seth shook Lars off. "That's easy for you to say. You got to fuck her last night. I want my fucking mate."

Lars shook his head. "We didn't. As much as both of us wanted to, needed to, we didn't. Last night she needed to feel warm and safe. She slept between us, and we both held onto her all night. I don't know about Damien, but my dick was hard all night long. But we want her to trust us. She thinks all we want is sex and to boss her around. If that's all you give her, that's what she'll continue to think."

Seth shook his head. "So because Damien thinks he's in love with her, he's going to let her walk all over him?"

Lars chuckled as the knot in his stomach eased. "No. If anything, Damien will be the first to look forward to punishing our mate if she defies us, but for now, he's had his legs knocked out from under him."

"And you didn't? I thought you were falling in love with her, too."

Lars grinned, love for their mate nearly overwhelming him. "I am. But I always expected to fall in love with my mate. Damien didn't. And for this to work with her, we're all going to have to present a united front. She needs strength and, if not love, affection. She knows we all want to bed her, but she also has to feel that we care for her. She has to feel safe with us, and that she's our priority. We can't be what she needs if we don't stick together."

Wes stood. "And if we keep fighting, she'll never let any of us close to her."

"Exactly."

* * * *

Damien stood just inside the French doors and listened as his mate asked whoever the hell she was talking to on her cell phone, how a woman could disappear without a trace. Absorbing the kick to the gut, he fought the urge not to go out there and grab the cell phone from her hand.

Rethinking his strategy, he strolled outside and sat at one of the tables, waiting for her to finish. She flicked a glance at him and lowered her voice even more. She obviously didn't know he could still hear her. She hurriedly thanked whoever she spoke to and ended the call, promising to call back. Maybe if he and his brothers each spent a little time with her, one on one, they could get her to trust them a little.

His reasons were a little more selfish than that, though. He just wanted to be with her. He sat back, his legs stretched out in front of him and tried to appear relaxed, when he really wanted to carry her to bed and spend the day making love to her.

Trying to appear as non-threatening as possible, he smiled and watched her walk toward him. But if she thought she could get away with running away from them, she had a lot to learn about her mates.

* * * *

Lacey walked toward Damien, thankful that she'd been able to finish her call before one of them came looking for her. Leaning back in his chair, wearing only jeans and a black t-shirt, his feet bare, he looked sexy as hell. His long hair had been left loose and she itched to run her fingers through it.

"Good morning, baby. Can I have a good morning kiss?"

Expecting him to pull her onto his lap as soon as she got near, she stopped between his splayed thighs and leaned down to kiss him. His lips felt firm and soft and she let hers linger. Surprised and disappointed when he didn't pull her onto his lap or try to deepen the kiss, she straightened and stared down at him. "Good morning. What are you doing out here?"

He put his hands behind his head, leaning back further, the move pulling his t-shirt tightly across his chest. "I just came out to see you. If you're not going with Wes and Seth to the studio, I thought maybe you'd like to come with me. Lars and I just finished setting up the equipment in our new office. I thought maybe you'd like to see it and see what kind of gambler you are."

Lacey had trouble focusing on his words. He looked so relaxed and laid back and so damned *hot*, she just wanted to curl into his lap and feel his arms come around her. She knew if she laid her head on his chest, and tilted her head back, he would give her one of those devilish grins and kiss her until her head spun.

"Lacey?"

Lacey tore her eyes from his chest and blinked, her face burning at being caught staring. "Sorry, I was thinking about something. What did you say?"

Damien stood, towering over her. "Come on, I want to show you how I make my living."

Lacey grinned. "You mean how you keep the wolves from the door?"

Damien chuckled and tapped her nose. "Cute."

She took the hand he offered and followed him inside. Heat trailed up her arm where he touched her, which she tried to ignore. Obviously he wanted to spend some time with her. As much as she had the hots for him, she really appreciated the gesture. She'd like to get to know them better.

Damien led her to the second floor and down another hall. "This is the master's wing. Our room is the room at the end."

Lacey blinked. "Our room?"

Damien smiled. "Come on. Let's take a look. They should be almost done."

Before Lacey could object, he pulled her down the hall to the room at the end. The double doors stood wide open and she could see a lot of activity inside. Several men smiled at them as they painted, moved furniture, and from the noise coming from the adjoining bathroom, she assumed someone worked on the plumbing. Her eyes widened when she saw the size of the room. "This is huge. It's at least four times the size of the other room."

"There'll be five of us sharing this room, baby. We need a lot of room. The bed they're setting up in the middle there will be for you and two of us. Two more beds will be set up on either side so that even though we can't all sleep together, we'll at least be in the same room."

"Damien, I told you—"

His kiss cut off the rest of what she'd been about to say. He touched her lips lightly, fleetingly before nuzzling her jaw. "We'll go slowly, I promise. Come on, I want to show you my office."

Lacey allowed him to lead her down the hall. "I know you went to a lot of trouble to do this but—"

"Do you like the color? Wes picked it out, since he knows more about that stuff."

Lacey nodded. "Yes, it's a really nice green."

Damien opened the door to a room next to the master suite and grinned, ushering her inside. "Wes said he wanted green because of your eyes. We all agreed. Once we get settled, you can change whatever you like."

Lacey smiled up at him, her breath catching when she saw the tender look on his face. "Sometimes you make me think this could work."

"It will, Lacey. Just give it time."

A sudden thought occurred to her and she backed away from him. "I won't turn into a werewolf, will I? I mean, like, if you bite me or something? Damn it, you're always biting me."

Damien threw back his head and laughed, slowly stalking her around the room. "You've been reading too many books. You have to be born a werewolf, my mate. Our children will be weres." He grinned devilishly and looked down to where her nipples poked at the front of her shirt. "But I can't promise not to bite."

With a squeal, Lacey took off, giggling.

Damien backtracked, closing and locking the door. "Do you know how a werewolf's animal instincts are aroused when he has to chase his mate?"

Lacey eyes him warily. "What do you mean?"

"It heats his blood. Chasing a mate who is trying to escape, especially one in heat, can drive a werewolf wild."

Lacey gulped. "In heat?"

Damien's grin was pure sin. "In heat, my mate. You've had my brothers and me close to howling. Unless you're pregnant, you're going to have all four of us this way every month. We'll all be chasing you around the house, starving for a taste of that cream and doing our best to get into that tight pussy. If you're ever in heat during a full moon, you're in huge trouble, sweetheart."

Lacey felt that cream he talked about dampening her panties as he continued to stalk her around the room. She couldn't look away, mesmerized by the way his muscles bunched and shifted as he moved gracefully around the room, slowly closing in on her.

She knew damned well he could catch her whenever he wanted. The fact that he didn't told her that he enjoyed this game as much as she did. "What do you mean? What happens during a full moon?" How could she resist him?

He took another step closer. "Our baser instincts come out in force."

Lacey began unbuttoning the shirt she wore, thrilling at the flare of heat in Damien's eyes. "You mean worse than now?"

Damien licked his lips. "Much worse."

Sliding the last button free, she moved behind his desk as she reached for the front fastening of her bra. "Ooh, I'm scared."

Damien's grin flashed again. "No, you're not. You're aroused. I want that cream that's dripping from you. I'm going to bury my face between your soft thighs and drink my fill."

Lacey had never been so aroused by just words before. When Damien started throwing off clothing, she knew she didn't stand a chance of making this game last. Inch by inch, he revealed his leanly muscled body, making her mouth water. To think that all he revealed belonged to her made her giddy with need. "You'll have to catch me."

He lifted a brow and growled. "Lose the shirt."

Lacey froze as the last of his clothing came off and he stalked toward her, slowly stroking the thick cock that rose magnificently toward his flat stomach. Her pussy wept even more with the need to have that incredible thickness inside her. She raised her eyes to his. "Make me-oh!"

He'd come over the desk and pulled her against him in a move so fast, she'd only seen a blur. Ridding her of the shirt and bra, he reached for the fastening of her cotton pants. "What were you saying, my mate?"

She stepped out of her pants and reached up, grabbing fistfuls of his silky hair. "I don't remember. Kiss me."

He ripped her panties from her and sat down, pulling her onto his lap. "With pleasure."

His hot hands moved over her as his mouth took possession of hers, kissing her deeply, his tongue sweeping through her mouth repeatedly and tangling with hers. He tasted like sin and she knew she would never get enough. When his hand covered her breast, she moaned and arched into him.

He lowered his head, taking a nipple into his mouth and scraping his teeth lightly over it. His mouth moved all around her breast, nipping the delicate underside and making her jolt. The sting only sensitized her breast even more. Amazed at the height of her arousal already, she cried out when he cupped it, stroking her nipple with his rough thumb. His growls began, thrilling her even more and making her tremble. The hard cock against her bottom had her squirming restlessly.

She broke off the kiss, panting. "I want you inside me. Please tell me you have a condom with you."

He grinned and opened a desk drawer. "We all keep them everywhere now. But before I fuck you, I'm eating that pussy."

Lacey gasped as he lifted her onto the desk and slid his chair close. After helping her to lie back, he lifted her thighs over his shoulders.

The first swipe of his tongue made her jolt. He firmed his grip and ate at her, his low growls vibrated against her slit, his mouth hot and hungry as he feasted on her and drove her quickly to the edge and over.

She screamed as she came, the pleasure so intense it took her breath away.

Damien lifted his head long enough to flash a grin at her. "Mmm, more cream." He lowered his head again.

Lacey dug her heels into his back as his tongue plunged deep. "Oh God."

She writhed on his desk as his devious tongue went back for more.

Her body shook as her orgasm had barely ended before he threw her into another.

He sucked her clit hard into his mouth, scraping it lightly with his teeth and making her scream once again. Her clit had become so sensitive, even the slightest touch became too much.

"Please, no more, oh God, it's too much."

He stood, and she could see he'd already donned a condom. Between one breath and the next, he plunged deep, and she gasped as he filled her, giving her just what she needed. He began stroking immediately, his groans and growls blending together into a sound so primal, she went wild beneath him.

If not for his strong grip, she would have fallen off the desk as he bucked against him. Her throbbing clit became needy again and she reached down to stroke herself, cut short by a slap on her hand.

"No."

"Damien, I need—"

"Hands over your head, or I'll stop."

She raised her hands over her head, gripping the edge of the desk. "Don't stop. Don't stop."

"Your pussy's milking my cock so good. So fucking good. Soft little ripples."

Lacey arched on the desk as his cock rasped repeatedly over that spot inside her. "Damien, oh God, I'm going to come again. Please. Please."

He roared and pushed deep, pinching her clit erotically. "Come with me, baby."

Lacey soared once again, crying out brokenly as his cock pulsed deep inside her. She loved those wicked growls he made as he pulled her against him and settled back in the chair with her straddling him. Her pussy still clenched on him, milking everything from him as she laid her head on his shoulder and struggled to catch her breath.

She caressed his chest, stroking the silky hair there and smiled when she felt the muscles quiver under her hand. Touching her lips to his throat, she sighed. "You wore me out."

Damien chuckled. "Ditto."

She lay limply against him. "Do you think if we just stayed here like this, the others would eventually find us?"

He ran a hand down her back and pulled her close. "Eventually. I just hope it's not Grandmother or Victor. I would hate to have to kill him for seeing you naked."

Lacey sat up. "Victor? I didn't think." She tried to scramble from his lap, but he held on. "Let go. I have to get dressed. What if he comes in?"

Damien chuckled and nuzzled her lips with his. "I'll hear and smell him before he gets here." He swatted her bottom. "Let's get cleaned up. I want to show you some things."

* * * *

Once they'd gotten cleaned up and dressed, Lacey sat on Damien's lap at his desk looking at his computer screen as he tried to explain the ins and outs of the stock market to her. "I can't pick stock until I see who runs the company," Lacey said for about the tenth time.

"I guess we got dressed just in time. Honey, you can't buy stock in a company based on the CEO's looks."

"Why not? You just guess."

"But they're educated guesses."

"Well so are mine. Look, if you want me to try this, I'm doing it my way. That other guy had beady eyes."

Damien's lips twitched as he stared down at her. "Okay. I'm going to set you up with an account."

Lacey started to jump up, but Damien held her in place. "I don't want your money."

Damien sighed. "Okay, I'll set up another computer for you. It'll be a fake account. I have a program that will do that. Then, you can pick the stocks you want to buy however the hell you pick them and we'll see how you do."

Intrigued, Lacey tilted her head to look at him. "But how will we know who wins?"

"Competitive little thing, aren't you? I just wanted you to get a feel for what I do every day. But if you want to compete, I'll set up another fake account for myself. We'll both start with the same amount of money and see who makes the most. What's the time frame?"

Reality came crashing back in. "Damn, I forgot. Maybe we'd better just forget it."

"Lacey, I—"

A knock at the door interrupted whatever Damien had been about to say.

"Come in."

Victor came through the door closing it behind him. "Agent O'Reilly is downstairs. He wants to see everyone. Your grandmother and brothers are waiting in the study."

Damien stood setting Lacey on her feet. "Damn it. O'Reilly's becoming a real pain in the ass."

Victor nodded. "He sounds more upset than usual."

Lacey and Damien followed Victor downstairs and went into the study. Everyone had gathered, looking none too happy as they all shot dirty looks at Agent O'Reilly.

The agent stood when Lacey came into the room and watched her as she seated herself on the sofa next to her godmother. "Well, Miss Roberts, it seems you lied to me when you told me that you didn't know of anyone who would want you dead."

Chapter Nine

Lacey groaned, burying her face in her hands as everyone started yelling at once.

"What do you mean, someone wants Lacey dead? Who is it?"

Lacey lifted her head, wincing at the ice in Lars' tone. "No one. It couldn't have been him. Damn it, Agent O'Reilly, couldn't we have talked about this alone?"

Nana reached for her hand. "Oh, Lacey. What's going on?" She looked at the agent. "You must be mistaken. Why would someone want to hurt Lacey?"

Damien gripped her arms and lifted her until they were eye level, surprising her once again with his strength. His eyes flashed dangerously. "If you don't spill it right now, you're in big trouble."

"Put me down."

When Wes came to stand beside them and touched Damien's arm, he lowered her to her feet, but the fire in his eyes remained. "Talk."

Damien blocked the agent's view of her, so she leaned close and whispered up to him. "Can we see what Agent O'Reilly says first?"

Wes leaned down to brush his lips across her cheek. "We'll talk when O'Reilly leaves."

Lacey nodded, taken aback when Damien inclined his head. *He'd heard that?* She sighed. Of course he'd heard that. She wondered if she'd ever get used to this.

Wes sat on the arm of the sofa next to her while Damien moved behind her with Lars. Seth remained seated in the chair next to their grandmother, watching all of them closely. Lacey smiled reassuringly at Nana before she turned to face the agent.

Agent O'Reilly watched all of them warily.

His eyes slid from one to the other as though trying to figure something out. He stood stiffly, his hands loose at his sides. After a few minutes, he appeared to relax somewhat, his attitude changing from wary to almost pleasant in a heartbeat. "I just spoke to your former employer, the principal at the school where you taught."

Nana gripped her arm. "Lacey, what's he talking about? Former employer? You quit your job?"

"No, she got fired."

"Fired? No, not my Lacey. You must have gotten your information wrong, as usual, Agent O'Reilly."

Lacey sighed. "No, Nana. He's not wrong. I did get fired, shortly before coming here." Lacey grinned at her godmother. "It was worth it."

When Agent O'Reilly smiled and pulled a small pad of paper and a pen out of his pocket before sitting, she glanced up in time to see the brief look of shock on Wes's face.

The agent flipped through several pages before stopping. "I talked to Thomas Shultz, the principal at the school. He seemed very anxious about how you were doing and also sounded like he's a little afraid of Ted Johnson."

Lacey sighed. "Everyone is."

Wes tangled his fingers with hers and pulled them onto his thigh. Lars' hands on her shoulders tightened. "Who the hell is Ted Johnson and why is everyone afraid of him?"

Agent O'Reilly's chuckle sounded rusty, as though from lack of use. "Apparently Miss Roberts isn't. She reported him for child abuse. I checked. It took three reports before someone finally showed up to investigate him."

Lacey shot to her feet. "That's because he bribes and threatens everyone. I had to go to the newspaper to get him investigated. After that, they had to or face public outrage." She sighed and moved to look out the window. "His little girl, Christina, was one of my students. She was very quiet, and at first I thought she was just shy. At recess, she stayed by herself and wouldn't run or jump or play with the others. Once, I had to tie her shoes for her and I saw the bruises on her leg."

The men cursed behind her and she turned. "I started really paying attention to her. I spoke to the nurse and together, we got her to show us her injuries. The nurse photographed them and we called the child protection services. We got her to tell us, a little here and there, what had happened."

Seth stood, his hands clenched into fists. "He beat on a little girl? Did you tell the mother?"

Lacey nodded. "Yes, I had someone cover for me one day so I could speak to the mother, Sarah, while he was working. She came to the door with a black eye and a broken wrist. He beat her, too."

O'Reilly looked back at his notes. "When you reported him, he came after you."

Lacey nodded, smiling reassuringly at Nana. "He's a big man in town, rich, powerful. A lot of people in Millville depend on him for their paychecks. He had no problem getting people to harass me. He put enough pressure on Ted to make him fire me. He contributes to the school, you see."

Agent O'Reilly looked down at his notes. "He slashed your tires, made sure you couldn't buy groceries in town, threw rocks through your windows and made threatening phone calls. Didn't you go to the police? I couldn't find a report."

Lacey laughed humorlessly. "They're in his pocket, too. The newspaper is investigating the entire thing. When Ted fired me, the reporter thought the best thing I could do would be to get out of town. There was so much pressure on the mayor, he had to have Ted arrested. I understand he was free an hour later."

O'Reilly smiled, something it appeared he seldom did. "What an amazing coincidence that in that hour, Sarah and Christina Johnson and Lacey Roberts all disappeared."

Lacey grinned. "She wanted to get away, but was afraid to do it on her own. I took her someplace safe. She's trying to divorce him."

"Has she contacted you?"

"Yes."

"Has he?"

Lacey hesitated.

"Lacey!"

Lacey looked up, wincing as Lars approached, looking madder than hell.

"Is this fucking asshole still threatening you?"

Lacey sighed and patted his chest to calm him. It didn't appear to help. "By email. He must have gotten my email address from Ted and has been sending me threatening emails. The threats are very vague, not something that would ever stand up in court. Mostly name calling." Trying to play it off, she grinned. "He thinks I'm a bitch."

Her godmother gasped from across the room. "Lacey, is this what's been bothering you. You sounded so strange on the phone and then said you might not be able to come."

"She probably had to make sure she didn't end up with any more cuts and bruises before she committed herself," O'Reilly offered helpfully. "She couldn't very well show up here all beat up, now could she?"

Lacey glared at him. "That's enough. There's no reason to worry Nana."

Her godmother stood, making Lacey groan. Damn, Nana could be quite formidable when it served her purpose. "I want to know what happened. Everything."

O'Reilly, the bastard, seemed only too happy to help. "One day after school, when she first reported him, she was jumped and beaten in the school parking lot. Even the principal watched, afraid to get involved." He looked down at his notes. "She had to go to the emergency room for x-rays. I have the ER report here."

Wes leapt forward and jerked it out of his hand. He read for a minute or two before folding the paper and sticking it in his pocket, his eyes telling her that this conversation was far from over.

Lars' jaw clenched and she smiled up at him, trying to diffuse some of the tension. "I'm fine. You can see that for yourself."

He smiled coldly back at her and leaned down to whisper in her ear. "When O'Reilly leaves, we're going to have a nice little talk, my mate."

"Johnson is staying in the media light, going to charity functions and the like," Agent O'Reilly continued. "If I were a suspicious man, I'd say he wanted to be well alibied. He's been asked about his wife and is telling everyone she's out of town visiting a relative."

Lacey turned away from Lars to face the agent. "She's divorcing him and won't be back."

"He's got people looking for her." O'Reilly shook his head. "That's what he gets for enlisting amateurs to do his dirty work. Word is that he's hired someone to take care of her, but he's bullying people into finding her for him." He paused a beat. "And he's looking for you."

Damien shot forward. "Why don't you go tell this bastard where she is? I would love for him to show up here."

O'Reilly smiled smugly. "What are you going to do, rip his throat out?"

Lacey put her hands on her hips and scowled at him. "You're not going to go into another werewolf story, are you? Damn it, someone killed that poor woman and, according to you, it's because they mistook her for me. I'm trying to help a woman get away from this other lunatic who beats women and children. I can't say I have a lot of faith in your help if all you're going to do is make up stories. Can you please take this seriously?"

O'Reilly stood, pocketing his pad and pen. "Miss Roberts, I do take all of this very seriously. I'll be back when I get more information. When I find proof that these men are werewolves, and that when they shift, they kill people, believe me, I'm going to make sure they stay in a cage for the rest of their lives."

* * * *

Lacey watched Agent O'Reilly roar down the drive before turning back to the others. "I don't know about you, but I'm starting to get hungry." She started from the room, but Lars stepped into her path, blocking her exit. His eyes glittered dangerously, never leaving hers. "Grandmother, will you excuse us for a bit? Victor, will you please see to it that we're not disturbed?"

Lacey plopped on the sofa, curling into the corner as Nana and Victor left.

"I don't know what you're so mad at. I took care of it and I'm here now. It's not like I'm in any danger. Besides, he's a business man, not a killer."

Wes stopped pacing long enough to glare at her. "If he had someone beat the hell out of you just for reporting him, don't you realize what he'll do to you now that he's lost his wife and daughter because of you. He's got to know that you're the one that helped them get away, damn it."

"Which is why I can't stay! I've been telling you all along that I would be leaving here. I wanted to see Nana before I disappeared and wanted to assure her that I'm okay. Her birthday was the perfect opportunity. I promised Sarah I would help her. I've already started that. As soon as I have what I need, I'm going to her. Once I get her settled, I have to go back and get the rest of my things before I can move on."

Lars bent down and nipped her shoulder warningly. "No, you're not. You're our mate and you'll stay here where we can protect you."

Lacey jumped up again. "I told all of you that I can't be your mate. I gave you all my reasons except this one. With all that's going on right now, I can't make a decision like that. I have to finish what I started." She laid a hand on Wes's arm. "Try to understand. They need my help. Sarah's so scared."

Wes's brows went up. "Do you think I don't know that? Do you really think we're going to leave that woman and her daughter out there defenseless? You have a lot to learn about your mates—and if you say we're not your mates once more, you're going over my knee. You've been warned. But you've lied to us since you got here. Do you really think you're going to get away with that?"

"I haven't lied. What was I supposed to do, walk through the door and say? 'Oh, I need help. Some lunatic is after me.'"

"*Yes!*" Four deep voices answered as one.

"Better yet, you should have called when you first had trouble with him back home," Seth added.

"I didn't even know you. The same applies to when I first got here. Then you start talking all this mate stuff and demanding that I stay. I can't *believe* I actually had sex with all of you."

Damien gripped her chin. "We didn't just have sex, Lacey. We mated you. Do you remember how your pussy burned as our seed mixed inside you? Now you carry our scent. Soon you'll carry our child. You're our *mate*, and we're not about to let anyone hurt you and we're not going to let you go. If you ever need our help, you're supposed to come to us and ask. You are *not* to keep secrets from us, especially regarding your safety. If there's ever *anything* wrong, whether it's a threat, or you're just not happy, you *come to us*."

"Damn it, I don't live like this. In case you haven't noticed, I'm a big girl and I can take care of my problems myself. I don't need the four of you to do it for me."

Lars leaned back in the leather chair behind the desk. "Whether you want our help or not, you're getting it and before we leave this room, you're going to learn that we mean business. This isn't some kind of game to us, Lacey. You're our mate and we need to protect you and make you happy. We won't put up with you keeping secrets from us." He held his hand out, waving his fingers. "Let me see that doctor report."

Wes drew it out of his pocket and handed it to his brother. "I admire your independence, Lacey, and your strength. But you have mates who need to take care of you, and we can't do that properly if you're going to keep things from us. That won't be allowed."

Lacey blinked. "Won't be allowed? Have you heard anything I've said at all? I'm not staying. You're not—"

Wes raised a brow, daring her to finish. "Go ahead. Finish that sentence. I'm dying to put you over my knee. You've already racked up a lot of offenses that won't be tolerated. Lars and Damien have kept Seth and me from punishing you so far because they think you're not used to all this yet. But you're pushing it. Badly."

She walked past the sofa and, Damien, who'd sat there with her earlier, reached out to grab her and pulled her to stand between his knees. To her amazement, he lifted her by the waist and placed her on his lap, straddling him. "You're awfully strong, aren't you?"

His lips twitched as his hands moved over her hips. "Werewolves are a bit stronger than your average man, honey. Which makes it even worse when you won't let us protect you."

Lacey sighed. "I'm not used to having someone telling me what to do or protect me, but I have to help Sarah and Christina. I guess it would be nice to have some help with them."

Damien lifted a brow. "You'll accept help for them but not to protect yourself." He pushed her hair back as the others moved forward, all talking at once. Lacey closed her eyes tiredly and they all became silent.

"I don't want to feel like I'm an obligation to you. I'll agree to try to have a relationship with all of you, but I can't promise anything. I really don't think it'll work. There's already been too much fighting, and like I said, we don't really know each other very well."

Lars sat next to them on the sofa and took her hand in his. "That's all we can ask for, but no holding back. It's just as new to us to have someone to care for and protect, especially since we learned we'd be sharing a mate. This is new territory for us, just as it is with you, but you have to understand that we're not about to let anyone get away with threatening you or allowing them to hurt you. If you try to hide things from us, it's just going to piss us off."

He held up a hand when she would have interrupted. "We're bigger and meaner than you could ever be. There are four of us with an entire pack behind us. Let's face facts, honey. We're a lot better equipped to take care of this than you are."

"I hate feeling like a burden."

Wes leaned over the back of the sofa and touched her cheek. "You're not at all. You've brought us all together when nothing else could have and we all care for you very much. We all have big shoulders that you can lean on whenever you want. That's not being a burden Lacey."

Damien grabbed the ends of her shirt, pulling them apart and sending buttons flying. "You're a pain in the ass, that's what you are. Not only do we have to protect you, we have to make sure you're nice and warm at night and keep you satisfied. It's a tough job all right."

Lars removed her shirt while Damien quickly dispensed with her bra.

Naked from the waist up, Lacey gripped Damien's shoulders as his hands covered her breasts. Between moans, she asked, "Are you sure you're up to the job?"

Damien raised his hips, pressing the huge bulge there against her center. "I'm up to it all right. Keeping our mate happy is going to be a full time job."

She shuddered when Lars moved in behind her, pushing her hair aside to sink his teeth erotically into her neck, his hands going to the fastening of her jeans. "Do you know how hard it was to lie next to you last night, all soft and warm and not make love to you?"

Lying back against Lars as he slid his fingers inside her panties, Lacey gasped. "Why didn't you?"

Damien's hands moved on her breasts, stroking and teasing her nipples as Wes and Seth stood behind him, watching everything.

Lars kissed her shoulder. "Because that's not what you needed. You needed to feel safe after what happened, and we made sure you did."

"That's the only reason you got to keep the nightgown," Damien added, lightly pinching her nipples.

Lars lifted and turned her so the others could rid her of her jeans and panties before settling her once again to straddle Damien's lap.

The feeling of vulnerability at being totally naked while the men remained fully clothed made her even hotter. She closed her eyes when Lars pulled her back against him again, his hands cupping her breasts and teasing her nipples. When Damien moved, she looked down to see him sliding his jeans down his hips. Her breath caught as Lars' hand slid over her stomach and continued downward. Parting her folds, his fingers slid through her slit and into her pussy.

Lacey gripped his forearms, her body bowed as his thick finger stroked her. His thumb flicked teasingly over her clit as Damien's hands came up to cover her breasts again.

Lars scraped his teeth over her neck again. "Have you ever been taken in your ass, my mate?"

Lacey's eyes popped open. "Of course not. I'm, ohh God, I'm not very um, ah, experienced."

Lars bit her earlobe. "You will be. You have four mates to see to your education. Seth, Wes, would one of you please go get the lube?"

"Oh, God, I'm not ready for something like that. And I'm not ready to get pregnant."

Seth grinned. "I'll get the condoms, too."

Lars nuzzled her neck as he continued his erotic stroking. "You'll be ready for me to take your ass before I do, gorgeous."

Damien glanced at Lars. "Hold onto her. I have to taste her pussy again."

Lacey thrilled at the way their voices became deep, growling whenever they became aroused. It aroused her even more. "I love how you growl. It's so sexy."

Damien waited for Lars to withdraw from her and, holding her tight bottom in his hands, lifted her to his mouth. "The scent of your cream brings out the animal in all of us."

Lacey had never experienced this kind of erotic word play and didn't want it to end. "I thought only cats, ohh, liked cream."

Damien slid his tongue through her slit, from anus to clit, making Lacey cry out as she jolted in their arms. "Werewolves love their mate's cream and feast on it every chance they get. Especially when they're in heat. Cream for me, my mate."

Lacey bowed against Lars as Damien held her to his mouth and feasted. Aware that Lars and Wes watched what Damien did to her only added to her pleasure. Wes came around the sofa to sit next to Damien, stroking her stomach and breasts and teasing her nipples until she thought she would go mad.

Feeling hands on the other side, she opened her eyes to see that Seth now sat next to Damien, seemingly enthralled at what his brother did to her.

Lars' erotic growl in her ear only sent her higher. "I can't wait to taste that sweet cream. Next time, it's mine."

"Oh God."

Wes leaned down to nuzzle a breast. "Look how beautiful she is, all pink and flushed." He flicked a nipple with his tongue. "Look at these pretty, little nipples."

"Sensitive, too." Seth lightly pinched the other.

Lacey held on to Lars as Damien's tongue thrust into her again and again. The growls he made vibrated against her slit erotically as did his groans of appreciation. Their hands and mouths moved over her, touching her everywhere. The desperate cries and pleas that filled the room astounded her. She'd never sounded like that before, never felt like such a sexual being before.

With them, all she could do was *feel*.

The sounds of the other's praise and encouragement and Damien's growls of appreciation, made her feel like the most desired and wanted woman in the world.

Lars nipped her neck sharply. "Hurry up, Damien. Go slow when you're alone. We can't wait any more."

Damien's lips surrounded Lacey's clit, and using his teeth, he sucked it sharply into his mouth as he had earlier.

Lacey screamed as fire raced through her. Her body jolted as electric flashes of pleasure hit with a force that stole her breath. They radiated from her clit outward and touched every inch of her, until even her fingers tingled. He kept her there, not allowing her to come down until she thought she would die from the pleasure.

Just when she thought she would, he released her, licking her clit lightly to bring her down slowly. Still trembling, she allowed them to adjust her to their liking, trusting their strength as they repositioned her against Damien's chest.

He slid down, lifting her to straddle his stomach. She heard the rip of foil and felt his hands brush her bottom as he donned a condom. When he lifted her, she grabbed on to his shoulders as he positioned her over his cock.

She shuddered as he filled her, inch by incredible inch, while Lars, Wes, and Seth murmured to her, using their hands and mouths everywhere. Her head fell back as his cock slid along delicate tissue, causing delicious little tingles of pleasure.

"You feel so fucking good, baby. Hot and tight."

Lacey had never made love to anyone so vocal before and couldn't believe how much his words turned her on. All four of them whispered erotic things to her during lovemaking, but Damien was by far the most talkative.

Lars growled the most. He did so now, running his hands over her bottom as Damien buried his cock deep inside her. He ran his lips over her neck as he pressed her down onto Damien's chest, his lips moving slowly down her back. When he got to her bottom, he scraped his teeth over the sensitive flesh.

Lacey jumped, unable to sit up as Damien's arms came around

her. She lifted her face to his. "Lars bit me. All of you bite me." Her voice came out in a moan as Lars ran his thumbs down the crease of her bottom.

Damien's laugh sounded tortured as he smiled down at her, cradled against his shoulder. "Werewolves bite when they're aroused, especially with their mate."

Lacey shuddered as he scraped an especially sensitive spot on her neck with his teeth. She moaned and gripped him tighter, trying to rock her hips when Lars pressed down on her lower back to hold her still. She groaned and pulled at Damien's hair until she lifted his head. "I want to move."

Instead of helping her, his grip tightened. His eyes looked even darker than before. "Stay still. Lars is going to lube that tight ass so he can fuck it while I'm fucking your pussy. Stop clenching on my cock. It's hard enough to hold back. Just stay still and we'll make it so good for you."

Lacey moaned again as Lars touched a finger, covered with the cool lube to her bottom hole. "It's already good."

"We'll make it better," Damien growled and she looked up to see him looking down at what Lars did to her.

Seth and Wes both rubbed her back and buttocks, their low growling words, alternately praising and demanding.

Wes turned her to face him as he began throwing off clothing. "We're going to watch Lars open that tight hole of yours. At one time or another, each of us will take you there. But for now, I want to feel your mouth."

Lacey watched mesmerized as Wes finished undressing, watched how his cock sprang up when he shucked his jeans. She cried out and bucked in Damien's arms as Lars pushed against her opening.

Damien's arms tightened. "Easy, my mate. Lars has to work a lot of lube into you, so he doesn't hurt you."

Lars caressed her buttocks with his other hand. "That's my girl. Try to relax your bottom a little. I'll go nice and slow."

Wes's cock jumped as he watched what Lars did to her. "I've never seen anything so fucking sexy in my life."

Lacey felt two more hands on her bottom, spreading her cheeks wider and knew they had to be Seth's. She couldn't believe how wanton and sexy she felt as four pairs of hands touched her. She never thought of herself as being such a sexual creature before.

Wes touched the side of her face as he stroked his cock with the other hand. She had trouble taking her eyes from it and watched as it got closer and closer until it brushed her lips. "Take me into your mouth, my mate. I need to feel your mouth on me."

Lacey opened eagerly, dying to taste him. Wes slid the head of his cock between her lips as Lars slid a finger deep inside her anus.

She jolted, moaning around Wes's cock as Lars and Seth rubbed her bottom.

"She's so fucking tight," Lars growled in a voice almost unrecognizable. "Fuck her. It's going to take some time to open her up and you'll never be able to hold off that long."

"Fuck," Seth continued to rub her bottom. "She's got the most gorgeous fucking ass."

Damien's grip tightened as he began to rock her on his cock, simultaneously moving her on Wes's. "Jesus, I can feel you stroking her. Her pussy keeps clenching. Fuck. I'm never going to last with her."

Lacey's system went on overload. With a cock in her mouth and one in her pussy, and Lars thick finger moving in her bottom, she became nothing more than a creature of need, shivering and trembling as her peak soon approached. Cool shivers and hot jolts of pleasure raced through her body at the same time, creating sensations in her that she'd never before experienced.

"Give me the lube, Seth. I need to add more to get two fingers inside her."

Lacey shuddered as Lars' finger slid from her bottom, greedily sucking harder on Wes, and using her grip on Damien's shoulders to try to move harder and faster on him.

Wes hissed. "Easy, Lacey. Shit. Damn it, I want to come in your pussy, not your mouth."

Damien continued to rock her on his cock, giving her enough friction against her sensitive flesh to keep her climbing higher, but not allowing her to go over. He reached up to grip her wrists and, pulling her hands behind her back, held them in one of his. "No, Lacey. Let Lars get two fingers into that tight ass and I'll fuck you good."

She moaned around Wes's cock, causing him to curse and pull from her mouth.

"That mouth is deadly." He took a shuddering breath and lowered himself beside her again. "You wouldn't believe what that tongue feels like on your cock," he told his brothers.

"I can't wait to find out what this ass feels like on my cock," Lars rumbled as he worked more of the lube into her.

Damien held her still and she turned her face into his neck as Lars began to push two thick fingers into her.

She whimpered, panting as shivers racked her body. "It burns. It doesn't fit."

Damien's lips brushed her hair. "Relax your bottom, baby. Let Lars make you feel good."

"I can't. Help me. I don't know how to do this."

He released her hands and cupped her head, angling her for his kiss. "I'll help you, baby." His smile looked pained as he lifted her from his chest and began to thrust into her.

Lacey balanced herself with hands on his chest, loving the feel of the spattering of silky chest hair. His hands on her hips helped her move into his thrusts. Lars kept his fingers poised at her puckered opening, caressing, but not pressing, and she relaxed, caught up in the sensations bombarding her.

Wes and Seth ran their hands over her back, each caressing a breast as they watched her, running their lips over her shoulders.

Lacey's eyes locked with Damien's fierce ones. His hands, hot and firm on her hips, guided her and helped her to move on him, harder and faster. It felt incredible. His thick heat thrust into her over and over, each thrust taking her closer and closer to the edge. She cried out, moaning loudly, encouraged by their own low growls, praise and groans of their own pleasure.

"It's too good. Oh God." The pleasure kept mounting and she closed her eyes, throwing her head back as it started. The devastating tingles began, warning her that she was about to go over. She felt everything at once, all sensations combining into one.

Damien thrust wildly now, just what she needed. Her orgasm slammed into her just as Damien growled and thrust deep.

Suddenly, two lubed fingers thrust into her bottom and she screamed.

The erotic burn and the pure sexual feeling of having Lars' fingers in her bottom, made her orgasm even stronger. The spasms that racked her body forced her muscles to clench on both of them, the fullness making her burn even more.

Lars wrapped an arm around her waist from behind as he moved his fingers inside her bottom. "That's it, my mate. Clamp down so I can stretch you good."

Every erotic thing they did to her drove her to want to do even more. Every inhibition melted away as they touched her, did whatever they wanted to her and made her love it. She'd never even imagined feeling so sexual, so desired. It was a heady feeling.

Their obvious need for her made her feel powerful while at the same time, the way they controlled her filled her with a deep sense of vulnerability. She had no defense against the potent combination.

When she finally began to come down, Damien pulled her down onto his chest. "Do it now, Lars."

Lars' fingers slid out of her and when she felt the head of his cock push at her forbidden opening, she scrambled to sit up.

Damien tightened his hold. "Easy, Lacey. It'll feel good. I promise."

Wes and Seth both ran their hands over her, soothing her as Lars began to press into her. They both murmured to her, biting out curses and comments as they obviously watched what Lars did to her.

Lacey panted and grabbed onto Damien as Lars pressed against her opening. "It hurts. Ohh. Oh God. Don't stop. It's inside me."

Lars' curses filled the air. "Fuck. She's so damned tight. Easy, baby. Let me get some more into you. She's squeezing me so fucking hard. Oh, fuck. Nice easy strokes, okay, Lacey? Try to relax your bottom a little, honey."

Lacey squeezed her eyes closed as an unbelievable and totally foreign sensation stole her sanity. Nerve endings came alive as Lars stroked into her, each stroke seating his cock a little deeper inside her anus. Shaking, she held on tight to Damien as she fought to adjust to it. "It's so big. It's going deep. Oh my God."

Lars held her cheeks parted wide as he continued his strokes. "A little more, my mate, just a little more. She's got the tightest fucking ass. I'm never going to last. As soon as I get inside her, we'll change positions."

Lacey couldn't believe that, after the orgasm she'd just had, she was already on the verge of another. The burn of her bottom being stretched took her somewhere else, somewhere she'd never been before. The need inside her blossomed almost out of control as she marveled at how carnal and primitive she'd become. She pushed back against Lars, aiding his invasion and shuddered when she felt his sack against her bottom.

"I'm in. Fuck, she's tight," Lars groaned in a voice so deep and formidable, it startled her.

Once again their strength amazed her as he wrapped an arm around her waist and pulled her back against him, and stood, all in one motion, sliding her off of Damien's cock and pushing his even deeper.

Damien slid a hand over her as he stood, allowing Lars to sit with her in the spot he'd just vacated.

Lacey moaned and whimpered as Lars settled her on his lap, his cock deep inside her.

His hands came around her as he nuzzled her throat. "You're so damned tight. So hot. Are you okay?"

Lacey groaned. "It burns but it feels, it feels so full."

Wes donned a condom and knelt between her splayed legs. He ran his hands up her thighs as he leaned down to kiss her deeply.

She grabbed onto his shoulders as he began to press into her, groaning at the incredible fullness as he lifted from her and began to thrust. She cried out as Damien and Seth both began to caress her breasts and pluck at her nipples while Wes's thrusts increased in both depth and speed.

She couldn't believe how full she felt. How taken. Her anus burned even more, setting off a series of mini orgasms and tightening her on both cocks inside her.

Wes held onto her hips firmly, his eyes almost black as he took her. "So fucking tight. So good. So hot."

"So beautiful, too," Damien murmured as he turned her to face him.

"Perfect," Lars rumbled against her neck as his hands slid over her stomach and down to her abdomen.

Lacey's toes curled as Wes dug at that sensitive place inside her and those warning sizzles began just seconds before she went over. She thrilled at Wes's loud growl as he joined her and Lars' bit off curses as he nipped at her neck. She couldn't keep from clenching on both of them and raw cries tore from her throat as it set of a new series of mini orgasms. "Oh. I can't. I can't."

Lars buried his face in her neck. "You can. Your mates all want you so much. Just let us make you feel good."

Lacey groaned as Wes slid out of her, and Seth took his place. "You're going to kill me."

Lars' cock jumped in her bottom. "Once more. Come once more, my mate."

Lacey had no choice as Seth and Lars set up a rhythm that robbed her of all thought and turned her to jelly. She cried out weakly as Lars and Seth both roared out their own completion.

She didn't expect the level of warmth and caring they showered her with afterward. Seth went into the adjoining bath and came back with a warm damp towel for her, cleaning her gently as they held and caressed her. Each kissed her gently, brushing their lips over her face and shoulders before releasing her to another. Damien bundled her into his shirt before Wes picked her up, holding her against his chest and carrying her from the room.

"How about a nice hot shower before dinner? Then we'll talk about your friend."

Lacey smiled up at him, cupping his jaw. "I don't know if I can stand up."

Wes smiled at her, more tenderly than he ever had before. "You can lean on me, sweetheart. Always."

"On all of us." Seth came up beside them as Lars and Damien followed them up the stairs, all in various phases of undress and each carrying armfuls of clothing.

Lacey giggled and whispered, "I hope you got everything. It would be very embarrassing if you missed something."

The men chuckled. At the top of the stairs, they turned left and headed toward the room they would share. "I think Victor and our grandmother are going to have to get used to it."

Lacey sobered as Wes carried her into the bedroom with the others. "I'm really starting to believe this can work."

"It will work. We'll make it work." Wes set her on her feet, glancing at the others, who all nodded in agreement.

Lars came forward and led her to the bathroom, the others close behind. "We don't want you to worry about it at all. Let us take care of everything."

Lacey slipped off the shirt Damien had bundled her into as Wes's jeans hit the floor. "If this is going to work, you guys can't be so bossy. I'm a big girl and I can take care of myself." She stepped into the shower. "And I need to know more about this werewolf business. Do you turn into werewolves when there's a full moon?"

Seth smiled. "Yes. Werewolves can change at will, but the *need* to change is more prevalent during a full moon." He wagged his brows. "That's when our primal urges come out."

"And since we now have an Alpha female," Wes added as he joined her in the shower, closing the door behind them, "the weres will be watching the house even closer to protect you."

Lacey closed her eyes and stood under the warm water. "As long as you *Alphas* don't boss me around, we'll be fine. If you try to tell me what to do, we're going to fight."

She frowned at the laughter coming from the other side of the door.

The cool air made her shiver as the door opened, and Damien leaned in to smack her bottom. "Oh, we're going to fight. Then you'll learn how a werewolf punishes his mate."

She laughed and splashed water at him, feeling more lighthearted than she had in a long time. For the first time she had hope that this might just work.

Chapter Ten

Lacey couldn't keep from smiling as she ate her dinner. Her godmother and Victor kept exchanging glances and smiling, so Lacey knew they had to know what she and the men had been doing earlier.

It wasn't as if the men did anything to hide it. The four of them looked more relaxed and kept grinning at her and each other all through the meal. They touched her often, reaching out to stroke her arm, her cheek, her hair. No man had ever made her feel so cherished before. To have the attention like this from four of them brought tears to her eyes.

They'd already talked about Sarah. She'd even called when Lars insisted on speaking to her. Even he couldn't convince Sarah to come to the mansion. Once Lars had been assured of her safety, Lacey told Sarah she'd get back to her about the papers, not wanting to discuss Steven's part in it around the men.

"Did you tell Lacey about tonight?"

Lacey turned to her godmother. "What about tonight?"

Nana patted her arm and laughed delightedly. "There's a full moon tonight."

Remembering Damien's earlier words, Lacey spun to him, her eyes widening at his devilish grin. Oh Lord. Her pussy clenched in anticipation. She turned back to Nana, trying to feign only mild interest. "Um, there is?"

"Yes, it's so exciting, isn't it?"

Lacey felt their eyes on her and kept her gaze averted. Hearing a low chuckle, her face burned as she looked back up at her godmother. "Exciting?"

"Yes, they'll shift tonight, and for the first time in years, the entire pack will be together again. I'm sure we'll see everyone tonight."

Lacey frowned in confusion. "I thought we just saw everyone together for your birthday."

"We did, sweetheart. But this time they'll be gathered as wolves. And they'll all come to pay homage to the Alphas' mate."

Lacey's fork clattered onto her plate. "What? What are you talking about? What do I do? They're coming to see me? A pack of werewolves?"

Nana patted her hand again. "There's nothing to worry about. I remember the first full moon after mating with their grandfather. It was so beautiful. All the wolves gathered together out back and serenaded me. Their howls filled the air and they all came up to me, one by one."

"Is that what they're going to do to me?" At her nod, she looked at the men. "What do I do?"

Lars reached over and circled her wrist and pulled her toward him, settling her onto his lap. "The wolves will approach you and lower themselves in front of you. Their tails will be lowered and their backs arched as a sign of submission, acknowledging your rank within the pack."

He smiled at her tenderly and dropped a kiss on her nose. "All you have to do is smile and thank them for welcoming you."

Intrigued, Lacey looked at the others. "Is that how they greet you?"

Wes chuckled. "Only if they've done something that made us angry. If we're really mad, they'll roll over onto their backs."

Lacey realized she had a lot to learn. "What does that mean?"

Seth leaned forward. "It's an even higher level of submission. Exposing their bellies or throats means they'll accept whatever punishment we deem necessary. A wolf exposed in such a way is easy to kill."

"Kill? You wouldn't actually kill one of them, would you?" Lacey stiffened when they all looked at her incredulously.

Lars turned her to face him, his tone colder than she'd ever heard it. "If warranted, yes."

* * * *

Lacey sat in a chaise lounge next to her godmother, both gazing out into the yard. The full moon illuminated the night sky so brightly, they could plainly see the hundreds of wolves approaching.

Still shaken by what Lars had said at dinner, Lacey wrapped her arms around herself as a chill went through her. "Nana, I can't believe they would actually kill someone. I would have a hard time living with something like that."

Her godmother nodded. "I know, sweetheart. You've been raised with good moral values. But you're new here and will have to learn another set of rules to live by. We're always threatened by rogue werewolves, who for some reason thrive on attacking and killing others, usually the weak and the helpless."

"Oh my God! That's terrible."

"Yes it is. Horrible. They usually go after the younger wolves and the females. They kill the sick or elderly without a qualm. You really don't expect Lars, Damien, Wes and Seth to turn a blind eye to it, do you? Some weres get sloppy and expose themselves, risking all the others. They would be warned, but if it continued, the pack leader would have no choice but to make them leave the pack. Sometimes, they get angry and come back for revenge." Her eyes hardened. "The one that killed that poor woman is a danger to their mate. You really don't expect them to let him live, do you?"

Lacey had trouble absorbing it all. "How did Agent O'Reilly find out about them?"

"One of those rogue wolves I just told you about killed his wife and two small sons."

Lacey gasped. "Oh my God. That poor man."

Her godmother patted her arm. "That compassion is going to make you a great Alpha female, but never forget that O'Reilly would take my grandsons, and all the others, even the elderly, and lock them away for the rest of their lives if he had proof of what they really are. Or, he may just kill them and be done with it. The younger ones would be lost. They don't change until they hit puberty and would have no one to guide them. They would all lose parents, some of them, both. They'd been vulnerable to other packs."

Horrified, Lacey spun to her godmother. "The children would be unprotected?"

Nana nodded sadly. "Exactly. The Tougarret pack is a peace loving pack that takes in those who aren't happy elsewhere and my grandsons keep them all safe. There are good and bad, Lacey. The good do their best to keep the bad in check. Sometimes, killing them is necessary. Stand up. They're all assembled to greet you."

With a sense of unreality, Lacey stood and moved forward to the edge of the patio as the wolves began to howl. Four black ones, larger than the others came to stand next to her, their deep blue eyes glittering in the moonlight.

One licked her ankle, making her giggle. "Stop it, Damien." The wolf looked up at her and she could have sworn he smiled.

Nana laughed from behind her. "Good. You're able to tell them apart."

Lacey shook her head. "No. That just seemed like something Damien would do."

She looked out to see them all as Lars had predicted, their tails lowered as they howled to her. Suddenly, it got very quiet as all of them stiffened. Lacey watched, fascinated, as their ears went up and their tails pointed straight back.

The black wolves growled and looked up at her. One of them sounded a series of short howls and the others all took off for the woods. The four black wolves raced around the corner of the house and disappeared from view.

"What is it? What's wrong?"

Her godmother moved back to her seat. "Sit down. Lacey. Someone's here. Probably Agent O'Reilly. He likes to drop by when there's a full moon. He likes to think he's going to catch them in the act."

Smiling at her godmother's sarcasm, Lacey hurriedly took her place back in the chaise lounge and tried to appear relaxed. Leaning toward Nana, she whispered, "Where did they go?"

"My grandsons ran around to the side entrance that is kept open for this very reason. The others scattered into the woods until our company leaves. They'll be watching."

Lacey would swear she could feel the wolves' eyes on her and looked out to see if she could see any of them. Deciding she was being fanciful, she attempted nonchalance. "It's really nice out here at night, especially with all the candles. It's really peaceful here."

"Yes, it is nice. I can't tell you how many times I've sat out here and just looked up at the stars."

Lacey adjusted Nana's blanket around her legs. "It's especially nice when the moon's as bright as it is tonight. You can see everything."

"I'm surprised the men allow you two ladies to sit out here all alone when there's a killer wolf close."

Lacey and her godmother turned to see Agent O'Reilly approach from the opposite end of the house from where the others had disappeared. His hard features looked menacing in the bright moonlight.

Before either of them could say anything, Seth came through the French doors, carrying thin blankets. He'd thrown on jeans, but nothing else and looked sexy as hell. "They're not alone at all, O'Reilly." He shook out one of the blankets and placed it over Lacey's legs. "They were getting cold, so I went in to get blankets. What are you doing here?"

Lars came through the open door. "There's a full moon.

O'Reilly's looking for werewolves again." He moved to Lacey and lifted her, sitting down on the chaise lounge and settling her onto his lap. She smiled her thanks as Seth came over and wrapped another light blanket around her shoulders and dropped a kiss on her hair.

Lacey smiled. "That's nonsense. He can't really be serious about that." She looked up at the agent. "Did you bring any news? Did you find out who killed that woman?"

Agent O'Reilly moved onto the patio, his jaw clenched in anger. "No, we don't have any new leads. But I don't expect to get any until this werewolf kills again. Let's just hope he doesn't get his real target this time, huh?"

Wes came out onto the patio. "I don't care for the fact that you keep coming around here and scaring the women. If you want to talk about werewolves instead of trying to find the killer, then do it when the women aren't present."

Taken aback at Wes's brusque tone, Lacey could only stare at him. Wes had to be the most laid back of all of them. For him to sound that way, O'Reilly must really be getting to him.

Lars' hand slid under the blanket and the loose sweatpants covering her legs and began to work its way up her calf. The words the other men spoke dimmed as her attention drifted to what Lars did to her.

She slid a glance at him, but other than a twitch of his lips, he betrayed nothing. Shifting on his lap, she tried to appear as though moving into a more comfortable position, deliberately moving her bottom over the bulge in his jeans.

His head whipped around. His look of surprise made her smile. She arched a brow and drew a small smile from him as he turned his attention back to the others. The hand on her leg slid upward, his fingers lightly teasing the back of her knee. His other arm tightened around her, pulling her against his chest. Hidden by the blanket, his hand slid under her shirt and traced the curve of her breast as his other continued to move lightly over the back of her knee.

She'd never thought of the back of her knees as erogenous zones, but Lars quickly taught her differently. Leaning against his shoulder, she jumped when O'Reilly raised his voice.

"One of these days I'll catch you and put all of you in a fucking cage where you belong!" He stormed out the way he'd come and disappeared around the side of the house.

Nana shook her head and blew out a breath. "Well, that was fun."

Damien came out to join them as they heard the agent's car squeal down the drive. "He won't give up. He's determined to catch us and I'm afraid that one day he will."

Lars leaned down to whisper in Lacey's ear. "We'll continue this later. Tonight, instead of my hand, I'll use my mouth and finish working my way up." He stood with her in his arms and deposited her back onto the lounge chair. "It's safe to go back out now."

In a flash all four shifted and raced into the woods.

"They'll gather again and come back up here," Nana said as she settled more comfortably. "What do you think of all this, Lacey? I know it's a lot to understand, but do you think you can be happy here?"

"Oh, Nana. I *am* happy here. I like being here with you and I have to admit, this," she waved a hand, "has me more than a little intrigued."

The older woman smiled at her. "That's not what I'm talking about and you know it. Do you think you can be happy with my grandsons?"

Lacey smiled. "I'd like to think I can. I can't believe how much I've fallen for them already, but I'm just not sure. They seem to, well—"

"Want you?"

Lacey nodded, her face hot, not used to talking this way with her godmother. "But I'm not sure how they really feel about me. I mean, they say I'm their mate, but I can't be with them just because of pheromones."

Her godmother smiled. "How could they not fall in love with you, sweetheart?"

Lacey smiled at her. "You're prejudiced. Nana, I can't make any decisions right now. Too much is happening and I'm afraid to make a decision until things are more settled. But I do know that I could never stay with someone who doesn't love me. And they're awfully bossy. I'm not too good at taking orders. I don't like that they think they can tell me what to do."

The older woman laughed softly. "Their grandfather was the same way. You're just going to have to teach them differently. Don't let them get away with it. You're a woman, sweetheart, the 'weaker sex'. Use it."

Lacey groaned. "But you had one. I have four to deal with."

"You're stronger than I was at your age, Lacey. You'll do fine. I have no doubt you'll have my grandsons eating out of the palm of your hand."

They both sat silently for several minutes. Finally Lacey asked. "Do you really think they like me for me? I mean, not just because of the way I smell?"

Her godmother stood. "Yes. I do. My grandsons wouldn't be so crazy about you otherwise. Recognizing a mate and staying with someone because of their scent are not the same thing, darling. Your scent just helped them to realize that you're the woman for them, that you're the woman they *will* fall in love with."

Lacey thought about that for a minute. "Is it ever wrong? I mean, has anyone ever thought someone was their mate and it turned out they couldn't stand the other person?"

"No. Nature is very wise. In all the years I've seen it happen, I've never known it to be wrong. That's why werewolves are generally happy. The others, like my son who don't wait for their true mates, are the ones who end up miserable. None of the rogues I told you about had settled with a mate. Now, I'm going to bed. You should, too. They'll be out for hours yet."

Lacey stood and followed her godmother inside. "How long was it before your husband told you he loved you?"

"Almost three months."

"Really?"

Nana started up the stairs. "Really. They're not very talkative about their feelings but werewolves are very physical. Did you notice on the patio that each of them touched you at some point, even if it was only a hand on your shoulder as they passed you? They show their affection more than they talk about it, which was something that was very hard for me to get used to. It's one of the things I miss the most."

When they got to the top of the stairs, Lacey hugged her, her eyes stinging. "Oh, Nana. I'm so sorry you have to be alone."

Her godmother smiled at her tearfully. "But I'm not alone anymore. Now that you're here, and my grandsons have moved in, the house is filled with laughter again. And when you all start having babies—"

Tears streamed down Lacey's face when Nana's voice broke. "I love you, Nana. I'll always be there for you."

Nana kissed her cheek. "I hope you'll always be *here* for me."

Lacey watched her godmother walk down the hallway to her room. Deep in thought, she turned and went to her own bed. She loved her godmother dearly, but she wouldn't let herself be pressured into any decisions right now.

An hour later, she still couldn't sleep. She'd spent her entire life sleeping alone until this week, but couldn't fall asleep now because the bed felt too lonely. The bed had definitely been made for more than one person.

Lacey got up and went back downstairs and straight out to the patio. Hearing the distant howls comforted her, and she smiled as she settled back onto the chaise lounge. Maybe if she just sat here for a while she'd be able to sleep.

* * * *

As they came out of the woods Lars caught the scent of his mate. Hurrying across the lawn, he saw her bundled in the blankets right where they'd left her hours earlier. Love engulfed him as he moved close.

He and his brothers all shifted as they reached the edge of the patio, while Victor continued inside. The men all thought nothing of their nudity, but Victor had always been more reserved and would never have appeared naked with a woman present.

Lars grinned. Even if she was sleeping like the dead.

He bent and lifted her slight weight, pausing as she moved in his arms.

"Lars," she breathed, and snuggled against him, her breathing evening out once again.

Lars froze, nearly brought to his knees by emotion as he looked down at her incredulously. "Did you hear that?"

Damien dropped a kiss on her hair. "She knew who you were." He adjusted the blanket over her shoulder. "She knew who I was in wolf form."

Lars started inside with his mate held securely against him. "That's only because you licked her ankle and she knows how kinky you are."

Damien chuckled. "She loves how kinky I am. Our mate loves to play."

When they got upstairs, Wes opened the door for him. "I wonder if one day she'll be able to recognize all of us in wolf form or when sleeping."

The uncertainty in Wes's voice and the longing on his face as he helped tuck Lacey between the sheets, had Lars offering. "Why don't you take my place with her tonight?"

Wes's head shot up. "You don't mind?"

Damien started toward the bathroom, yawning. "Of course he

minds, dumb ass. But we all have to give her a chance to be close to all of us." He slid a look at Seth. "Don't even think about it. The other side is mine as soon as I take a shower."

Chapter Eleven

Wes hung up the phone and stood, anxious to get back to Lacey. It seemed impossible that she'd been here such a short time. She'd quickly become the center of the household, and everyone, him included, seemed to gravitate to her whenever possible.

Grandmother looked happier than he'd ever seen her. She had the chance to be with her beloved goddaughter and her grandsons every day now. Even Victor had mentioned, on several occasions, just how much joy she'd brought to all their lives.

As though they didn't know it.

He and his brothers talked more than they ever had before, their main focus on finding out who wanted to hurt Lacey. Their fiercest enemy, the Galbraith's pack, lived the closest and since their scent had been on the dead woman, they'd arranged a meeting with the pack leader, Aaron Galbraith, for tomorrow morning. They all strongly believed that either he or his son, Steven, wanted Lacey dead.

He didn't want to think about that now. Right now, he just wanted his mate.

Following her scent to the studio he shared with Seth, he grinned when he heard the heated discussion from inside. Their grandmother had been more than happy that each of them worked from home and encouraged them to all appropriate rooms for their work space.

Lars and Damien shared the office upstairs while he and Seth shared the studio in the back. He never would have believed that they would be able to share workspace and found they'd all been surprised by just how well it worked out.

Chuckling at the frustration he heard in Seth's voice, Wes opened the door and walked in. The reason they'd chosen the room, the huge wall of windows let the sun shine in, all of it appearing to be drawn to Lacey. He smiled inwardly. Just like everything else.

Her hair looked even redder in the bright beam, glowing like fire around her flushed face. Not at all surprised that his cock came to life, he leaned against the wall and watched them.

"Lacey, you're using too much water."

"Do you want me to sculpt wood, like you do?"

"No, the tools are too dangerous. The clay is better for you."

"Then why don't you leave me alone and let me do it?"

"I am, it's just that if you use that much water—"

"It'll dry." She looked up at Wes and smiled. "It looks good, doesn't it?"

Wes couldn't help but smile at her. Dressed in jeans and wearing one of their shirts as a smock, with smudges of clay on her cheeks, she looked adorable. They'd each lost shirts to her, teasingly complaining to her about it but they all loved seeing her in their shirts.

Every time he saw her, the love he already felt for her weakened his knees. He stood, just staring down at her as it hit him yet again, still surprising him as it grew more every day. "It's beautiful, darling."

She grinned and lifted her face for his kiss. "You're not even looking at it."

He laughed and kissed her again, wiping the smudge from her soft cheek. "I was looking at you."

Seth shook his head and kissed her hair, grinning, before going back to his work in progress. "She's a damned minx today. She already has Damien nuts because she's making more money in the account he set up for her than he is."

"It's not my fault. I told him that he couldn't trust the guy with the beady eyes."

"She rearranged all of Lars' papers on his desk."

"I was only trying to clean up."

Seth sighed. "She's using too much water."

"It needs to be softer."

Wes grinned. "I think it looks beautiful. It's the finest bird I've ever seen."

Seth threw back his head and laughed as Lacey frowned up at him.

"It's a turtle."

Wes bit the inside of his mouth to keep from laughing. "I see it now. It's a beautiful turtle. Can I have it when you finish?"

Lacey's eyes narrowed. "You're just saying that. Besides, I'm making this for Lars, for his desk. It's kind of an apology for messing up his papers. But I'll make you something the next time."

Wes glanced at Seth, to find him watching Lacey as though transfixed. It had taken longer for Seth to realize his feelings for their mate, but now that he had, it shook him almost as badly as it had shaken Damien.

Wes walked around Lacey's sculpture. "You're really good at this. Tomorrow, do you want to try your hand at painting again? And I still want you to sit for me."

Her grin had his groin tightening even more. "Yes, I'd like that."

Working from home gave each of them more time with their mate. They saw each other all the time, ate together, hell they made love to their mate together and all slept in the same room. The camaraderie between he and his brothers surprised the hell out of him and, for the first time in his life, he could say he was truly happy.

They all were, and it all revolved around a little redheaded minx.

Seth watched Lacey, sighing when she doused the clay with water again. When he looked back at him Wes saw the question in his eyes and nodded.

Both glanced over to see Lacey watching them.

"What was that all about? I thought you said no secrets."

Wes sighed heavily. "We have a meeting tomorrow with the

Alpha of another pack, the pack we think is behind killing that woman."

"What? You can't go. It's too dangerous. Let's just call the police. Or O'Reilly."

The panic in her eyes and the scent of fear that emanated from her had him groaning as it brought his primal instincts to the surface. He knew damned well there was no threat to her, but just the scent of fear from their mate had a growl rumbling from his chest.

Seth's body tightened, too, and he could see his brother's struggle to contain it. He didn't feel the least bit surprised to hear Lars and Damien racing down the stairs.

He knew Lacey couldn't hear them and didn't want her to be startled when they rushed in. "Lars and Damien are going to burst through the door."

He'd no more than said it, when they did. Both zeroed in on Lacey, their gazes sweeping the room, searching for a threat.

Wes shook his head. "It's nothing. I told her about our meeting tomorrow and she's afraid that we'll get hurt."

Damien's brows went up. "That we'll get hurt?" He went to Lacey and pulled her into his arms, kissing her hair. "Baby, you *do* remember what we are, don't you?"

Lacey gripped his arms. "Yes, but so are they. They could hurt you. I don't really understand all this werewolf stuff. Sometimes I actually forget it. It just doesn't seem real to me."

Lars went to her and kissed her hair. "It's real, sweetheart. We're going to have to spend some more time as wolves around you to get you used to it."

"But in the meantime," Damien added, kissing her lightly, "we are perfectly capable of taking care of ourselves."

Wes grinned, as a real sense of brotherhood washed over him. "And each other."

Lars studied Lacey's sculpture. "What are you working on?"

Lacey grinned. "Seth wanted me to stay in here with him while he worked on his sculpture, so he gave me something to do. It's a present for you, an apology for messing up your work space. It's supposed to go on your desk. How do you like it?"

Lars grinned. "It's beautiful, darling. The cutest little bird I've ever seen."

Wes couldn't catch his breath, as he, Seth, and Damien laughed hysterically as they watched Lacey storm out of the room, while Lars stood shocked, staring after her, with a clump of wet clay sliding down the side of his head.

* * * *

Lacey knew she owed Lars an apology. Her temper had gotten the best of her once again. She'd never before had so much trouble controlling her temper as she did with the four of them. She smiled as she remembered their lovemaking this morning. It appeared *all* of her passions ran deep where they were concerned.

She couldn't believe that the relationship they'd begun showed signs of actually working. Even with trouble surrounding them, Lacey felt happier than she'd ever been. Lars, Damien, Wes and Seth appeared to be happy. She'd met their mothers and even they had commented on their sons' happiness.

She combed her damp her, having showered after working with the clay. She'd been so busy since she'd come here that the days seemed to fly.

Each of the men had shown her what they did for a living, and it amazed her that all four of them could actually work from home. She'd also learned that they hired other werewolves for any work they wanted done, such as the ones who'd finished the bedroom and the landscapers.

They each had to be available for problems within the pack and it was up to them to handle all disputes that couldn't be worked out otherwise. They also took a great interest in their pack members.

She'd heard them discussing upcoming marriages and sickly pack members. The doctor that they sent was also a pack member.

It appeared to be a close community, and the men had told her that once she settled in here and the threat to her no longer existed, she would have her own duties. She didn't quite understand them yet. She just knew that she would be called on for advice and would be asked to help with some of the problems the women of the pack needed help with.

She had no idea what kind of advice she could give and worried that she wouldn't be the kind of mate they needed. What the hell did she know about being a werewolf?

But, if this continued to work, she would try her best to fit in. Maybe she could check out the local school and see if she could find a job teaching. Tugging a tangle, she thought about back home and wondered if she would even be able to get a reference.

Maybe once this business with Sarah had ended.

She hated keeping secrets from the men, but she just had to talk to Steven. He'd agreed to handle the divorce for Sarah and do all the paperwork necessary to file for custody of Christina. He'd collected all the doctor and hospital reports as well as those he could get from the child protection service.

She'd called to check on Sarah earlier and to assure her that she would take care of everything. Sarah trusted no one and wouldn't allow Lacey to give Steven her number, so everything had to go through her. She wouldn't come to the mansion unless she had to. She'd gotten a job washing dishes in the diner next to the motel and could take Christina with her. She didn't want to leave it.

In the meantime, Lacey still got emails from Ted. She hadn't told the men about them, knowing that there would be nothing they could do about it and it would only anger them. The threats had been subtle, nothing that couldn't be interpreted another way in case she turned them over to the police, but they were there nonetheless. If he didn't know her whereabouts, he would soon. After she'd dropped Sarah off, she'd changed directions, but she hadn't planned to be here this long.

With all the assets at his disposal, she had no doubt he would eventually find her. But Sarah would be the one he would really go after.

With that thought in mind, she went to their bedroom and used her cell phone to place a call to Steven.

"Lacey, I've been waiting for you to call. I have most of the information together. I need Sarah to sign a few things so that I can proceed."

Lacey smiled. "Really? You have everything you need?"

"Almost. I'm still waiting for a few more of the doctors' reports. I can't believe how many times Sarah and Christina had to go to the hospital, and no one investigated."

Lacey plopped onto the bed and traced a pattern on the quilt with her finger. "Ted's a bastard and has everyone in his pocket. There's no way anyone in town would go against him. He bribes or threatens everyone. Lars and the others all have a meeting tomorrow morning. Can I meet you at your office about nine? I can pick up the papers and mail them to her while I'm in town."

"Sure, nine would be great. Lacey, I, uh—"

Lacey frowned at Steven's hesitation. "What is it?"

"Well, I just wanted you to know that the meeting your men have tomorrow is with my father. He's the leader of the Galbraith pack."

Lacey jumped to her feet. "Your father is their worst enemy? Why?"

His sigh carried sadness and regret. "It's a long story. I can't get into it over the phone. I'll explain when I see you tomorrow."

"Steven, they won't be in any danger, will they? Wait! Your fathers a—"

"Yes."

"Are you?"

"Yes?"

"Steven, do you know who killed that woman?"

The sigh that came through the phone sounded defeated. "I'm not sure, Lacey, but if I had to guess, I would say it was my father."

"No. Why?"

"My father hates the Tougarrets, Lacey. He has for years."

"Why?"

"Not over the phone, Lacey. O'Reilly has ears everywhere. I'll see you in the morning."

Lacey stared down at the phone once he'd disconnected. Lars, Damien, Wes and Seth would be meeting with a man, a werewolf, tomorrow, one that even his own son suspected of murder.

She dropped the phone and went in search of Lars. She would apologize and find out if he realized just what a threat this pack leader could be.

Walking down the hall, she saw the door to the office he shared with Damien standing open and heard his voice coming from inside.

She slipped in just as he hung up the phone and a glance at Damien's desk told her that they were alone. Closing the door behind her, she walked toward his desk, hiding a grin as he leaned back and steepled his hands over his flat stomach, staring at her coolly. "I came in to apologize."

He raised his brow arrogantly. "Really?"

* * * *

Lars struggled to let only mild interest show on his face as his cock came to full attention. He could see her struggle not to laugh as she faced him and found himself torn between bursting out in laughter or turning her over his knee and paddling her ass.

He and his brothers had become spoiled, he knew. Because of their looks, their money, and their positions as Alphas within the pack, women had thrown themselves at them ever since he could remember. He knew they'd all long ago grown tired of fawning women.

It appeared that fate had a sense of humor, and thought fit to see that the woman they would take to mate would be a handful.

God, he loved her.

"Really. I didn't mean to throw the clay at you."

"Whether you meant to or not, I still got hit with clay. The clay you were using to make me a gift to apologize for messing up my desk, I believe."

Damned if she didn't look sexy as hell when she blushed. "Yes, well I'll make you another one."

"And do you really believe you're going to get away with that, just by making me another sculpture?" Christ, if they let her know just how much she could really get away with, they would all be in big trouble.

"What can I do to make it up to you?"

"Do you know how a werewolf punishes his mate?" He'd kept his voice cool, while inside the beast clamored to get free.

"Why would a werewolf have to punish his mate? That's not right."

"Werewolves aren't politically correct, my mate. The main priority for a male werewolf is to protect his family. If you ever do anything to endanger yourself, we, as your mates, would have no choice but to punish you, for your own good. You'll never be allowed to put yourself in any danger. You must tell us about any danger or threat to you so that we can handle it. If you don't, you'll find yourself in big trouble."

Lacey gulped. "What kind of punishment?"

Lars was happy to see her trepidation. He wondered just how stupid she thought they all were that they wouldn't know that the threats to her had continued. Did she really think they would believe that after what she'd done to Ted Johnson, that bastard would stop?

He wanted her to understand just what would be in store for her if she kept lying to them. "First you would be stripped. Then you would be turned over one of our laps and be given a spanking assuring that you won't sit comfortably for quite a while."

He ignored her gasp and continued. "Then you would be taken from behind. Your ass. The ultimate submission. The ultimate domination. Your ass would be fucked long and hard until you see the error of your ways. You would not be allowed to come until you plead for mercy and apologize profusely for daring to endanger our mate."

"That's, that's—"

"Inhuman? Barbaric? Chauvinistic? Mean?" He smiled coldly. "You're mated to werewolves, Lacey. Not puppies. With enough provocation, we can be all of the above."

She looked ready to bolt, and he caught the scent of fear, so he decided to let her off the hook. "But just throwing clay and messing up my desk doesn't warrant a punishment like that."

She gulped. "It doesn't?"

He'd give her one more chance to come clean. "Of course not. But if any of us find out you're getting threats from that man back home and you don't tell us about them, well, that would be different."

* * * *

Lacey swallowed the huge lump that had formed in her throat and did her best to plaster on a smile. Shit, she would be in real trouble if they ever found out about Ted Johnson's emails or the meeting she had scheduled with Steven. She would just have to make sure they didn't find out. "So if I make you another turtle, you'll forgive me for messing up your desk?"

Lars smiled warmly. "Of course. I would love to have one of your sculptures for my desk." He raised a brow at her grin. "But that doesn't forgive having clay thrown at me just for admiring your work."

Her smile fell. "It wasn't a bird, damn it. It was a turtle. How come everyone thought it was a bird?"

Lars settled back, smiling. "I found out about that after I got hit with the clay and you stormed out." He tensed as she came closer, a soft growl coming from deep in his throat.

"Down boy," she teased, moving closer. "How can I make it up to you?"

"How badly do you want my forgiveness?"

"Really badly. I would hate it if you didn't forgive me for hitting you with that clay." She shrugged. "I have a temper."

"Really?" he asked dryly. "I never would have guessed."

"I usually don't lose it, but since coming here..." She shrugged again.

"Imagine that. Well, you're going to have to learn that when you lose it with me, you'll have to make up for it. First, I want to feel that soft mouth on my cock. Then, I want to taste that sweet cream I smell coming from you. Then I'm going to fuck you. That's how you can make it up to me."

She smiled at him coquettishly. "That's seems like an awful lot for just a little lump of clay."

"It hurt my feelings. Plus, I have to wait longer for my sculpture. Is that my shirt?"

She shrugged. "I didn't think you'd mind. It's really comfortable."

Lars firmed his voice. "Give it back."

"Now?"

"Right now."

Lars groaned when she started unbuttoning her-his shirt. She hadn't worn a bra. When she finished unbuttoning it and hesitated, he wagged his fingers. "Come on. I want my shirt back."

Lacey moved closer as she let the shirt drop from her shoulders.

He accepted the shirt she handed to him, tossing it onto his desk. "Now the jeans."

Lacey reached for the fastening of her jeans, lust racing through her at the look on Lars' face.

His heavy lidded gaze never left her as she slid her jeans down and kicked them to the side. "Give me the panties."

Lacey shivered at his tone. "They're wet."

"Yes, I know. I want them. Now."

Lacey gasped as he reached out and ripped them off of her, his hands so fast, they'd just been a blur. Before she'd recovered, he pulled her between his thighs and took a nipple into his mouth, reaching out to grasp the other between thumb and forefinger. She cried out at the exquisite sensation, tangling her hands in his hair and pulling him closer.

His hands gripped her buttocks, squeezing erotically, spreading her cheeks just enough to cause an amazing little sting at her bottom hole.

She moaned, gripping him tighter, marveling yet again at how very sensual all four of the men were. It never failed to surprise and excite her. By the time he lifted his mouth from her breast, she trembled and would have fallen onto his lap if he hadn't held her steady.

"I want to feel that mouth on my cock."

He brushed a hand lightly over her mound, making her tremble even more. As she dropped to her knees, he unfastened his trousers. He lifted up as she took hold of the sides to pull them down, reaching for his cock as soon as it appeared.

Running her hands over his thickness, she thrilled at the velvety texture and steely hardness. A drop appeared at the tip and she licked it off with her tongue, his hiss of pleasure exciting her even more.

Encouraged, she licked him all over, from base to tip and all around, her hands gripping his taut thighs as she opened her mouth wide and took him inside. The muscles under her hands hardened to rock as she used her mouth on him. He tasted so good. She couldn't get enough of him.

She sucked him lightly, using her tongue to please both of them. When she stroked the underside, his thighs tightened impossibly and a growl erupted as he reached for her. Encouraged, she did it again.

Those growls did her in every time.

Within only a few strokes, growls and bit off curses filled the air. "Fuck, Lacey. That tongue. Stop. Stop."

His hands tightened on her hair as he lifted her head away from his cock, before pulling her onto his lap. Burying his face in her hair, he growled against her neck. "That fucking mouth is incredible."

She moaned as his hands went to her breasts. "When you growl, it drives me crazy. What's wrong with me that your growls turn me on?"

Lars lifted his head and turned her to face him, smiling. "You're mated to werewolves, sweetheart."

Lacey arched into his hands as he tugged at her nipples, keeping her eyes on his. "I love you."

His eyes flared as he cupped the back of her neck and pulled her face even closer. "Say it again."

"I love you."

"Oh, my mate, I love you so much it sometimes overwhelms me."

"Oh, Lars."

His mouth covered hers, sweeping it possessively as he pulled her impossibly close. With his mouth still on hers, he stood and settled her on her back on the desk. Ending the kiss, he used her shirt to pillow her head before he straightened.

His hands moved over her, from her shoulders downward until her reached her mound. Playing with her curls, he smiled. "My hot tempered redhead. I'm going to lap you up."

He seated himself once again, this time between her thighs.

Lacey shuddered as his lips brushed the inside of her thighs as he worked his way to her center, lifting each over his broad shoulders. When he parted her folds, she dug her heels into his back, lifting her hips in offering.

At the first swipe of his tongue through her slit, Lacey jolted at the hot velvety friction on her delicate flesh. Her moans became continuous as he fed on her in earnest now, as though to steal every drop of her cream.

The low growls he made as he pressed his tongue deep, vibrated through her and quickly pushed her over the edge. Her whimpers and cries blended with his harsh groans as more of her juices flowed. He ate at her as though hungry to get every drop.

Finding nothing to grab onto, she twisted frantically on the smooth surface, the pleasure almost too much to bear. His long smooth licks devastated her senses, and she began to climb once again.

Lars gripped her thighs, pressing them back against her and outward, spreading her wide and open for his ministrations.

She gripped his forearms, holding on tightly as his tongue ventured lower and licked at her puckered opening. She jolted, crying out at the erotic pleasure, but he held her firmly.

"You're delicious, my mate," he rumbled against her in that voice she loved. "But I can't wait any more. I have to take you."

"Yes, oh God. Yes."

She barely heard the rip of foil before he thrust inside her, and she went over again. Her flesh heated and tingled around him, gripping him tightly as he stroked her.

His hands tightened on her hips, holding her firmly in place for his thrusts.

The fire in his heavy lidded gaze made her even hotter. Those low growls coming from deep in his throat thrilled her.

"My mate. My mate. So fucking hot."

Her breathless moans became hoarse as he dug at the sensitive spot inside her. Her orgasm built slowly, each deliberate thrust taking her closer and closer. Little sizzles grew stronger and spread, inch by inch, all through her body.

Slow, hot waves of pleasure washed over her as she came. Lars' thrusts slowed as he stroked her inner flesh deeply, dragging out her orgasm longer than she could have imagined.

She couldn't stop coming.

She gulped for air as the waves continued, the heat and tingles ran through her body and stole her breath. The long, smooth strokes never faltered as he worked that secret place inside her until she thought she would die.

"Lars, I, oh, I can't, so good."

"Yes," he hissed as those devastating strokes continued. "Keep coming, my mate. Those ripples are killing me." His thrusts became harder and faster.

Lacey screamed, her voice nearly gone as one giant wave of heat washed over her. She clenched hard on Lars' cock as he held himself deep, and shivered at his loud roar as he came.

He covered her body with his, his face against her neck as they both struggled to catch their breath. After several minutes, he lifted his head to look down at her. "I love you, Lacey." Brushing her damp hair back, he smiled so tenderly, she wanted to cry. "I've waited forever for you, and I'm so glad you're finally here."

She touched his lips, tracing them with her finger. "I love you, too. It would break my heart if this didn't work."

"It is working, love. As soon as we find out who's causing trouble, we'll have to start on making some babies. What do you think?"

Lacey frowned up at him. "But how will we know—?"

He kissed her. Hard. "All of your babies will belong to all of us." He grinned. "Grandmother will be impossible, you know that, right?"

Lacey smiled as a flood of happiness washed over her. "Yes. Between Nana and Victor, we may never even get to hold them."

Lars smiled and looked at the papers strewn all around them. "Now, every time I work at this desk, I'll be thinking about this, and smelling you. I'll never get any work done."

She laughed as Lars helped her from the desk, papers sticking to her back and bottom that he had to peel off. "I guess I messed up your desk again. But this time it was your fault."

Lars chuckled and bent to kiss her lingeringly. When he lifted his head, her breath caught at the love shining in his eyes. "It was worth it."

Chapter Twelve

Seth and his brothers, along with about a dozen others raced through the woods adjoining the Galbraith property. The morning air felt cool, but their fur kept them plenty warm enough. Not knowing how many pack mates Aaron would have with him, they hoped they had enough. More had wanted to come but they'd told them no, not wanting to appear as though they wanted trouble. He hoped they didn't regret it. Meeting with anyone from the Galbraith pack had always been a dangerous business.

He caught the scent of the other pack and slowed as did the others. With Aaron Galbraith, one never knew if they would be walking into an ambush or not. Looking over his shoulder at the wolves behind them, he growled a warning at them to back off. They'd agreed before starting out that the others would stay hidden unless needed. They all knew Aaron and the others would know of their presence, but wouldn't know just how many of them watched from their hiding places in the woods.

They may just need any advantage they could get.

When the small clearing came into view, he and his brothers stepped forward. They usually handled all dealing with their fiercest enemy together, but this time felt different. Since Lacey had come into their lives, they'd talked to each other more than they had in all the years before and had begun to build a close relationship they hadn't had in the past.

They paused in the clearing. He knew the three other wolves standing next to Aaron wouldn't be the only ones he'd brought with him, but understood his need to have these three close. He would have known that all four of the Alphas would come.

Recognizing the three others, he wondered again why Aaron never brought his son. He would think it important for the next leader of the pack to be present and wondered if Aaron worried that his son would get hurt. It always put him on alert, wondering if this would be the chance Aaron had always been looking for to attack. Keeping his son out of the line of fire would protect the next pack leader.

When Aaron finally stepped forward and shifted, he and his brothers did the same. The others with Aaron waited until they shifted before doing so. Smart. Aaron had trained them well.

Aaron stepped forward. "What the fuck do you want?"

They'd all agreed to let Lars take the lead. He folded his arms across the chest. "I know you've heard we've found our mate."

"Yeah, I heard. So?"

"Someone wants her dead."

"Yeah, I heard you had a little trouble at your party. What's that got to do with me?"

Lars jaw clenched. "Someone killed an innocent bystander by mistake. Her throat had been ripped out. The scent on her was Galbraith and Tougarret. Apparently someone we both know. When I find out who in my pack betrayed us, I'll deal with it. But apparently someone in your pack is dealing with the traitor in mine. Any idea who?"

Aaron looked surprised at first and then thoughtful. Seth kept an eye on him as he watched the others.

"Well, well, well. I didn't think he had it in him. Good. You deserve to lose your mate. Then you'll understand just how I've felt all these years because of the Tougarrets."

Lars frowned. "You've hated the Tougarrets ever since I can remember. You even killed our father for chasing your mate. Don't you think you got your revenge?"

"It wasn't enough. I won't be happy until your fucking pack is destroyed. Believe me, if I get a chance to fuck your mate, I will.

With or without her consent. Then you'll know hell."

As Aaron turned away, Seth called after him. "Are you saying that our father raped your mate?"

Aaron turned back, his face tight with fury. "It would have been better if he had."

Damien stepped forward. "What the hell do you mean by that?"

Aaron turned to his men, who nodded and back away. "Your father fucked my wife with her cooperation. I caught him and killed the worthless piece of shit. She wasn't my true mate, and I knew it, but I wanted an heir. Imagine my fucking surprise when it turned out that she was *his* fucking mate."

"Jesus," Lars breathed.

Aaron shot him a disgusted look. "Yeah. And when my son was born, imagine how I felt when he came out carrying the stench of your father."

Lars shot forward, grabbing his arm. "What are you saying?"

The men behind Aaron came to attention and moved forward. Seth shifted his weight, ready for an attack.

Aaron waved them back. "I'm saying my son isn't my son at all. He's your father's whelp and your half brother." He smiled coldly. "Steven has heard about your mate. Maybe he wanted to see if she's his mate, too. If he picked the wrong woman, he could have killed her to cover his tracks. Or, he knew it was your mate and killed her to keep you from having it all. You see, my wife is Galbraith. Steven carries the scent of both packs."

* * * *

All four men shifted as soon as Aaron had dropped his bomb shell. Racing back to the mansion, Damien could still hear Aaron's laughter and knew he'd never been so scared in his life. Fear had them running back to Lacey as fast as they could, hoping that they would find her warm and safe in their bed as they'd left her a short time ago.

It seemed to take forever to get back to the grounds and when they did, they shifted again on the run as they raced inside and almost into Victor.

"She's gone."

Damien felt the bottom drop of his stomach. "What do you mean she's gone?"

She left shortly after you did. She tried to sneak out, so I didn't know about it until she started her car."

Damien and the others quickly donned the clothing they'd left behind. "Where did she go?"

"Don't worry, she's being guarded. I called Ethan. He and the others are following her. He called a few minutes ago. She's at Steven Galbraith's law office."

* * * *

Lacey stared at Steven, shocked. "You're really their brother?"

Steven's lips twitched. "Half brother."

"And they don't know it?"

"No."

"And they hate you and your pack because your father killed their father."

"Exactly."

"And you've never met?"

"No, I knew they wouldn't want anything to do with me, so I didn't bother. We've always known about each other, but they don't know we're related. We've been very careful to avoid each other all these years."

Lacey reached out to touch his hand. "You have to tell them, especially if your father, uh, step father hates you as much as you say he does."

Steven shook his head sadly. "They'd never believe me."

"You'll never know if you don't try. Why do you stay with your pack if they're all against you? Why don't you leave and join the Tougarret pack. I hear them talking sometimes about taking in werewolves that are shunned from other packs. I'm sure they'll take you and your mother in. After all, you're family. Oh my God! Does Nana know?"

Steven sighed. "No. She knows that her son and my mother were caught together and that's why my father killed him. She doesn't know I'm her grandson. I'd love to meet her. I hear she's a hell of a lady. But Lacey, I don't think they'd want me in the pack. I would be a constant reminder of what their father had done. I can't leave my mother alone. She's had it even harder than I have all these years. The pack has more or less turned their backs on her, but my father won't let her leave. He's dedicated his life to making her as miserable as he can. She's nearly broken. The only thing that keeps her going is me."

Tears pricked Lacey's eyes. "Steven, that's terrible. Your poor mother. You have to get her away from there. You have to talk to Lars and the others. They'll help you."

Steven sighed. "I'd love to be able to get my mother away from there, but she won't go. We've spoken of it before and I know that if I took her away, she'd just go back. She loves my father, as fucked up as that is, and still does anything to please him."

Lacey put her hand over his again and started to speak, but froze when the door burst open and Lars, Damien, Wes and Seth barged in, every line of their bodies tight with rage. She jumped up and stood between them and Steven. "What's going on? Why are you all here? Has something happened? Is Nana okay?"

* * * *

Damien saw red, actually saw red. The fear he'd felt for her safety had been replaced with an anger he'd never known. His mate had actually been holding hands with Steven Galbraith, the man they suspected of trying to kill her. Aaron hadn't lied. Steven did carry the scent of both packs.

Livid, he grabbed her and pulled her away from the other man, baring his teeth. "What are you doing? Why the hell are you touching him? You are in so much trouble, my mate."

With Damien holding onto Lacey and keeping her out of the line of fire, Lars approached Steven. "You touched my mate. You're dead."

Steven sat back and let his arms drop to his sides, leaving his chest and throat vulnerable. "There's nothing going on between your mate and me except friendship."

Lacey struggled against Damien's grip. "Are all of you crazy? Steven's helping me with Sarah. You've got a lot of nerve barging in like this."

Damien swatted her ass. "Be still. We think he's the one who killed that woman, thinking it was you."

"What?" Lacey shrieked. "You're crazy. Steven would never harm me."

Lars leaned over Steven's desk. "Is she your mate?"

"What?"

Damien swatted Lacey's ass again. "Stay out of this. He's our brother."

"I know."

They all whirled to look at her. "You know? How?"

Damien's teeth ground together when she smiled sweetly at Steven.

"He just told me. That's what we were talking about when you bullies barged in. I've been trying to talk him into coming to tell you."

Lars whirled back on Steven. "Is she your fucking mate?"

Steven shook his head sadly. "No, she's not. When I heard about what had happened with you, I followed her to the diner to find out. Right away I knew she wasn't. I'm drawn to her—"

Damien and Wes both growled menacingly as Seth moved

forward.

"Like a sister," Steven finished.

Seth moved to the desk. "So, because she isn't your mate, you tried to kill her. If you couldn't have her, you didn't want us to have her either. Repayment for what our father did to your family?"

Steven stood. "Think about it. I already knew her scent. If I'd have tried to kill her, I would have done so. I wouldn't have mistaken that other woman for her. Now, if there's nothing else, get out of my office." He picked up an envelope. "Lacey, here are the papers for Sarah to sign. Get them back to me as soon as possible."

Damien eyed Steven thoughtfully. What he said had been true. He had already met Lacey. He wouldn't have mistaken that other woman for her. If he and his brothers had taken the time to think about it, they would have come to the same conclusion.

Fear for Lacey had scrambled their brains.

Lacey glared at him and tried to pull out of grasp. He let her go so she wouldn't hurt herself. As long as she kept her distance from Steven she would be fine. She had no idea just how fast and deadly a werewolf could strike.

He hoped like hell she never found out.

Lacey smiled at Steven apologetically, ignoring the threatening growls from Damien and the others. It appeared they'd been too lenient with her if their growls didn't even faze her.

They were the fucking Alphas, damn it!

Their mate would damned well learn that they were in charge. After they took her home and showed her just what would happen every time she defied them, they should no longer have to deal with this shit again.

"Steven, I'm so sorry about these assholes. Thank you so much for helping me. At least you're willing to listen and have compassion for others."

Damien couldn't believe it. Even his brothers looked shocked at her audacity. He couldn't wait to have her bare ass over his lap. She'd scared the hell out of all of them and had the nerve to blame all of this on them.

Fucking unbelievable!

His temper spiked even higher when Steven smiled at her. "Don't worry about it, honey. Let me know when you have those papers signed. If they won't let you bring them to me, I'm perfectly willing to come to the house to get them." He raised a brow at Lars. "That is, if it's all right with you."

Damien saw Lars' inner struggle reflected on his face. None of them wanted Steven anywhere near Lacey, but if they said no, it would look like they didn't want to help Sarah and her daughter, Christina.

Lars' eyes promised retribution, but Steven didn't look as afraid as he should have.

"We'll let you know. In the meantime, stay away from our mate."

Damien had had enough and pulled Lacey out of the room. "Come on, my mate. You're going to pay for scaring the hell out of us."

* * * *

Lacey shot another apologetic look at a grinning Steven before Damien stormed out of the building, dragging her behind him. "Let go. You're pulling my arm out of the socket."

Damien's answer was to bend and lift her over his shoulder.

"Damn it, Put me down."

He slapped her bottom again. "Be still. You're not going anywhere but home."

"Stop hitting my ass."

"Wait until I get you home. Your ass is going to be bright red before I'm through with you. How dare you lie to us and put yourself in danger. You're our mate, damn it."

Lacey lifted enough to see that the other three looked furious. "I was never in any danger, you idiot. Steven would never hurt me. You have to tell your grandmother about him."

Seth opened the car door so Damien could put her inside. "You're going to learn not to take chances with your safety and tell us about any fucking meetings you have."

Wes got into the other side of the back seat and pulled her to the center. "You don't leave the fucking house without permission."

Incredulous, Lacey gaped at him. "If you think I'm going to ask you for permission for anything, you're delusional. If that's what you want in a woman, you've got the wrong one."

Damien gripped her chin as Lars shot down the road. "We've got the right woman. We've just got to teach her a lesson."

"Teach me a lesson?" Lacey was so mad, she could barely get the words out. "You're the ones who need a lesson if you think you're going to get away with this."

Lars met her eyes in the rear view mirror. "I warned you, my mate, what would happen if you put yourself in danger or didn't tell us about any threats. Do you think we don't know about the emails you're still getting?"

Lacey gritted her teeth. "How did you get into my email? It's password protected."

Lars looked back at her coolly. "Child's play."

Lacey lost her temper. Big time. Beating on Damien's chest, she screamed her fury. "I can't believe you would do that. I can't believe your nerve. I won't be treated this way."

Damien caught her hands in his, the ease in which he did so infuriating her even more. "Easy you little hellcat. We only did it to protect you!"

Wes wrapped his arms around her from behind and pulled her against him. "We can't let anything happen to you. Don't you fucking get it? You're everything to us, Lacey. We'll do whatever we have to do to keep you safe!"

No amount of arguing changed their opinion. When they pulled up to the house, Lars hadn't even put the SUV in park before Wes got out, pulling her out behind him, throwing her over his shoulder and starting toward the house.

Lacey fought, kicking and screaming as he carried her in and up the stairs, the others trailing close behind. She looked around as she bobbed on Wes's shoulder, but Victor and Nana didn't appear.

"Put me down. You're not going to boss me around, damn you." Grabbing the back pockets of his jeans, she pulled. Hard.

Wes slapped her ass again. "Fuck. Get her hands. She's fucking squeezing my balls."

Lars grabbed her hands in his, forcing her to let go. "You're a damned wildcat. Let's see if we can make you purr."

"Not until I paddle her ass," Damien growled.

"And she begs," Seth added.

Lacey continued to curse and scream at them as Wes dropped her onto the bed and they all began pulling at her clothes until she lay naked in the center. They surrounded her, throwing off clothing as they touched her. Having already learned all her weaknesses, each stroke had an extraordinary erotic effect. She had an idea what they would do because of Lars' threat, but the experience of being so completely vulnerable nearly overwhelmed her.

Hands touched her everywhere, and she found herself flipped onto her stomach with a huge pillow under her hips. Her legs were spread and someone moved between them and under her, but with her shoulders held down, she couldn't tell who it was. She kicked her legs, trying to inflict damage where it would hurt the most, fear, anger and unwilling lust each scrambling for dominance. They chuckled, making her even angrier.

"I'll get even for this. You're not going to tell me what to do."

Damien low rumble sounded close to her ear. "We'll see about that, my mate."

With tensions so high, it didn't take long for her anger to turn into need. The growls filling the room told her that the men had also been swept into it, the highly charged atmosphere igniting their primal urges, which in turn, aroused her even more.

As helpless as she felt, she knew they would never hurt her and had become just as helpless to the passion as she had.

Still cursing at them steadily, she felt a hot tongue swipe her slit and a sharp slap on her bottom simultaneously. The startling contrast of sensations stole her breath.

The sharp sting of the slap quickly gave way to heat, blending with the talented hot tongue moving on her slit. Her pussy wept with the need to be filled as the velvety strokes continued, pressing inside to gather her juices, only to come out and lick her clean again. She struggled uselessly at the hands holding her in place, needing her clit to be stroked.

She never felt such a thing. "Oh God. It's too much. More, damn it."

Another slap landed, spreading more of the heat and making her bottom burn. The touch of a lubed finger to her puckered opening made her jolt, but several strong hands held her in place.

Another swipe on her slit and a cool thick finger invading her back passage sent a shudder through her, so close to coming she knew she would go over at any second.

A heated slap.

More cool lube.

The burn of two fingers pushing deep.

Another swipe of a hot tongue.

They were killing her. "Let me come. I need to ahh, oh my God. More."

Lacey couldn't keep up with all the sensations. Hands ran over her continuously, long, smooth strokes as though to calm the rest of her while igniting an inferno in her bottom and slit.

Her entire being became focused on the heat at her center, sizzling tingles radiating from there all throughout her body. She panted. She whimpered. She begged.

Her throat had become almost raw from her hoarse cries of need.

Still, they wouldn't allow her to go over. Just when she thought one more stroke of that devastating tongue would send her over, it slowed. Another slap landed, two firm hands caressing the heat into her. The thick fingers imbedded in her anus moved, demonic strokes waking nerve endings and making them quiver and tingle.

"Please do something. I can't stand it."

Another swipe of a tongue.

Gripping handfuls of the bedding, she struggled against the hands holding her in place.

Other than their deep growls, the men remained silent as they drove her to the edge and kept her hanging there.

Lacey kicked. She screamed. She fought. She needed to come more than she needed her next breath. Still they denied her.

The bed shifted and Lars turned her to face him. His eyes blazed as his gaze traveled down the length of her body. He pushed her hair back from her face and lowered onto the bed next to her. Tears spilled from her eyes, her need had become so great.

"Promise you'll tell us before you leave the grounds again."

Lacey struggled just to breathe as the fingers in her anus stroked deep. It was no longer enough. She craved that burning, too stretched feeling. She needed it now. But she couldn't give up her independence. "You c-can't b-boss me ahh!"

The thick fingers withdrew from her abruptly, leaving her grasping at emptiness. Whoever had been between her legs moved away. The bed shifted again as one of them moved beside each hip, hot hands on her inner thighs holding her spread wide. The other moved between her legs and she groaned when the head of a thick cock began to push at her forbidden opening.

More growls sounded as the tight ring of muscle gave way and steely heat pressed deep inside her.

Her toes curled as she cried out at the carnal sensation, of the pure dominance of the act. Her body had a will of its own and kept clenching on the unyielding thickness that stretched her so tremendously.

She heard groans and bit off curses amidst the growls but couldn't make sense of any of them, all her focus on the sensations washing over her and the sound of Lars' voice.

"Say you'll behave and do what you're told, and we'll let you come."

Lacey scrambled to assemble a coherent thought. "I'll be, ahh, move, please move." She reached for her clit, knowing the slightest touch would send her over.

Lars caught her hand before she could reach her destination. "No. You can come as soon as you promise to behave. No more secrets. No more leaving the house without telling anyone."

"I swear I'll make you pay for this." Lacey bucked as the cock in her ass withdrew slowly, only to press, just as slowly, back into her.

Talented fingers played with her folds, almost, but not quite touching her clit. The growls and moans continued behind her.

"So fucking tight. I can't last Lars." Seth's voice sounded tortured.

"She's drenched. All this fucking juice. The scent is driving me insane." Wes growled.

Damien's deep voice came from her other side. "She's shaking like a leaf. She's going to come any second."

Lars held onto her hand as he reached under her to tug at a nipple. "Say, 'I promise', and you can come."

"Damn you. Damn you," she whimpered. "I promise. Let me come. Let me come."

The strokes in her bottom came harder and faster. A firm stroking began on her clit and Lacey soared.

Spasms of indescribable bliss racked her body as everything exploded. Her screams went on and on as the pleasure raced through her, and the cock in her ass plunged deep.

"She's fucking milking my cock so hard. Jesus. Too good. Too good."

The only sounds in the room, harsh breathing, groans and low growls gradually lessened.

When she finally began to catch her breath, warm hands caressed her as tremors continued to rack her body. She shuddered as Seth slowly withdrew from her. They surrounded her, speaking softly and caressing her, but she didn't know what they said.

She jolted when a warm cloth touched her, relaxing again as they cleaned her and covered her with the blanket. Surrounded by their soft voices and heat, she drifted in a fog. Warm, firm strokes on her back melted her bones.

I'll get even for this, was her last conscious thought.

* * * *

Lars sighed and continued to rub her back. "She's asleep."

Damien leaned down to kiss her shoulder before covering it with the blanket. "I've never been so scared in my life. Hopefully, she learned her lesson and we won't have to go through that again."

Wes ran a hand over her bottom, looking down at her lovingly. "She's so damned passionate. Every time we touch her she goes up in flames. I have to go jerk off. Next time, I get to punish her."

Lars looked across his mate to Damien. "She's incredible, isn't she? I'm already deeply in love with her."

Damien looked up at him in alarm. "Are you sure it's love?"

Lars grinned and touched Lacey's hair. "I'm sure. You love her, too. So does Wes. Seth isn't there yet. But he's falling."

Damien looked more than a little alarmed. "I don't know about love. She's our mate. We care for her and take care of her. She'll have our children and be with us forever. I have strong feelings for her. Shit. I don't know what the hell I feel. Maybe—I don't know."

Lars chuckled, careful not to wake their mate. "You never expected to fall in love with your mate, did you?"

"No. I thought it was just that we would get along and the sex would be great. She has to obey me and I take care of her. I thought it was just chemistry."

Still smiling, Lars shook his head. "No. Pheromones are just the way of ensuring we recognize the right one sooner. Nature already knew she would be the one we would fall in love with. I have with no regrets. She's smart, funny, sweet, compassionate—"

"Bad tempered, hard-headed, sassy—"

Lars smiled broadly and nodded. "That, too. Makes life a hell of a lot more exciting, doesn't it? Can you imagine having a wimpy doormat for a mate?"

Damien stood and looked down at her. "Well, at least now she'll obey us."

Lars kissed her hair again before standing, and adjusting the blanket over her. "We'll see."

Chapter Thirteen

Damien scowled as Lacey walked out of the room he and Wes had just entered. Clenching his jaw, he watched her go and turned to his brother. "I've had enough of this shit."

It had been three days since they'd punished their mate and gotten her promise not to leave the house without permission and to let them know about any threats.

She hadn't spoken to any of them since.

When she'd come downstairs for dinner that night, they'd all been prepared for her to be repentant, begging forgiveness. Instead, she'd totally ignored them as if they weren't there, not even looking at any of them. She spoke to Victor and their grandmother but wouldn't say a word to them.

She'd gone up to bed early, and deciding to give her some time alone, they hadn't gone up right away. When they did, they'd found their bed empty. They'd tracked her to the bedroom she'd used when she'd first arrived. Damien had carried her sleeping form back to their bedroom and he and Wes had gotten in on either side of her.

They'd made love to her the next morning before she had completely awakened, taking her so slowly and sweetly, he thought it would kill him. Afterward, they'd gone downstairs, smug in the knowledge that all was well.

It wasn't.

Somehow, most of their shirts had disappeared. When Wes had walked into the family room to join her in watching a movie, she'd thrown her popcorn at him, bowl and all and stormed out. Seth's car keys had been taken and no amount of threats could get them back.

Papers had disappeared from Lars' desk and his desk chair had collapsed when he sat in it. Damien had expected something similar and had approached his desk carefully, checking everything.

Not knowing what she would do to get even with him stretched his nerves to the breaking point. Needing to get away for a little while, he'd decided to go for a ride on his motorcycle. When he pulled his favorite pair of boots on, it had almost been a relief to find them full of chocolate pudding.

Their mate in a temper was a force to be reckoned with.

She never left the house, but stood looking out the windows until they all felt like heels. They'd come to realize she wouldn't go outside without permission, but only because she'd promised.

And she wouldn't ask.

Although they took turns sleeping with her and making slow love to her each morning, she still hadn't forgiven them.

Wanting a reason to confront her, Lars had even logged onto her computer, thinking if they could find proof that she'd gotten threats that she hadn't mentioned, they could at least fight it out.

Her email box had been full, none of her emails even read.

They couldn't accuse her of receiving threats and not telling them when she wouldn't even open the emails to read them, thereby having no knowledge of the damned things.

Lars and Seth came into the room and shut the door behind them.

Lars poured himself a drink. "Anyone have any bright ideas?"

Damien paced. "She our mate, damn it. Our word is law. She has to obey the fucking rules. It's only to keep her safe."

Wes moved to the window and looked out. "She is. She's doing just what she promised to do."

Seth plopped onto the sofa. "We can't live like this. She's miserable, and she's making the rest of us miserable. I thought when men shared a mate, they were all happy. What the fuck?"

A knock at the door interrupted them, and Victor stepped inside. "May I join you?"

Lars nodded. "If you'd like. We're not very good company at the moment. Lacey's still pissed at all of us."

Damien sighed. "She hasn't even been on the program I installed for her to check her fake stocks. She loves beating me at that."

Seth shook his head. "I went out and got her some more clay. When I told her about it, she didn't even acknowledge me."

"She won't paint, either. I even asked if she would sit for me so that I could paint her portrait. I thought it would look nice hanging over the fireplace in the living room. She left the room." Wes paced beside Damien. "She talks on the phone to Sarah and Steven. I heard her laughing at something Steven said to her yesterday, but when I walked into the room, she took the phone and left. Grandmother looks worried."

Damien poured his own drink. "She deserved to be punished. She had to learn that we won't put up with her risking her safety in any way. If she's pissed off, too bad. At least she's pissed off and safe." He hated that she looked so sad. Damn it. They hadn't done anything to her she hadn't deserved.

Lars scrubbed a hand over his face. "But like Seth said, she's miserable. I want Lacey to be happy again." He sighed and leaned back in his chair, looking incredibly tired. "What the hell are we supposed to do about it?"

"Grovel."

All four men spun and stared at Victor incredulously.

Lars recovered first and sighed. "You're right of course. We didn't handle it very well. There had to be a better way to get her to understand what we needed from her."

Damien shot to his feet. "She's our mate! We're supposed to protect her. If she's pissed off, she's just going to have to get over it. I want her safe, and I don't care what I have to do to make sure she stays safe."

Victor raised a brow. "Even if it makes her unhappy?"

Damien slumped back in his chair. "Fuck. She stares out the

fucking window all the time. She wouldn't even go shopping with Grandmother."

Victor nodded wisely. "I remember when Victoria got mad at me, she would slam doors and throw things at me." He chuckled and shook his head. "There aren't many things worse than an angry mate. You'll learn that. Your grandmother asked me to speak to you about this because it's gone on long enough. You're going to have to learn to read your mate's moods. You'd better learn fast how to deal with those moods or you're going to end up in hot water all the time."

Damien's gut churned. "Then why the hell isn't she yelling at us and throwing things?"

"Because we hurt her," Lars said softly. "We hurt her feelings by not listening to her and for overwhelming her until she had no choice but to give in. It wasn't fair, and we shouldn't have done that to her. It was four against one and she didn't stand a chance. We should have listened to her and fought it out."

Victor nodded and smiled. "True. Werewolf punishment is used only when a mate deliberately defies you or does something inexcusable, such as having an affair or deliberately endangering her life or the life of your children. Drunk driving, going against a doctor's orders, not seeking medical attention, etcetera."

Damien felt like a lead weight had settled in his stomach. What the hell had they done?

Seth groaned. "She didn't do anything like that. But how were we supposed to know she wasn't in danger?"

Wes leaned back against the desk. "I can't stand to see her this way. We should have listened to her about Steven. She apparently trusts him. We wouldn't even listen when she tried to talk about him and when she mentioned telling our grandmother about him, we cut her off. She's right. Grandmother needs to know about Steven and have the chance to get to know him if that's what they both want."

Victor stood. "That sounds like the best way to start. Tell her that you're going to tell your grandmother about Steven. "

Lars nodded and smiled at Victor. "I think you're right. You're a very wise man, Victor. Of course, once we get her talking to us again, and apologize for not listening, we're going to have to deal with her temper."

Damien grinned, hearing the anticipation in Lars' voice. He agreed. He'd much rather have her angry at them then have her sad and hurt. "She's going to be really pissed."

Wes chuckled. "She's got a hell of a temper. We're going to have to watch each other's backs until she forgives us."

Victor left the room, leaving the four of them alone.

Seth laughed. "Our mate sure is a challenge, isn't she?"

Damien exchanged a glance with Lars. Seth really didn't get it yet.

Seth seemed more interested in playing and exerting control than anything else. Damien loved a challenge as much as the others, maybe more so and knew that dealing with his fiery mate in a rage would definitely be challenging. But his priority had become making his mate smile again.

He really couldn't stand to see her so unhappy. Victor had been right. Lacey's sadness and hurt had him floundering to know what to do to get back what they'd begun to build.

Oh God. He'd done it. Lars had been right. He'd fallen in love with her.

He glanced over to look at Wes, who looked thoughtful. Wes frowned at Seth. "Is a challenge all you can think of? It doesn't bother you that she's upset?"

Seth jumped out of his chair to confront him. "Of course it bothers me that she's upset. I don't like that she's been moping around the house or that she won't talk to us."

Wes nodded, still looking thoughtful and just a little worried.

Damien knew how he felt and wanted to reassure him, something completely out of character for their past relationship but completely fitting for their new one. Lacey had changed their lives. "I don't think

Seth has fallen in love with our mate yet. Don't worry about it. The rest of us already know we have."

Damien adjusted his stance when Seth moved on him, grabbing the front of his shirt.

"How I feel about my mate is none of your fucking business."

Damien broke his hold and shoved him. Hard. "That's where you're wrong, little brother. Anything that affects Lacey is my business."

Lars moved to stand between them, facing Seth. "Damien's right. I have no doubt that one day soon you'll feel for her what the rest of us do, but if you don't, she's still your mate. But the three of us won't allow you to hurt her, no matter what you say. We love her and have her best interests at heart. If we stop trusting your judgment concerning her, you won't have a say in how we handle her."

Seth sighed heavily and dropped into a chair. "You're right. Look, don't ask me what the hell I feel for her. She's got me so fucking scrambled, I just don't know. I won't hurt her, though."

Wes nodded and dropped onto the sofa. "We need to go talk to Lacey. We'll have her with us when we tell Grandmother about Steven. At least we can get her talking to us again."

* * * *

The sound of the rain beating against the window depressed her even more. Unable to concentrate, she closed the book she'd been trying to read. Turning away from the window, she gazed around the room. She loved the comfortable informality of the family room, even though she could see the room didn't get a lot of use.

She'd had Victor mail the papers Steven had prepared to Sarah. When she'd spoken to Sarah a few hours ago, the other woman told her that she'd already signed and mailed them back. Once they arrived, she had to somehow get them back to Steven.

She'd stopped checking her email. Most of them had been from

Ted Johnson anyway. The others, from Tom Shultz, made her see just what a wimp her ex-boss had become. He deferred to Ted, and had been helping him to get his child back, claiming that Sarah had been the one to abuse Christina.

With the information Steven had already gathered, Ted didn't stand a chance.

Lacey had already paid for the private investigator that Steven had contacted, grateful that she'd managed to save enough over the years to help. With the house she'd grown up in for sale, she should quickly recoup enough to build her savings again.

Not knowing how the relationship she'd begun with the men would work out, she would be more comfortable if she had some money put aside.

Thinking about Lars, Damien, Wes and Seth depressed her one minute and made her furious the next. She had no idea what to do about them. She only knew she wouldn't be able to resist them much longer.

She hadn't been able to resist their lovemaking at all. Every time they touched her, she simply melted in their arms and had no defense against them. Their scents, their sounds, their heat, their touch never failed to turned her into a quivering mass of need.

How the hell could she have fallen in love with *four* men?

Because she loved them, their unwillingness to listen to her had sliced her to the bone. Knowing she could never last in a relationship with men who wouldn't listen to her and who blew off her feelings made her incredibly sad.

The way they'd used her passion for them against her infuriated her and saddened her even more.

The way they bullied her and tried to tell her what to do made her want to hit them over the head with something.

Avoiding all of them had been difficult, even in a house this size. But she knew if she stayed in the same room with them, or God forbid, tried to speak to them, she would break down and cry, something she vowed not to do. Once she got over the hurt, she looked forward to a good fight with them. She had no problem giving them hell for what they'd done to her but couldn't do it until she was sure she could do it without tears.

She couldn't believe how much it had *hurt*.

When they walked into the room she stood, preparing to leave. She couldn't face them, not when she still hurt so much.

"Please stay. We'd like to talk to you about Steven."

Lacey looked up to see Lars watching her closely. "I'm tired. I don't feel like talking about it."

Damien came close and touched her arm. "We want to tell Grandmother about Steven. We want you to be there when we do."

Lacey sank back into her seat. "You're really going to tell her? Why?"

Seth and Wes sat while Lars and Damien remained standing close to her. Lars touched her other arm. "We realized that you were right. Grandmother has the right to know about him."

Lacey stared at him shocked. "You admit I was right?"

Lars smiled at her so tenderly, it brought tears to her eyes. "We made some mistakes with you, my mate, and I hope you'll forgive us."

She eyed him suspiciously. "Why are you saying this now? Because you want me to help you tell your grandmother about Steven? Have you spoken to him?"

"No, we want to tell Grandmother first. I don't want to get his hopes up of meeting her if she needs some time to adjust to it." He took her hand and sat, pulling her onto his lap. "We know we hurt you by not listening to you."

Lacey sat stiffly. "I don't like the way you used sex against me to get what you want."

Damien moved closer. "You're right. The punishment was extreme for what you did." He lifted her chin until she looked up at him. "But don't think it won't happen again if you do anything to risk yourself ever again."

Lacey jerked away from his hold and jumped up. "You'd better *never* do that to me again."

Damien snarled. "We will if you put yourself in danger. We didn't realize that you trusted Steven so much. We didn't trust him at all and thought he was the one trying to kill you."

"What? Why would Steven want to kill me?"

Damien sighed. "The Galbraith pack have always been our worst enemies, and we didn't know why until that morning. Aaron Galbraith told us the truth about Steven and that Steven carried the scent of both packs."

Lacey blinked. "What does that have to do with anything?"

"He might have decided that we don't deserve to have a mate after what our father did to his family. The Galbraith pack is not happy that, because of you, our packs have been reunited. Whoever killed that woman carried the scent of both packs. We still don't know who it is."

Lars clasped her hand in his. "We didn't know of anyone else who carries the scent of both packs. No one in our pack does, so it has to be someone from their pack."

"Or she could have been killed by someone from each pack so their scents were both on the body," Wes added. "Whoever it is won't be happy until you're dead. When we found out about Steven, we raced home to find you gone. When we found you with him, we went nuts. That's no excuse, but we were so scared that we'd lost you, we snapped."

Lacey glanced at each of them. They actually believed their actions had been justified. "I was fine. I knew Steven wouldn't hurt me. I don't have the senses you have, but I have one none of you can claim. Women's intuition. I am not going to live my life in a bubble. If you expect me to stay here with you, you'd better learn that. I'm not stupid, nor would I take unnecessary risks. I won't put up with your bullying and I won't ask for permission to leave the damned house. If you can't deal with that, I'm leaving. And if you ever try to *punish* me again, I'll feed you your balls."

Seth surged to his feet. "You're our mate, damn it and you'll do as you're told."

Lacey threw her book at him and stormed out of the room.

* * * *

Seth caught the book before it could hit him in the chest and started after her.

Wes caught his arm. "Let her be. At least she's angry now instead of sad." He shook his head. "Everyone apologizes and you have to lay down the law again. We need to keep her close, asshole. We're not going to be able to do that if she keeps avoiding us." Ignoring Seth's glare, he looked at the others. "I guess one of us has to go get her and get Grandmother. After we tell Grandmother about Steven, we're going to have to do what we can to calm her down."

Seth threw the book onto the sofa. "We did the right thing and I'll be damned if I'm going to promise never to do it again. We still have no idea who's trying to kill her. She has to learn to trust our judgment."

"Did we trust hers?" Wes asked softly.

Damien grinned. "I guess we can find an outlet for all that passion. I don't think we've gotten to the mother load of all that anger yet."

Lars chuckled. "Yeah, but we'd better protect our balls."

* * * *

Lacey went to the kitchen and got herself a glass of juice, feeling for the first time in days as though she no longer had a lead weight in her stomach. She knew she still had a long way to go in teaching her *mates* a thing or two, but at least they'd admitted they'd been wrong in what they'd done to her.

She had no doubt that they would fight in the future. Couples fought but to have four of them to deal with would definitely be a challenge.

She understood some of their thinking because of the talks she'd had with her godmother. They felt perfectly justified in coddling her and doing their duty as, not only her mates, but the Alpha males to keep her safe. Double the chauvinism, times four. It was a wonder she was ever allowed out of the bedroom.

She appreciated that her safety was important to them, just as theirs was to her, but she couldn't live her life wrapped in cotton. And like her godmother, she had a mind of her own and fully intended to use it.

She smiled when she thought about some of the stories Nana had told her about the fights she'd had with her husband regarding the same thing. It would take patience and she knew she'd have to put up with their chauvinistic attitudes to get what she wanted, but she felt confident that she could do it.

Her mates, always used to being in charge, would have to learn to compromise.

That should be fun, she thought to herself with a grimace.

A hand on her shoulder made her yelp and she almost dropped her juice glass. Wes managed to pluck the glass out of her hand just in time. She skewered a finger into his hard chest. "Can't you make noise or something instead of sneaking around?"

Wes grinned. "I didn't sneak in, I walked."

He leaned down to kiss her nose and she pushed him away. "I'm still mad at you."

His smile never faltered. "I know, honey. We'll fight later. O'Reilly just pulled up. We're going to go talk to him in the study. As soon as Grandmother and Victor get back from shopping, we'll talk to her about Steven."

Lacey nodded. "Okay. She's really going to want to meet him."

She touched his sleeve. "His father is awful to him and to his mother. I told him you would let him join the pack. I know it's not my place but—"

Wes ran a finger down her cheek. "You still don't get it, do you, sweetheart. You're the Alpha female of the pack. You have a lot more power here than you think you do. Unless it's something my brothers and I are dead set against, your word is law, too."

Relieved, Lacey slumped against him. "So you're not against him and his mother becoming part of the Tougarret pack?"

Wes nuzzled her hair. "We'll have to all sit down and talk about it. Steven and his mother might not want to join. If they do, we'll talk about it with them. But your wishes carry a lot of weight. I can't promise anything until we've talked to Steven, but I don't think there'll be any problem with it. Okay?"

Lacey smiled up at him, lifting her face for his kiss. When it ended, she pushed him away again. "Go talk to O'Reilly. Get him out of here before Nana gets back. He upsets her."

Wes grabbed her around the waist and lifted her against him. "I had to go jerk off after I watched Seth fuck your tight ass. Tonight, it's my turn. I want my cock in that gorgeous ass." He kissed her again and set her on her feet, and laughing, strode out of the room.

Lacey just stood there, staring after him as lust slammed into her. Weak kneed, she dropped into a chair. Damn, what they did to her should be illegal. He'd aroused her so easily, and she knew it would be hours before she could find relief. Bastard.

Then she remembered that the scent of her arousal drove them crazy. She smiled to herself. Good. She would think lascivious thoughts all day, imagining what they would do to her later. By the time they went to bed, they would all be in fine form.

Her cell phone on the counter rang, and she was still laughing to herself when she went to answer it.

* * * *

Wes walked into the study to find his brothers and Agent O'Reilly already waiting.

"The medical examiner's report confirms that it was an animal bite that killed Bonnie Hancock. He's pretty sure it was a wolf. What do you have to say to that?"

Lars, who'd been leaning back in his chair behind the desk, sat forward. "What the hell am I supposed to say to that? There are thousands of acres of woods behind the property. We hear them all the time, but I have no idea how one got close enough to the party to attack someone, especially with nobody seeing it. I have no idea why it would even attack her. Wolves don't usually attack unless provoked."

"Maybe it was rabid," Wes told the agent, taking a seat on the sofa. Thinking about whoever had killed that woman and wanted to kill his mate enraged him. Whoever had done this *would* be considered rabid and dealt with accordingly. "Most of the neighbors were here that night and are aware of the danger. If we find the wolf, we'll kill him."

O'Reilly leaned back in his chair and raised a brow. "Funny how you don't say it. You say him. How do you know it's a male instead of a female?"

Wes looked at his brothers in horror as the truth finally hit him. He carefully schooled his features, but he could see that his brothers had come to the same conclusion. "You're right, of course. It could very well be a female. But females only attack to protect their young."

Lars stood. "If that's all O'Reilly, we each have work to do and need to get to it. Our businesses don't run themselves. We'll let you know if we learn anything."

Wes stood, impatient for the agent to leave.

When he finally did, they watched until he drove away. Wes turned to the others. "It's Steven's mother, isn't it? Aaron told us himself that she was father's true mate. She gave birth to his child.

She would carry his scent, along with the Galbraith scent. She's the only one other than Steven that would carry both scents."

Damien paced. "It *has* to be one of them. There's nobody else. Didn't Lacey say that Aaron treated her like shit ever since she had Steven?"

Lars nodded. "Aaron told us himself what a disappointment she was to him. We have to call Steven. She would have heard about Lacey like everyone else but she wouldn't have gone after her if she thought she might also be his son's mate. We have to find out what Steven told her."

Wes started from the room. "I'll go find Lacey. She has his number."

He strode quickly to the kitchen only to find it empty. He started to leave in search of her when he saw a piece of paper lying on the table.

Steven's mother, Dolores called. Husband hurt her. Needs help. Went to go get her. Be back soon. L.

Panic stricken, Wes raced to his brothers. "Look what I found. We've got to go find her. Where's that fucking number? We've got to see if Steven knows where she'd take her."

Damien cursed a blue streak, fear in his own voice. "She had a card. I'll look in the bedroom. See if we can find her purse. Shit, she doesn't know enough about all this to realize that she would be the last person Dolores would call."

They found the card on the dresser in their room and quickly placed a call to Steven. When Wes told him what they thought had happened, they were met with dead silence.

Wes shouted into the phone, so scared, he shook with it. "Damn it, Steven. Where would she take Lacey?"

"I can't get in touch with her. She called me earlier and I was busy and told her I'd call her back. No one knows where she is."

"Did you tell her about Lacey?"

Steven sighed. "Yes."

"What did you tell her?"

"She knew about Lacey coming here and that she was your mate. She seemed upset that your pack reunited but not really mad. I told her that I wanted to see if Lacey was my mate, too. That made her happy."

"What did she say when you told her that Lacey wasn't your mate?"

"She wasn't happy about it. She said it wasn't fair that you and your brothers got everything while I had nothing, but for her to do something like this— Look, I'll leave and go get my father. My mother never goes anywhere. My father won't let her. The only place she knows is here. She would never leave the area. She usually— shit, she'll be in the woods. I'll get my father and meet you there."

Wes slammed down the phone and kicked off his shoes. "The woods."

Lars and the others threw off their own. "Let's hunt."

Chapter Fourteen

Lacey groaned as the pounding in her head made her nauseous. She was freezing and realized she lay sprawled on the cold ground. Shivering, she curled into a ball, trying to get warm, wincing at the sharp pain in her head. *Where the hell was she? Why did her head hurt so much?*

"If you try to escape, I'll have to hit you again."

"Dolores?" Lacey sat up painfully and leaned back against a tree, wincing as the rough bark scraped her back and shoulders. "What happened?" She looked around, careful not to turn her head quickly, to see nothing but woods all around them. It had to be the woods that bordered both properties, but she had no way of knowing how far they'd come.

"You're a present for my husband. When he sees what I got for him, he's going to be so pleased with me."

Finding it hard to focus on the woman, Lacey frowned. "I don't understand. You said you were hurt. I came to help you. You hit me?"

"Of course I hit you. You came just like I knew you would. Steven said you were one of those people who went out of their way to help others. Idiot. My Steven was right. He's a very smart boy." She jumped up and down, clapping her hands together. "It worked just like I planned it. You're just the thing I've been waiting for. Aaron will love me again."

Dolores had obviously lost all grip on reality. A big woman, she danced around, speaking in a sing song voice. "Aaron's going to rape you, then he's going to kill you, then he's going to love me."

Lacey finally managed to focus but darkness had started to fall, and the way Dolores danced in and out of her vision made it hard to watch her. "So you killed that woman at the party because you thought it was me?"

Dolores stopped her dancing and came to kneel in front of her, her face tight with anger. "That was *your* fault. Steven told me that you had red hair. I watched and saw that woman going around and talking to everyone the way you should have been doing. It's not my fault you weren't there. When I lost sight of her, I asked one of the children where the Alphas' mate had gone, they told me that you went around the side of the house. When I snuck around, she was there. How was I supposed to know it wasn't you?"

Lacey shook her head and immediately regretted it. "I was on the other side of the house. With my mates. I wish you had come that way. They would have killed you."

"They would never have caught me. I was so happy when I thought you were dead. I was just waiting for Aaron to mention it and wonder who did it. I couldn't wait to tell him that I was the one who killed you. You ruined that for me."

Lacey knew her men would be looking for her. She just had to wait for them. But what if Dolores's husband was on his way? "Does your husband know that you're doing this?"

Dolores stood and started dancing again, looking very pleased with herself. "No, it's a surprise. I left him a note. I was there when he met with your mates, but I stayed upwind so they wouldn't know it. But I heard Aaron tell them that if he could rape you, he would and that they didn't deserve to have you. He thought Steven was the one that killed that girl and he sounded so proud. I want him to be proud of Steven."

Lacey moved slowly, trying to get her legs in position so that she could jump up and run when she got the chance. "Does Steven know about this?"

Dolores whirled on her. "No. He likes you. I can't believe it. The whore of the Tougarret pack. I thought about getting him to help me, but I knew he wouldn't. Aaron was so proud when he thought Steven had killed that woman. I wanted him to be the one to take you to his father, but it wasn't to be." She began dancing again. "But when Aaron sees what I've done, he'll be proud of me and then he'll like Steven."

"You're crazy." Lacey stood slowly, fearing she would pass out as the world spun crazily. "You're going to let your husband rape and kill me so that he'll like you?"

"It's the only way! Nothing else has worked. He's hated me for years."

Lacey moved slightly away from the tree and glanced around. She had no idea which direction to run and looked for a clue. Trees, trees and more trees. It all looked the same to her. "That's because you had an affair. What did you expect him to do?" She had to get out of here before the Alpha of the Galbraith pack appeared. She knew the only way she would have some time to wait for her men would be if he decided to rape her first. If he decided to pass on the rape and just kill her, she knew it could be over at any second. Lars and the others had stressed over and over just how quickly a werewolf could attack.

Dolores moved closer and looked at her beseechingly, as though needing Lacey to understand. "I loved Roland. He was my mate. But I didn't find him until after I married Aaron. I should have waited." She walked away again, glancing around the clearing. "Aaron is close. He'll be here soon. When he kills you, it will fix everything."

Lacey felt a warm presence, a tingling awareness, and prayed it was the mating bond her men had told her about and not the presence of the other pack. "I'll bet your husband wasn't happy when you gave birth to another man's son."

Dolores whirled on her, her eyes hard as stone. "You bitch. You know nothing about it."

"I know you cheated on your mate."

"He's not my mate. Roland was. But his other sons got everything that should have been Steven's! They have to pay for that. I won't wait for Aaron. I'll kill you myself, you bitch. I'll make your men pay for stealing everything from my son."

Lacey blinked as Dolores shifted, becoming a gray wolf before her eyes. She charged, her jaws open as she leapt at Lacey. It happened so quickly, she knew she would never escape and braced herself for the attack.

A black blur leapt between them as the woods exploded. As her knees gave way, another black wolf stood in front of her, pushing her back against he tree. A brown wolf and a dark gray one took positions on either side of her.

Loud growls sounded from all around her and she stood again shakily, afraid that someone would get hurt. The wolves surrounding her closed in, not allowing her to move.

Dolores, still in wolf form fought with the black wolf and even Lacey could see she was outmatched. The black wolf moved too fast for her and Lacey could see Dolores's frustration grow.

With sudden insight, Lacey realized that the black wolf that faced off with Dolores and who'd jumped between them was Seth. Wes stood at her feet.

A huge red wolf jumped between Seth and Dolores, growling threateningly and baring its teeth at Seth. Lars and Damien, in wolf form, leapt forward, flanking Seth. Wolves came out of everywhere, baring their teeth and growling, but none attacked, all eyes on the Alphas.

The red wolf had to be Aaron.

Dolores's growls chilled Lacey's blood and she watched, mesmerized at the scene in front of her, hardly able to believe her eyes.

Aaron turned to Dolores and nipped her, growling as another black wolf came forward. Steven. Oh God. This could get ugly.

She could see the rage of the Alpha, the bared teeth and menacing growls toward the gray sending a chill down her spine. Dolores backed down, rolling onto her back and baring her vulnerable belly.

Lacey held her breath, scared of what Aaron would do to her. When he moved toward her, Steven leapt between them in what Lacey recognized now as a threatening stance, which Aaron quickly mimicked.

Seth, Lars and Damien leapt to Steven's defense, forcing Aaron to face all of them.

The tension grew as wolves raced forward, and Lacey braced herself for an all out battle. Fear for her men had her automatically trying to move toward them, but the three wolves surrounding her pushed her back again.

"Wes, they're going to kill each other," she cried fearfully.

She watched the growling wolves fearfully, proud that her men stepped forward to protect their newly found brother but was so scared for them she could hardly breathe. Her chest hurt as she gulped in air, biting back the screams that threatened for fear it would distract them.

To her amazement, Aaron stopped growling and turned his back on both Steven and his mother and walked away. All growling stopped as wolves looked at each other as though not quite sure what to do.

Aaron stopped and turned, shifting into human form. "I never knew." He looked at Lacey. "I never knew she felt this way. You're safe from my pack." He raised his voice, as though to make sure that everyone heard. "I will personally deal with anyone from the Galbraith pack who threatens or harms you."

Lars, Damien and Seth shifted and Lacey couldn't help but admire her men as they stepped forward and extended their hands.

One by one they all shifted, shaking hands all around. If anyone thought it strange for hundreds of naked men to be shaking hands in the middle of the woods, she couldn't see it. Wes shifted in front of her and turned, kissing her deeply. "Are you okay, my mate?"

"I'll be fine."

He narrowed his eyes. "You forget I can smell your lies and your pain. I'll be right back. Victor, Ethan, stay with Lacey."

She looked up to see a naked Dolores running into the woods carrying her clothes.

Tears ran down Lacey's face when she saw Aaron put his arm around Steven. "Let's get your mother home. She needs us. I'm sorry, son. For a lot of things."

Steven shook hands with the men and waited with Aaron for his mother to get dressed and join them.

As the men approached, she saw the others had shifted again. Happy that she wouldn't have to travel back to the mansion with a bunch of naked men, Lacey smiled tearfully at her men as they came back to her.

"Seth, you jumped in front of a crazed wolf to protect me. Oh my God, you're hurt." She pulled his collar aside to look for the source of all the blood soaking his shirt.

He smiled and wrapped his arms around her. "What can I say? I'm in love with my mate. Let's go home."

Passed from one to the other, Lacey snuggled against each of their men as they headed for home. Her legs felt like cooked spaghetti. "How far is it?"

Seth lifted her into his arms. "Don't worry. You have your mates to take care of you. Just relax and go for the ride."

Wes came up beside them. "What the hell did you think you were doing, going off by yourself that way? You scared the hell out of us. When we get home, I'm turning you over my knee."

Remembering her godmother's warning about getting around them, Lacey kept her face carefully blank. "I know. I deserve it. Just let me take care of this horrible headache and wash and disinfect the scratches on my back first."

"What?" Seth froze in his tracks as four voices exclaimed simultaneously.

Lacey's head really did hurt so she had no qualms about lifting her hand to her head and groaning. Since it did hurt, she didn't lie.

"She knocked me out. It's getting easier to focus now. I just need a couple of aspirins."

Lars moved in front of Seth. He pushed her hair back, examining her head, and she winced when he hit a particularly tender spot. "She's got a fucking knot on her head. What about the scratches?" He took her from Seth's arms.

"On my back and shoulders. They'll be fine. I know it's more important to you to do your punishment thing." She grimaced. "Maybe my spanking can wait?"

Damien examined the knot. "Nobody's spanking you. You're going to see the doctor and go to bed." He turned to the gray wolf walking beside them. "Victor, can you get the doctor? Have him meet us at the house. Let grandmother know that everything's fine."

Lacey hid her face in Lars' neck so they wouldn't see her grin. When they continued walking, Lacey sighed and looked over at Seth, "Isn't it nice that the two packs aren't enemies any more?"

Seth nodded. "Yes, I just hope Dolores gets the help she needs. Aaron told us that he's going to take care of her. He seems repentant when he realized just how bitter and demented his wife has become. As the Alpha, and her husband, he should have noticed."

Lacey smothered a moan. Even though she didn't walk, the uneven ground they moved over juggled her head and she felt like little knives stabbed her temple. She leaned against Lars' shoulder and closed her eyes as the nausea threatened again. "It seems funny to say her husband instead of her mate."

"They can still make it work if they try," Wes told her. "Not every werewolf is lucky enough to find his mate."

Seth moved close and touched his lips to her forehead. "And some are too stupid to realize that they've fallen madly in love with their mate, until it's almost too late."

* * * *

The doctor and Nana met them as they stepped into the house. By this time, Lacey wanted to scream from the pain in her head. The men wouldn't even have to smell it, she knew they could see it.

She wouldn't let the doctor look at her until she'd showered, over the men's protests. "I'm freezing, and I'm dirty. I want a shower first so that when the doctor's done, I can go right to sleep."

Lars got into the shower with her. "You look like you're going to fall over."

"It's just my head. As soon as I get rid of this headache, I'll be fine."

"You've probably got a concussion. I know your scratches will heal by tomorrow, but I have no idea about a damned concussion. Let's get you cleaned up. The doctor's waiting."

They hovered as the doctor examined her and gave them instructions for her care, assuring them that she would heal by morning. Victor appeared with an offer for food, which she rejected. She still felt nauseous and knew that anything she managed to eat would come right back up again. Whatever the doctor had given her had worked so at least the pain had eased. When her godmother came in, Lacey looked over at Damien questioningly.

He shook his head. "No, but we should now."

As they'd expected, Nana cried when she learned about Steven and wanted to meet him right away. After they'd explained all that had happened, her godmother smiled tremulously and dried her tears. "It's wonderful that the Tougarret pack and the Galbraith pack are no longer enemies. Please tell Steven that as soon as he's ready, I'd love to meet him. Another grandson, I can't believe it. I knew what had happened with Aaron Galbraith and your father but I never suspected that Steven was your father's son. Your brother."

Lacey reached for her godmother's hand. "He's a good man, Nana. You'll like him a lot."

"The poor thing. All these years of being resented by the man he looked up to as a father and a mother demented by bitterness. If only she hadn't had the affair with your father—"

Wes put his arm around their grandmother. "It looked like Aaron had a rude awakening. It shook him that his wife killed thinking it would make him love her again."

Lacey leaned against Lars, letting his heat seep into her. "I hope they'll be okay. But what's going to happen with Agent O'Reilly? He's not going to stop until he finds whoever killed that poor woman. How can we keep the truth from him?"

Lars lifted her chin. "Pack business, Lacey. It'll be taken care of within the pack. We can't have a crazy woman in jail, shifting every time someone makes her mad. It'll be up to Aaron to deal with it. If he doesn't, we will."

Wes sighed. "I think that's what's weighing on him the most. As the Alpha, it's his responsibility to deal with her. She brought attention to all of us, and Alphas all around the area will be watching him to make sure he handles it."

"You mean there's more of you?"

Lars chuckled. "Of course, darling. All over the world."

The doorbell rang, and Wes squeezed his grandmother's shoulder. "That's Steven."

Nana's eyes widened and shimmered with tears. "I'll go down. Maybe he needs me. I can't wait to meet him."

The bed shifted as Seth joined them. "You didn't think there were only two packs of werewolves in the world, did you?"

Lacey shrugged. "I really didn't think about it. I guess I have a lot to learn."

He smiled and patted her hand. "You have plenty of time. Sleep now."

Lacey jumped as her cell phone rang. Lars bent and retrieved it from the back pocket of her jeans. "Do you want me to answer it for you?"

Lacey reached for it. "No. I'll take it."

* * * *

Seth couldn't help but notice how tired his mate looked. The pain in her head had eased but hadn't completely disappeared.

He would have nightmares about how close she'd come to being killed earlier. He doubted if she even knew how close. He ran a hand over the bandage on his shoulder.

When Wes found the note she'd left, his heart had stopped. It hadn't started again until they'd found her. It had almost burst from his chest when Dolores had shifted and attacked.

Love for her had slammed into him with the force of a freight train. Terrified for her, he'd leapt between her and the powerful jaws of another werewolf, praying he would be in time. He could no longer imagine a life without her.

"Sarah? Calm down. I can't understand you."

Seth exchanged a look with Lars as Lacey scrambled from the bed, nudging Lars out of her way as she started getting dressed.

"Okay. Calm down. Go to the other room. I'm on my way." She looked around the room, her eyes touching on each of them. "No, I'm not coming alone."

She disconnected. "Ted found Sarah. The motel manager told her that some men were asking questions about her. We've got to go get her. Can we bring her back here?"

The men were already moving. Damien nodded. "We should have made her come here days ago. Let's go get them."

Lacey noticed that the men stayed close as they started down the stairs. "I'm fine. Whatever the doctor gave me helped. I should have brought Sarah and Christina here. But I didn't know you and didn't want to make trouble." She grimaced. "You've had nothing but trouble since I got here."

Lars squeezed her hand as they moved. "None of this is your fault."

They got to the foyer in time to see Steven embrace their

grandmother, tears in both their eyes. Seth patted Steven's shoulder. "We'll be back." He explained what had happened.

Steven nodded. "I'll come with you. I'd like to help." He turned back to his grandmother. "I'll be back and we'll talk."

Grandmother nodded. "I'd like that."

* * * *

Lacey prayed all the way to the motel where she'd hidden Sarah. "We have to get there in time."

Steven frowned. "She's only been ten miles away the whole time?"

Lacey nodded. "Yes, I didn't want her too far in case something happened, but I didn't come see her after we dropped her off in case I was followed. I hid her west of Nana's house and went east to use my credit card to buy gas before I went to Nana's."

Wes rubbed her arm. "What did you say to her about going to the other room? What was that all about?"

Lacey watched out the windshield, silently urging Lars to go faster. "When we got to the motel, I had Sarah check into a room. Once she and Christina got settled, I went to check into another. I paid cash and told the manager that I was there on a business trip and would be keeping strange hours, and I didn't want to be disturbed by housekeeping. I paid for two weeks in advance and got a room a few doors down from Sarah's."

Damien turned from the passenger seat to face her. "So you gave Sarah the key to that room in case of an emergency? Pretty smart."

Lacey nodded. "That way she could get there quickly and be able to look out and see whoever came to the door of the other room."

Seth squeezed her hand. "You're something, my mate. A perfect mate for an Alpha."

"Or four?" Lacey asked, squeezing his hand. "There's the motel. Hurry."

* * * *

The room that Sarah had been staying in stood empty, but their belongings had been scattered everywhere.

Seth searched the bathroom. "It looks like someone searched the place."

Lacey turned and raced to the other room as the men all stood guard. She banged on the door. "Sarah, it's me. It's Lacey. Oh, Sarah, be here. Sarah. Christina. It's Lacey. Open up."

The door opened and Sarah came out, throwing herself in Lacey's arms. "They were here. They went to the other room and left just a few minutes ago. Oh God. Lacey, behind you!"

Lacey turned, staying in front of Sarah, to face the two men coming toward them, both with guns.

Seth moved to stand in front of her. "Lacey, you and the others get inside."

"Move away from the door. Mr. Johnson wants his wife and kid. This is none of your business, man."

At the sound of the young man's voice, Sarah gripped Lacey's arm. "I'll never get away from him."

Lacey looked around. Not seeing the others, she smiled. "Everything will be fine, Sarah. I promise. Take Christina and go into the bathroom. I'll come get you in a minute."

After Sarah rushed Christina into the bathroom, closing the door behind them, Seth spoke softly over is shoulder. "You too, Lacey."

Lacey moved to stand beside him. "And miss this? You've got to be joking."

Seth pinched her bottom and pushed her behind him. "Behave."

He turned to the thugs. "If you're smart, you'll put the guns away and leave. Go tell your boss he's not getting them back."

Lacey peeked around Seth, keeping her eyes on the men, not wanting to give away the positions of the black wolves moving in around them.

The two men stopped and pointed their guns at Seth. "Get out of the way. We'll shoot you if we have to."

Two of the wolves leapt onto the men and their guns went flying.

Lacey pointed. "That's Damien on the right and Lars on the left, right?"

Seth laughed and kissed her forehead. "So much for you being scared. Yes, it's Lars and Damien. You're learning, my mate."

Lacey moved to stand in front of him, aware of the menacing growls from behind her. Laying her hands on his chest, Lacey looked up at him. "I want to learn. I want to be a good mate to all of you."

Seth's eyes flashed. "You're staying? No more talk about leaving?"

Lacey reached into his open collar and traced her fingers over the bandage there. "I'm staying. There's no place I'd rather be. I love you all so much." Her voice broke as Seth pulled her tightly against his chest.

"We love you, too, Lacey. So damned much."

The police pulled up as the manager of the motel ran out. "They're over there. They have guns."

Lacey turned in Seth's arms to see the police holding guns on the men now lying on the ground. Not seeing the wolves, she looked around. "Where'd they go?"

Seth rubbed her back. "They have to get dressed. That's the only downfall to being a werewolf. Every time you shift, your clothes come off. Uh, sweetheart?"

Lacey looked up at him and kissed his jaw. "Hmm?"

"What do I have to do to get my car keys back?"

Lacey backed away and put her hands on her hips, careful to keep her voice low. "Do you think I don't know which one of you was in my ass when you *punished* me?" She moved around him. "I have to get Sarah."

Seth followed her. "Come on, honey. Please?"

* * * *

They'd just finished packing Sarah and Christina's meager belongings when Steven walked into the motel room. He came to a halt, his eyes going wide as he stared at Sarah.

Lacey looked from one to the other, surprised to see a similar reaction on Sarah's face. "Sarah? Steven? Is something wrong?"

Damien came up behind her, chuckling. "Well, I'll be damned."

Lacey frowned up at him. "What? What's going on?"

Damien wrapped his arms around her and pulled her back against him. "It looks like Steven has finally found his mate."

Chapter Fifteen

Lacey moaned as warm lips captured a nipple and tugged. She reached up and tangled her hands in silky hair, gasping as teeth lightly scraped across the beaded tip. "Wes."

Her nipple was released as those wonderful lips captured hers. "You're learning your mates well, my love. Even in the dark."

Lacey opened her eyes to find the room in total darkness. Ever since the night they'd rescued Sarah two months ago, her men had been even more loving than before, and it was rare for a night to go by without at least one of them reaching for her in the dark. By the time she came awake, she was already aroused.

As Wes kissed her deeply, another warm mouth closed over her other breast. Seth. She'd fallen asleep between the two of them hours earlier.

Lacey moaned into Wes's mouth as Seth used his teeth. Wes ended the kiss to whisper in her ear. "Tonight I'm taking that ass."

Lacey's bottom clenched in response to his erotic promise. "Oh, yes."

Seth's mouth inched downward as Wes took a nipple into his mouth once again.

The bed dipped where Seth had been as Damien sat beside her. His hand cupped her other breast, stroking his thumb over her nipple. "Can anybody play?"

Lacey cried out as Seth spread her thighs and lowered his head to her slit. She would never get used to having so many hands and mouths touching her at once. Each time felt so familiar and yet so different. Her men loved to play and got more inventive all the time.

And bolder. Secure in their love for each other now, their lovemaking had gotten even more intense and erotic than before.

She felt a cock brush her cheek as Seth's tongue pushed into her. Opening her mouth wide, she took the head of Damien's cock into her mouth, cradling the tight sack beneath. His hiss of pleasure mixed with their growls creating the erotic sounds that always sent her higher.

Damien leaned over her and began fucking her mouth, each stroke taking him deeper to her throat. "Use that soft tongue, my mate. Suck me deeper. Ahh, that's it. Good girl."

A pinch of her nipple made her moan as the pleasure shot straight to her pussy.

Seth growled louder as more of her juices flowed.

Wes continued to play with her nipples as he took her hand in his and wrapped it around his cock. "Stroke me, honey. Then my cock's going right up your ass."

"Make room for me," Lars growled and Lacey felt the bed dip again.

She whimpered as Seth moved away and Damien and Wes withdrew their cocks from her mouth and hand. "Don't stop."

Wes chuckled and lifted her. "We're not stopping. You're going to take care of all four of us at once. And I'm going to heat that ass before I take it. I know how hard you come when you get spanked."

"Oh God," Lacey groaned as Seth lay down, and Wes positioned her on top of him.

Seth gripped her hips and together they lowered her onto Seth's waiting cock. Since they no longer used condoms, Lacey felt every bump and ridge even better as inch by thick inch filled her pussy.

She tried to move, but Seth stopped her by pulling her down onto his chest.

"Don't miss," he warned his brother. "If you hit me, you're dead."

Wes chuckled. "I won't miss. I can see that fine ass perfectly."

Lacey jolted when a sharp slap landed, followed by a firm caress, spreading that intoxicating heat. "More."

"Oh, yes, my mate. You're getting more." Another slap landed, followed quickly by another, until Lacey squirmed restlessly on Seth.

"Ahh! I want to come. Fuck me, damn it."

Lars lifted her hand and placed it around his cock, moving it over his thick shaft, reminding her of the way he liked to be stroked.

She groaned as Wes worked the cool lube into her and positioned his cock at her puckered opening. "Yes. Oh, it burns. More. Ohh!" She panted breathlessly as the large head popped through the tight ring of muscle. She felt hands in her hair as Wes began stroking shallowly, working more and more of his cock into her ass.

Damien's cock touched her cheek again. "Open. I want to fuck that mouth." He held her head in his hands as she opened wide and began to move, working his cock deeper. "That's it, baby. Use that tongue."

She felt full to bursting as Wes slid to the hilt inside her ass and held himself still. With a cock in her pussy, one in her ass, one in her mouth and her hand full of yet another, Lacey tried to concentrate on pleasing them all. But they had already gone well past the time when she could do anything but feel what they did to her.

Damien stayed with her as they lifted her slightly so Seth and Wes could establish a rhythm that would send them all over the edge.

Their primitive growls and coarse words only added to the savage need they'd awakened inside her. She couldn't help but tighten on the cocks inside her. Each time she did, both Seth and Wes groaned and cursed.

"It's like fucking hot velvet," Seth rasped.

"Her ass is incredible. So fucking tight. I'm so fucking close. Make her come."

"No," Lars barked. "She's not to come yet. Damien and I will take care of her. Open that ass up good, Wes. She's getting fucked there again."

"And I'm coming in her throat while Lars is fucking her ass,"

Damien growled.

Lacey groaned around Damien's cock, so close to coming she couldn't stand it. She would never be able to last. Those delicious warning tingles began just as Wes plunged deep, his cock pulsing and shooting his seed into her anus. A few more strokes. So close. So close.

Seth raised his hips and pulled her down onto his chest to stop her from moving as he came, roaring her name.

His movement had pulled her away from Damien's cock and she cried out, reaching for it as Lars took her hand away from his length.

"No, damn you. No. I'm so close. More."

Lacey struggled against Seth's hold as Wes withdrew from her. She tightened her bottom to hold him in but couldn't.

Kicking and screaming, she fought their hold as she tried to move on Seth's softening cock. "Damn you. Damn you. No." She reached for them in the darkness, but somehow they all avoided her hands as they repositioned her.

Seth slid off of the bed and Damien took his place. Taking her head in his hands, he lowered her mouth back onto his cock. "Suck."

Lacey needed no further encouragement. She attacked him, starving for his taste.

She sucked him greedily as Lars moved in behind her, a series of sharp slaps reigniting the heat in her bottom. She moaned on Damien's cock as Lars lifted her hips high and pressed the head of his cock against her forbidden opening.

She always struggled to relax her bottom in order to take them, but she could never quite accomplish it. Each time a cock entered her bottom, it burned. And each time it burned, it made her crave even more.

She felt those warning little tingles as Lars pushed into her, sucking Damien even more deeply as she felt her orgasm approach. She clenched on him, making it burn once again, Just when she thought she would go over, Lars stopped moving.

She kicked her legs, struggling as she tried to get him to move again.

Seth laughed and reached from behind to take a breast in each hand, rolling her nipples between his thumbs and forefingers. "I think she wants to come bad."

Damien smoothed her hair, cursing as she used her tongue on him. "I'm coming. Damn it."

Lacey thrilled as his thighs tightened under her hand as he exploded. She swallowed on him, loving the taste of him as Lars started moving in her ass once again, his strokes so deep she would swear she could feel it in her throat.

Lars froze inside. "Move, Damien. Do you want to feel how a werewolf loves to fuck his mate the most?"

Almost mindless with need, Lacey would have agreed to anything and wanted all he had to give her. "Yes. Fuck your mate."

Lars growled harshly and lifted her hips more firmly against him with a hand over her mound as he leaned over her, covering her back with his. His teeth sank into her shoulder, holding her in place for his thrust as his fingers parted her folds. A rough finger touched her clit, moving her over it in time with his thrusts.

She clenched on him hard as she came, screaming hoarsely as he continued to thrust into her. It felt so incredibly carnal to be taken this way, held in place for her mate's thrust as he took her in the most dominant way possible. His deep growls in her ear only magnified the sensation and she couldn't help but go over again.

Her clit felt so swollen and sensitive, that each thrust caused as much pain as pleasure, just like the thick cock moving in her bottom.

Lars released her shoulder, nipped it, and used his tongue to ease the slight sting before rumbling in her ear. "Again. Come again."

She couldn't deny him. His domination of her was complete.

Breathless, she came again.

Her body. Her mind. Her soul. Her heart.

He owned them all.

They all did.

Lars groaned his completion against her neck as he pushed deep, pulling her hips back against him.

Lacey trembled uncontrollably as she collapsed onto the bed.

Lars covered her body with his, pressing her into the mattress, lifting her hands over head and interlacing her fingers with his. Nuzzling her hair, he murmured in her ear. "I love you, my mate. I don't know how I ever lived without you."

He cuddled with her, speaking softly, loving words in the darkness.

"I love you, too. All of you. So much."

When Lars withdrew from her, running a warm hand over her bottom as he stood, Wes came out of the bathroom with a warm cloth.

She blinked, groaning when Damien turned on the light as Wes cleaned her.

When Wes finished, Damien lifted her against him, sitting on the bed with her cradled in his arms. Seth came to her other side, tucking a blanket around her. He leaned close to kiss her shoulder. "You do know how much we all love you, don't you?"

Lacey smiled and reached for his hand, snuggling deeper into Damien's embrace as she struggled to keep her eyes open. "Yes. I love you, too." She yawned, smiling as Wes and Lars came back. "Now that we all know that we love each other, can we go back to sleep?"

The men shared a glance and she felt her stomach drop. She sat up hurriedly, pushing away from Damien, looking from one to the other. "Oh God. You don't want me anymore. You've made a mistake. I'm not your true mate."

Damien pulled her back against him. "Are you crazy?"

Lars caught her hand. "We told you the first day we met you that we were sure about you. We just all told you how much we love you."

Wes smiled at her tenderly, stroking a hand over her arm. "We're doing this badly. We didn't mean to scare you."

Lacey watched them warily. "What's this all about? What's going on?"

Damien gathered her even closer. "We're trying to figure out a way to tell you that you're expecting our baby."

Lacey shot up, now wide awake. "What? I'm pregnant? How could you know that?"

Damien laughed. "Your scent, my mate. A woman's scent changes when she's pregnant."

Lacey laughed and cried at the same time, seeing the men's own grins through her tears. They took turns holding her, each kissing her and telling her how much they loved her. She wiped her eyes. "Can I assume you're all as happy about this as I am?"

Seth and Wes bundled her back into bed. Seth pulled her against him. "Very happy, my mate. We've known for a couple of days and waited to make sure."

Wes turned off the light and turned to lay a hand on her abdomen. "We're very excited about the baby. And we're very much in love with our mate."

Lacey giggled, happier than she'd ever been. "I can't wait to tell Nana. I'm so glad I came for her birthday."

They all chuckled. Wes rubbed her stomach. "We all are, my mate. We all are."

Epilogue

Adjusting the blanket over her legs, Lacey settled into the lounge chair and looked up at the full moon. Her godmother had gone up to bed a short time ago.

It had gotten even colder since she'd come out but she knew she would never sleep if she went up to bed. She could no longer sleep alone, having gotten used to her men holding her through the night. Besides, with all the blankets covering her, she'd gotten warm and toasty and didn't want to get up anyway.

Running a hand over her swollen abdomen, she couldn't help but smile at how wonderful life had become in the few months since she'd come here.

She'd sold her house and cut all ties with her hometown. Sarah and Christina lived at the Galbraith Estate, both happy and well loved. Sarah's divorce had been finalized, and they had all been invited to her and Steven's wedding which would take place in less than two weeks.

She smiled when she thought about how happy Steven and Sarah looked together. Steven absolutely adored his future wife and Christina. It had taken time, but the little girl had begun to relax around him, no longer afraid of being hit. She went to school where members of both packs taught and, although she probably didn't realize it, was constantly guarded. The packs both spoiled her rotten.

Aaron Galbraith had left the area, having heard from the pack doctor of a psychiatrist in Canada, a member of another pack, who might help his wife. Knowing what she was capable of, and afraid for Sarah and Christina, he'd taken her away, leaving Steven in charge of the pack.

The two packs got along famously now and gathered often. Even now they worked together, going after the two rogue wolves that had been causing trouble in the area.

Agent O'Reilly still showed up from time to time, but had gotten a lead on another attack somewhere up north and had left over a month ago to follow it.

She smiled at the tiny kick and smoothed a hand over her abdomen again. Lars, Damien, Wes and Seth had gone nuts over her pregnancy, and it was a wonder she ever even got to walk. They carried her every chance they could despite her protests and held her on their laps as much as possible.

When the baby had started moving, they'd been awestruck. Since then, it was rare for one of them to be near and not have a hand on her belly.

They'd appropriated a space for the nursery and already bought more stuffed animals than a child could ever use.

They spoiled her rotten, rubbing her feet and back and always trying to coax her into eating more.

She was guarded even more closely than before. The rogue wolves in the area had been moving closer, attacking Alphas and their mates. The men thought they wanted their own packs and attacked the Alphas in order to take over.

Lacey had watched them go, trying desperately to hide her fear for them as they'd shifted and started out. She knew they would be careful, but they took their responsibilities seriously and she wouldn't completely relax until they came home.

Knowing that Steven and his pack traveled with them eased her mind somewhat, but still—

Startled by a loud howl, one that sounded close, she tried to see into the trees. An answering howl sounded in the distance, followed by several others, coming from all directions. She knew they communicated that way but, having no idea what it meant, she started to get nervous. Wondering if they'd found the rogue wolves, she waited anxiously for any more sounds.

Several minutes went by, and hearing nothing, Lacey began to relax again.

"You fucking bitch!"

Lacey jumped and looked over to see Ted Johnson and the two men that had been outside the motel the night they'd rescued Sarah. Her hands went protectively over her abdomen. "What the hell are you doing here?"

"You really didn't think I would let you get away with what you did to me, did you? I had to leave Millville. You embarrassed me and after the arrest and the investigation, no one wanted to do business with me any more. And it's all your fault, bitch for getting into my business. I'm going to teach you a lesson about minding your own business. I see you're pregnant. Let's see how you feel when I take away your kid."

Out of the corner of her eye, Lacey could see the yard filling up with wolves. Five huge black ones ran silently toward her. "I think you'd better leave while you have the chance."

One of the men from the motel pulled out a gun. "Come on. Let's get this over with."

Lacey smiled at him. "Do you remember what happened the last time you pointed a gun at me?"

The five black wolves ran onto the patio, two lunging at the arm of the man holding the gun and knocking it away. The man went down and found himself surrounded by angry, snarling wolves. She recognized one as Ethan.

Ted started to back away, a look of terror on his face as he held his arms out as though to ward them off. "What the fuck is this? We're being attacked by wolves?"

With the wolves surrounding him, Lacey couldn't see the man on the ground, but the other backed toward his boss. "I told you. You didn't believe me when I told you that wolves attacked us in that parking lot. Holy shit!"

Lacey grinned as the other man caught sight of the number of wolves filling the yard. She pushed the blankets aside and stood.

Ted's eyes widened. "Don't move. You're going to make them attack."

Lacey laughed and reached out a hand to the black wolf closest to her. Wes turned toward her and licked her fingers. "They won't attack me, you idiot. Just anyone who threatens me. Or Sarah. Or Christina. Hmm, I wonder what they'd think of the fact that you wanted to take my child from me because I helped yours get away from you."

If possible, the growls became even more menacing as the black wolves closed in on him.

Ted looked at her pleadingly. "Call them off. I'm begging you."

Lacey petted the two wolves beside her. Wes and Lars. Seth stood in front of her. "They have your scent now, Ted. They can track you anywhere."

Ted gulped. "I'll go. You won't have any more trouble from me."

Lacey narrowed her eyes at him. "And you'll leave Sarah and Christina alone?"

"Yes."

"And you'll let Christina's new stepfather adopt her?"

"What?"

More menacing growls as the wolves moved closer to him.

"Yes. Yes. I'll do it."

"Don't change your mind once you get away from here. Remember, they can find you anywhere."

"I won't. I won't. Just call them off."

Lacey tilted her head. "You know, Ted, you're a pussy. What kind of man hits women and children? And you come here threatening a pregnant woman?"

The wolves from the yard, their teeth bared, continued to move closer, growling threateningly, poised as if to pounce.

When Ted tried to back away, a gray wolf behind him nipped his leg. "Oh, damn it, it bit me."

Lacey grinned at him. "You really are a pussy."

Ted's face got red and he took a step toward her. "You—"

That's as far as he got before Seth leapt at him, knocking him down and standing over him, sharp teeth and strong jaws moving closer and closer to his throat.

"I'm sorry. I'm sorry. Please tell them to let me go."

Lacey laughed delightedly. "You wet your pants! Oh God, this is priceless. Get up, you asshole."

When Ted got shakily to his feet, Lacey turned her back to him, letting him know that she didn't fear him at all. Settling back into the lounge chair, she petted the black wolf, Lars, who gripped the blanket in his teeth to pull it over her.

"Goodbye Ted. Don't forget to sign those custody papers or my friends and I will pay you a visit. You don't deserve to be a father."

Ted took off, sliding on the patio in his haste to leave. He scrambled up, leaving the others to follow and disappeared around the side of the house.

Lars, with his head resting on her swollen abdomen, shifted under her hand and reached for her. "Thank God we got here in time. Victor was watching the house and alerted us that someone was here. We thought it was O'Reilly and stayed back."

Lacey lifted her face for his kiss. "You got here in plenty of time. That was fun."

He lifted her into his arms and started toward the house. "I've had enough hunting for tonight. I want to make love to my mate."

"Amen to that," Seth added, coming up behind them. "Damien and Wes are talking to Steven and they'll be right in."

Lacey snuggled against Lars' naked chest. Eying her men's naked forms, she could already feel the moisture dampening her panties. "Did you find the rogue wolves?"

Lars nuzzled her hair as he started up the stairs. "We were chasing them, almost had them cornered when Victor sounded the alarm."

Lacey leaned back, staring up at him. "You didn't let them get away because of me, did you?"

Seth caressed her leg, making her shiver with need. "There isn't anything we wouldn't do to keep you safe."

Lacey smiled and reached for his hand as they entered the bedroom. Seth had changed so much toward her since she'd first met him. Still playful, he'd become more thoughtful, especially since learning of her pregnancy. Once, when they'd been alone in the studio, he'd confessed that he hadn't fallen in love with her as quickly as the others had and it had troubled him deeply.

Feeling guilty, he'd been almost reverent in his lovemaking and it had taken considerable effort on her part to get him to play again.

She'd returned his car keys, and he'd immediately gone out and traded his beloved sports car in for an SUV, claiming that he couldn't drive her and the baby around in something dangerous. His new vehicle had every safety feature money could buy and already had a child's safety seat installed in the back.

Lacey looked up at him now as Lars laid her gently on the bed and headed for the shower. "But I don't want them to get away."

"They won't. The others will track them and we'll keep an eye out. But I think they all understand that we want to be with our mate tonight."

Lacey sat up. "What did you have in mind?"

Since the night they'd told her of her pregnancy, they'd been so careful while making love to her that she wanted to scream. Not that they didn't satisfy her. They did. Completely. But she loved when her men got wild and hungry for her, so much so that they forgot everything else.

Seth reached for the buttons of her shirt. "Is this my shirt?"

"Do you want it back?"

Seth's cocky grin made her giggle, delighted when he played. "Yes, I believe I do."

He helped her undress, tossing her panties aside just as Wes and

Damien walked in, gloriously naked, closing the door behind them. Wes's brows went up. "It looks like we're just in time."

Lacey moaned as Seth covered her breasts with his hands. "Does this mean you're all going to take me tonight?"

Lars came out of the bathroom wearing only a towel. "Absolutely. One at a time. Slowly."

Lacey shuddered as Seth lightly stroked her nipples. "Sensitive, sweetheart?"

"Oh, yes. I won't break. Why won't you take me like you used to?"

Damien moved to her other side and laid a hand over where their baby grew and was rewarded with a kick. "We will, my mate." He bent to drop a kiss on the spot where he'd felt the kick. "As soon as you heal from giving birth."

Lacey moaned as the bed shifted and Lars took a nipple into his mouth. "But I want all of you. Oh, that feels so good."

Wes touched his lips to her belly and moved lower. "You have all of us sweetheart. Always."

Lars and Seth helped her to lie back as Wes's lips closed in on her center. Lars kissed her deeply, making her senses soar. "Don't worry, my mate. We'll satisfy you, you insatiable woman."

Lacey moaned. "You always do, but I want to satisfy all of you."

Lars' eyes flared. "You do, my mate. In every way."

THE END

www.Leahbrooke.net

ABOUT THE AUTHOR

When Leah Brooke isn't writing, she's mapping out new stories or spending time with her family. She's thrilled when a story comes together and falls in love with all of her heroes.

Siren Publishing, Inc.
www.SirenPublishing.com

LaVergne, TN USA
01 February 2010
171578LV00007B/5/P